DO NO HARM

Fiorella De Maria

Do No Harm

A Novel

IGNATIUS PRESS   SAN FRANCISCO

Cover images © iStockPhoto.com

Cover design by John Herreid

© 2013 by Ignatius Press, San Francisco
All rights reserved
ISBN 978-1-58617-724-9
Library of Congress Control Number 2012942822
Printed in the United States of America ∞

Acknowledgements

As I am neither a lawyer nor a doctor, I have many people to thank for providing me with the legal and medical details for this book, most especially James Bogle and Dr Philip Howard. All the characters and events of this book are entirely fictional, though in Britain today it would be possible for a doctor to face prosecution for saving the life of a patient in possession of a living will.

Prologue

Maria sat hunched over her computer, blinking sleepily at the gaudy colours of the news website. She had been checking the political news section all evening and had lost count of the number of times she had pressed the Refresh button in the hope that the "vote pending" story would magically change to "breaking news". Now that an update had finally appeared, she was almost too exhausted to react and glanced impassively over the contents of the page, with its hackneyed illustration of Parliament's green couches in the left corner and a neat central chart showing the way the MPs had voted. Maria took it all in, then picked up her mobile phone to send a text message to a friend: "Passed with a huge majority, bill cannot fail now. The lie did not come into the world through me." With that, she slipped her phone into her dressing gown pocket and got up with uncharacteristic weariness.

Maria's home was made up of two tiny interconnecting rooms in a smart London house owned by an elderly lady who had not been able to bring herself to move out of the family home where she had raised her children. Like many other elderly landladies dotted about London, she rented out the upstairs rooms to "nice girls", usually single twenty-something professionals like Maria, whilst she herself lived in the converted maisonette downstairs. Perhaps because she charged her girls the lowest rent possible, the house had not been decorated in many years and bore a feeling of faded grandeur as though the best times were long over and the whole edifice might crumble like the House of Usher when its owner died.

The bedroom resembled the cabin of a passenger ship, with its blue walls sloping inward, the floorboards bare and unvarnished and an ancient bed with brass bedsteads tucked cosily into a corner, swamped by a generous duvet. Through a narrow connecting door was a study lined with wallpaper that had been a rich green once but had faded to the colour of ochre. It contained the obvious articles—a desk covered in piles of A4 paper accompanied by a chair in desperate need of upholstering and a heavy old-fashioned bookcase crammed full of books and files. On the wall over the desk was a print of the Madonna and

Child next to a black-and-white picture cut out of a literary magazine of Alexander Solzhenitsyn staring pensively into the distance. Immediately below his picture, Maria had written her favourite quotation in her very best florid handwriting: "Let the lie come into the world, but not through me. Not through me." Solzhenitsyn was an odd choice of pinup for a twenty-two-year-old woman, perhaps, but Maria's tastes had always been what her friends would have called countercultural. There were no personal photographs.

Maria whispered a brief prayer in the direction of the Madonna and Child, wished Solzhenitsyn an affectionate goodnight and moved towards the small basin wedged into the opposite corner of the room. As she filled the basin with water, she felt the dull vibration of her phone springing into action and the tinny chimes of Big Ben muffled by the folds of her dressing gown. There was a short reply: "Be of good cheer. You were called to be faithful, not successful."

Maria switched her phone off and absorbed herself in the reassuringly mundane rituals of washing her face and brushing her teeth. Fidelity was all very well, of course, but for once, only for once, she would have loved to have found herself on the winning side. Just to know what it felt like.

1

"Darling, put the aliens back in their craters before they go in the box, could you?" called out a voice from the landing.

Dr Matthew Kemble was on his knees in his children's nursery, tidying up with them before bed. At least *he* was tidying up. Dominic, aged three, had eagerly started putting the books away only to be distracted by the gripping storyline of *The Tiger Who Came to Tea*, and he was now sitting on his bed with the book open at the part where the tiger drinks all the water in the tap. Little Angelina, adorable in her enormous pink dressing gown, had sat down in the toybox and was smiling endearingly at her father in the happy female knowledge that he was entirely under her control. It was seven o'clock on a chilly February evening, and the Kemble family—its younger members, at least—were winding down at the end of a busy day. A smell of baby powder and strawberry bubble bath pervaded the room, and Matthew could not help feeling a certain despondency that he would soon have to leave the warm chaos of his home for a night shift at the Accident and Emergency unit of the Edith Cavell Hospital. In the meantime, however, he searched for the last couple of squat plastic red-and-green aliens and placed them carefully into the craters of their Manic Martians moon base.

Thomas and Cecilia appeared in the doorway, Cecilia in her Beauty and the Beast pyjamas, Thomas still in his school uniform, waving a glossy textbook with a picture of the night sky on the cover. "Dad, is Pluto a planet or not?" he asked. "Mrs Saunders says it isn't any more, but the book says it is. I have to draw a picture of the solar system, and I don't know whether to put it in or not."

"When I was your age, it was a planet", said Matthew. "Do get out of that box, Angelina, darling—but I think scientists worked out it wasn't after all. The orbit is all wrong, elliptical unlike the others, and it's made of rock, when all the other outer planets are made of gas." He braced himself, grasped Angelina by the waist and lifted her out, causing her to start wailing indignantly as he had known she would. "It could be an escaped moon from another planet in another solar system, which I find rather fascinating, but then ..."

"Oh, Dad, do I draw it or not?" The textbook fell to the ground with a sad thud. "Did you know Dominic's taking his duvet cover off?"

Matthew turned around to find Dominic sitting swathed in a cloud-like duvet, with the vast blue Thomas the Tank Engine cover slowly wrapping itself around his head. He looked like a cross between a cartoon Aladdin and Cupid. At that moment, Matthew's wife, Eva, appeared before him like an avenging angel. "What on earth have you done to Dominic?" she demanded as though he had personally trussed the boy up like that. "And what's wrong with Angelina?"

Angelina, in the absence of any attention, was rolling around in a corner of the room building up to a nice little tantrum. "Stop it!" said Thomas. "That's bad."

"I not bad!" shrieked Angelina in high-pitched indignation. "I not bad! I not bad!" Every time she made the declaration, her voice became a shade higher, until the words were almost lost in an ear-piercing shriek. "I NOT BAD! I NOT BAAAAAAAAAAD!"

"I think it might be bedtime", said Matthew decisively, signaling for Thomas and Cecilia to take the toybox out of the room. He bundled Dominic's duvet back into its cover whilst Eva calmed Angelina down and coaxed her into bed. Somebody turned the lights down, sending out the silent signal that it was the end of the day and time for everyone to settle down.

Guardian angel from heaven so bright
Watching beside me to lead me aright . . .

It was Matthew's favourite moment of the day. He bent down and kissed Angelina's soft, fragrant cheek, provoking a broad smile, and traced a cross on her forehead. "Nighty-night." Then he stepped across the room to say goodnight to Dominic whilst Eva hustled the other children out of the way.

"Do you want a coffee before you go?" she asked, as Matthew emerged onto the landing.

"I'd better not. There was a weather warning about black ice on the roads. I don't want to be late."

They went downstairs together, and he heaved on his winter coat, then double-checked that he had everything he needed. "Drive carefully", said Eva, reaching up on tiptoe to kiss him. "See you in the morning."

"Goodnight, Evi."

Matthew stepped out into the darkness, and the bitter cold hit him full in the face, causing him to start shivering as he walked the short distance to his car. He was of a rather gloomy turn of mind at times, but could not quite understand why he felt more than usually down at the prospect of leaving the house for a night of heart attacks, black eyes and suicide attempts. He busied himself starting the car and drove away into the night.

"Do you remember anything of what happened?" asked Matthew. The casualty—a woman in early middle age—had been found unconscious on the concourse of a railway platform by a man who had just stepped off a train and had had the presence of mind to call an ambulance. The woman was now fully conscious, if a little confused to find herself amid the bright lights and noise of a busy hospital unit.

"I was running to catch the last train", she said, in the blank, disengaged tone of a person who has had a serious shock. "I think I must have lost my footing and hit my head on the way down. It was a bit slippery, I suppose."

"That would make sense."

"Yes, I think I must have knocked myself out. I can't really remember much until I was in the back of the ambulance." She paused. "I can't feel my fingers."

Matthew nodded. "It looks as though that arm's broken. Is it hurting?"

"It's just starting to."

"Well, we'll send you down for an X-ray now that we're happy your head's in one piece."

"I'm all right then?"

"15 out of 15 on the Glasgow Coma Scale, which means ..."

"Oh, I know", she interrupted with sudden eagerness. "I've heard about that on *Casualty*."

Matthew smiled. He had a quiet loathing of medical dramas, which had slowly turned a generation of Brits into a nation of hypochondriacs. Once upon a time, a person had a headache; now they had a brain tumour because they had seen it on *Casualty*. "You're very lucky someone got out at your station and found you at this time of night. You would have frozen to death if you'd lain there until the morning."

The woman suddenly looked alarmed. "Can't I go home? My husband will be frantic."

"We can make a call for you if you like, but I'm afraid you'll have to stay in tonight for observation. Just a precaution because you knocked yourself out."

The woman was about to start protesting when a young man appeared at Dr Kemble's side. He had the fresh, eager look of a newly qualified doctor who slightly fancies himself as the romantic lead of one of the aforementioned prime-time medical dramas. "Sorry to disturb you", he put in breathlessly. "There's a bit of a situation over here. I wonder if you could possibly ..."

"Yes, yes, just a moment." Matthew turned to one of the nurses. "Can you sort out this lady, please?" He nodded to the woman. "I'm afraid I've got to deal with an emergency. Nurse Deacon here will take care of you now."

"What is it, Harry?" demanded Matthew as he was propeled in the direction of another cubicle.

"Suicide attempt", said Harry. "Multiple drug overdose."

"What's so remarkable about that in a casualty unit?" Matthew asked impatiently. "You've dealt with them before; you know the procedure."

"Of course I do, Dr Kemble. I wouldn't have bothered you with it, but it's just a little complicated ..."

Matthew and Harry arrived at the cubicle and the all-too-familiar scene. A young woman, Matthew guessed in her mid to late twenties, lay unconscious in the bed, whilst another woman of around the same age sat at her side with that rather guilty air about her that so many accompanying friends and relatives had, as though she imagined herself to be personally responsible for the terrible predicament her companion was in. Matthew would barely have noted it if it had not jarred with her otherwise slick, professional demeanour. The companion did not belong by the side of a medical emergency somehow, so beautifully made up for an evidently quite different evening, not a carefully styled hair out of place. It only made the girl in the bed appear all the more pathetic: pale, disheveled and frail like a Victorian portrait of a consumptive waif. There was the offensive smell of alcohol and stale vomit all around her, with traces of it evident around the girl's mouth and on the tips of her hair where her body had rebeled against being poisoned before she had finally passed out. A sorry sight indeed, but a common one.

"I called the ambulance as soon as I found her", said the companion, standing up when she became aware of the doctors' presence. "I wasn't really sure what else to do. I kind of went into autopilot."

"You did the right thing", Matthew reassured her. "Have you any idea how long ago she poisoned herself?"

"No, I've no idea. She was already out of it when I found her. There was sick everywhere."

"Right, well, we'd better get to work. Do you know what she took?"

Harry intervened. "She's diabetic. According to her friend here, it looks as though she took an overdose of insulin, but there were other things. She found the remains of a bottle of vodka and empty packets of other pills—Tamazepam, paracetamol. It looks as though she just took anything she could lay her hands on."

"Right. She'll need a gastric washout." Matthew turned to the companion again. "You—erm—you might want to step outside. It can be rather distressing to watch."

"That's the problem, Dr Kemble", said Harry awkwardly. "This lady says she has a living will."

"I'm sorry, Doctor", the woman said. "I probably shouldn't have even called an ambulance. I just kind of acted on impulse. I thought maybe you could make her comfortable or something." She handed Matthew the advance directive, a crisp, formal legal document, neatly printed on good-quality paper. "She was always very adamant she would not want treatment in a situation like this; she's never liked doctors and hospitals. Sorry."

"No offence", promised Matthew. "What people say and what they want, though ..."

"The living will is quite specific, Doctor. She showed it to me when she made the thing."

Why does she have to sound so relentlessly cold? thought Matthew, then felt immediately guilty for thinking something so harsh as she was almost certainly in shock. What people failed to consider in situations like these was quite how traumatic it was to stumble unsuspectingly over a friend in such a horrendous state, and the woman might well not have had time to take in the enormity of what had happened.

"Would you excuse us a moment, please?" Matthew took Harry's arm and pushed him out of the cubicle. "If I didn't know better, I'd think you were passing the buck."

"Maybe we can get someone to look at this", suggested Harry. "There might be some loophole."

"There's no time. We've no idea how long it is since she took the overdose. She could be dead by the time we've finished looking for a way to cover our backs."

"These things are legally binding. We were warned about this. If you go against her living will, you could end up in really quite a lot of trouble."

"Yes, and if I don't, she will be dead by the morning. She's hardly made it easy for us as it is."

"If it's what she wants."

Matthew stood at the entrance of the cubicle, staring at the piece of paper that was causing all the trouble. The fact was that it was the first time he had ever been presented with such a thing, and he felt an unfamiliar sense of confusion overtaking him. The practice of medicine held very few surprises for a man his age, all those endless little disasters that brought men and women to this place, helpless and frightened. After a few years, it all became quite mundane and perfunctory, but this was different; this was repugnantly, terrifyingly different.

Matthew stepped forward and glanced through the gap between the curtains at the woman lying in the bed, happily unaware of his dilemma. He could hand the case back to Harry now, and no one would be any the wiser. They would keep the woman comfortable as her friend had requested, and in the morning, they would cover her in a sheet and take her to the mortuary. It was hardly as though he had never lost a patient before, and if she were really that determined, she might well be the type to make suicide attempt after suicide attempt until she was finally successful . . .

A second later, Matthew was glaring in Harry's direction, and he knew with the guilt of age and experience that he was going to raise his voice, not because he had anything particular against the man, not for that matter because he was actually angry, but because he would rather come across as the most monstrous tyrant in the patriarchal hegemony than admit he had considered abandoning a patient for a single second. "If she were my daughter, I would want someone to treat her. I wouldn't care about this piece of paper."

"She's not your daughter. You need to be a bit more objective."

Matthew wondered afterwards—and he was to have plenty of time to wonder—whether he would have hesitated just a little while longer if he had not felt so irritated at being lectured by a kid he had lectured himself not so long ago. "I did not train as a doctor so that I could stand back and leave a vulnerable patient to die. I'm sorry you do not feel the same way."

Harry looked away in evident embarrassment. "There is a small question of the patient's rights."

Matthew climbed down from his invisible podium. He knew he sounded like something out of a campaigning leaflet, but it was almost becoming a habit. "I don't have time to have an argument with you, Harry. Call a nurse. I'll need an orogastric tube . . ."

"Yeah. Like you said, I know the procedure."

2

Brookwood Immigration Removal Centre had claims to being one of the nastiest buildings in the whole of England, and it was up against some pretty stiff competition. Maria's heart always sank when her boss sent her to meet a client there, but something about the urgency of working on asylum cases appealed to Maria, with its palpable sense of racing against the clock and the knowledge that there was a human life at stake. When an asylum seeker's claim was turned down, there was usually only a matter of days in which to prevent his deportation and little or no warning beforehand that a decision was imminent. He would go unsuspectingly to the ugly municipal building to sign on as he did every week or every fortnight, only to be tapped on the shoulder by a security guard and informed bluntly that his case had been turned down and he was going to be thrown out of the country.

Before he knew it, and still in a state of shock, he would be locked in a room and allowed the luxury of one phone call—though he was often so distraught that the friend or lawyer at the end of the line would have little idea what he was talking about—before being bundled into the back of a van and driven sometimes for hours to a detention centre. The system was brutal and faceless. No questions would be answered, no reassurances given, no plea listened to. Reports of abuse by "escorts" employed by the private security firms who did the Border Agency's dirty work were common and met with total indifference from the authorities. By the time the unfortunate had arrived at the detention centre, been aggressively searched and locked in a cell, he was usually in no position to wonder how he had come to be sucked into this Soviet-style nightmare, when just a few hours before he had been walking contentedly down a busy London street, thinking about his plans for the afternoon.

Maria's client was one such unfortunate. She was a nineteen-year-old Chinese immigrant who went by the improbable name of Lydia, three and a half months pregnant and due to be deported in eight days' time. Maria knew Brookwood reasonably well and had left plenty of time to go through the tortuous security process before the planned meeting. It should have been almost second nature to her by now, but she never failed to be appalled and bewildered by the whole experience. Standing outside the forbidding concrete building with its razor wire and unmanned checkpoint, Maria always had the feeling that she was leaving her own country altogether and entering some hellish parallel universe without certainties or hope. So few people knew about the existence of these institutions that when she came away from them, she felt unable to speak about what she had come across without the sense that she was asking people to believe there were trolls at the bottom of the garden or that the moon was made of Edam cheese.

Maria braced herself and stepped into a dingy anteroom, where a sullen-looking receptionist fiddling with her nose piercing asked Maria what she wanted. "I'm here to see a prisoner", said Maria.

"You mean a resident", snapped the receptionist. "Stand in front of the camera, please."

"I'm on the system", answered Maria icily. "I should think you have all the biometric information about me you could possibly want."

The receptionist glared at her. "Name?"

Maria handed over her provisional driving licence, a discreet green card which contained all the identifying information she needed. The receptionist glanced at it, typed some details into a computer and pushed it back at Maria with visible contempt. "Through there, and don't forget to hand in your personal effects, including your mobile phone if it's got a camera."

Maria strode over to the lockers fixed to the opposite wall and threw her handbag inside an empty one, retrieving a handful of coins and a notepad and pencil. As she walked through the open door, she glanced back at the receptionist. "Don't want me taking any photos of the inmates then?" she asked.

A security guard marched Maria into a private room and frisked her, taking a particular interest in her hat, counted the coins in her pocket to ensure that she was not carrying more than the limit of £10, then led her through a series of heavy metal doors which opened only after her fingerprints had been scanned. "Terrible weather for the time of year", remarked the guard as they walked along the corridor. His manner was so unbearably congenial that he might have been escorting Maria for tea at Harrods.

17

"Freezing", she managed to answer, only to be struck silent again as they entered the dark, institutional world of the visitors' room. A row of plastic chairs lined one wall facing a security guard seated behind a counter, who scrutinised Maria carefully as she sat down. All over the walls, pinboards were covered with posters screaming official propaganda. One poster showed a picture of a young woman being embraced by an elderly relative beneath the caption "Thinking of returning home? Let us help you." None of the inmates here would have relatives to embrace them when they were thrown out of the country. Another, less colourful poster depicted an Iraqi man looking proudly into the distance and said, "Have you been denied asylum from Iraq or Afghanistan? Go home and help rebuild your country!"

Maria began to fidget, aware that she had not left the view of the CCTV cameras since she first entered the detention centre. The previous week, a planeload of Iraqi refugees had been forcibly dragged back to Baghdad in shackles, an act that had been vocally denounced by human rights groups but that had been largely ignored by the British media. Her eyes hovered over a small, inconspicuous banner in the middle of all this nonsense, printed in pastel shades. It was a quote from Saint Francis de Sales about the need to treat all men with gentleness and compassion. She thought of the dossier she had leafed through in the taxi on the way to this place, cataloguing a string of abuse allegations by former asylum seekers: severe beatings, nerve damage to wrists from being shackled for prolonged periods, the withdrawal of food, obscene verbal and sexual abuse, including young women being stripped to their underwear and chained before being forced onto aeroplanes. She wondered what on earth Saint Francis de Sales would have made of all of this.

"She's ready for you now", said the guard behind the counter. "Press your finger on that ..."

"I know", said Maria, pressing her forefinger on the tiny glass panel near the door. There was a small flash of red light, an unpleasant grating noise and the door heaved open, revealing a larger room, almost empty, furnished with small clusters of chairs positioned an exact distance apart and yet another counter, this time stationed by three guards. Sitting in a corner, as far from the guards as she could manage, was a diminutive girl, clasping and unclasping her hands in her lap. "Lydia?" Maria called, softly so as not to alarm her.

Lydia looked up abruptly and nodded in recognition. "You are from Adamston and Kirkpatrick?"

"Yes", said Maria, sitting opposite the girl and taking out her notepad. "You have asked Jonathan Kirkpatrick to take your case, haven't you?"

"Yes, one of the other inmates said he was good", Lydia said. She had a furtive, rather breathy way of talking, and Maria found herself straining to hear. "My first claim was rejected because they said that even though my father was imprisoned for his political activities, I couldn't prove that I was in any danger, and it doesn't matter if he told me to get out of the country if anything happened to him."

"How long have you been resident in this country?"

"Three years. I arrived just after my sixteenth birthday. I had an English boyfriend and everything."

"Where is he now?"

"He left me when he found out I'm pregnant. It changes everything."

"Hence the need for a new claim." Maria sat back and started taking notes, noticing as she did so that Lydia looked distinctly uncomfortable. "It's all right, I'm just sketching out the case. Your pregnancy will be regarded as unlawful because you are unmarried and also because of your age. If you are returned to China, there is a very high possibility that you will be forced to undergo an abortion or face punitive fines for having the child and be unable to register the child's birth."

"That's right. I don't think people here realise what it is like. The papers always say that the family planning laws are being relaxed, but it's not really true. I don't know what I'll do if they force me to go back. If we could simply delay my departure it would be something, just long enough for me to have the baby. At least the baby would live then, even if life was difficult . . ."

"Let's hope we can do better than that", said Maria, still scribbling. "The first thing we need to do is to get the removal orders canceled. That will give us time to make a fresh claim and put together a really strong case. We also need to try and get you out of detention. It's not a good place for you to be in your condition. Could you quickly tell me what the conditions are like? How have you been treated?"

Lydia glanced towards the security guards awkwardly. "I do wish we could speak somewhere else", she murmured. "This place is really meant for men. They only put me here because there was no room for me anywhere else. They said they would take me somewhere else tomorrow which is meant for women and children and it would be better."

"Try not to look at them. Tell me everything."

"The cell stinks of men. You know what I mean, sweat and smoke, and it wasn't cleaned properly between people. We are locked in all the time, twenty-four hours a day. The cell is terribly damp because the shower in the corner drips all the time, and the toilet makes it smell. There's no air . . ."

"Ventilation?"

"Yes, there's no ventilation. I'm sharing with another woman who's going to be moved with me tomorrow, and, you know, there's no privacy if I need to, you know, use the toilet or anything."

"What about food?"

"They open the door, throw it on the floor, and leave." Lydia's eyes began to glisten. "I mean, why do they have to do that? It's like they want you to feel like an *animal*." She stared down at her hands, which she still clasped and unclasped.

"What about your health? Have you seen a doctor?"

"I asked once, but it's hard to keep asking. Everyone shouts so much."

Maria closed her notepad. "All right, it should be better at the other place, but we still need to get you out." She stood up. "We should be able to get the removal orders stopped." They walked towards the door, but Maria found herself lingering, unwilling to walk away and leave the girl behind.

"You had better go", said Lydia finally, sensing Maria's reluctance. "I'll be all right. You'll be late enough home as it is."

The thought went around Maria's head, as she was walked back through the endless creaking doors, *but why can't I just take her with me? Why can't I just take her by the hand and walk with her out of this place? It ought to be so easy.*

Back at reception, Maria retrieved her personal effects from the locker and walked towards the door. "Ex*cuse* me", said the receptionist with an indignant squeak. "I need your ID." Maria walked back to the counter, rummaged in her purse and slammed her provisional driving licence onto the desk. She was greeted by a thunderous scowl. "And what exactly would you be wanting me to do with this, love?"

"I thought you said you wanted my ID?"

The receptionist rolled her eyes. "No, I wanted the thing around your neck, if it's not too much trouble." Maria glanced down at the label she had been given on arrival, with her name and photograph on it. "Yes, that's right." Maria felt her temper rising. She dragged the cord over her head and threw it onto the counter. "Well done, dearest. Didn't hurt, did it?"

Maria brought her fists down onto the counter with a crash—rather more loudly than she had envisaged—releasing an exhilarating wave of rage that had been building for the past hour. "Who do you think you're talking down to, you pathetic waste of space?" The receptionist shrank back in astonishment. "If you hate your disgusting little excuse for a job so much that you have to behave like that, *get another one! Get a life whilst you're at it!*"

As Maria leant over the counter, convulsing with pent-up frustration, she just had time to hear the sound of an alarm shrieking around her before two burly men pounced on her and wrestled her to the ground.

3

"You know something?" remarked Jonathan, as they clambered into the back of a taxi. "When I got the phone call from the police station this morning, I was half tempted to leave you there to cool your heels. What on earth were you thinking of?"

"I'm not sure I was really thinking", admitted Maria, shivering. She looked as though she had spent the entire night running through a howling storm: her hair was unkempt; the last traces of makeup had smudged, particularly her mascara; and her clothes were crumpled from having been slept in. "I'm awfully sorry."

"Awfully sorry is really quite inadequate", was the only response she could reasonably have expected. "I send you to a detention centre to interview a client, and you end up in shackles yourself. I'm not accustomed to having to bail out colleagues. Have you any idea— you're shivering, are you cold?"

"Not exactly. I just feel peculiar. It was freezing cold in that cell though. I ended up huddling up under pages of the *Financial Times*. Didn't sleep a wink." She closed her eyes. There had been many humiliating moments in little Maria's life; it was almost part of the job description. She could have recalled the drizzly morning she had been standing outside the Chinese embassy protesting against forced abortion and a policeman on a horse had clip-clopped up to her to ask her her business. The policeman had been in the process of relieving her of her permit to hold a protest when the horse had been caught short and relieved itself on her ... but nothing could beat the indignity of being thrown onto the floor by two security guards, having her wrists shackled behind her back in case she tried to make a break for it whilst the police arrived, going through the formalities of arrest and being bundled into the back of a waiting panda car. In case she had had any self-respect left by the time she arrived at the police station, she was then forced to remove her shoelaces and hair scrunchy in case she tried to commit suicide and—horror of unspeakable horrors—after a hellish night locked in a police cell, she had to face the sight of her smirking boss when he arrived to bail her out in the morning. "I got all the information you wanted if it helps."

"You mustn't let these people get to you", said Jonathan, refusing to be distracted. "You'll be qualified soon. How will you ever cope in a high-pressure situation if you're that easily riled?"

"Shall I get right to work on it? I won't feel relaxed about this case until she is out of there. It's a terrible place for a pregnant woman." Maria blinked blearily out of the window. "Where are we going?"

"You're in no fit state to start work", Jonathan said. "I'm having you dropped off at your house. Have a bath, have some breakfast and then get some sleep. I'll see you this afternoon looking a little more like a member of the human race."

"What about my case?"

"I shouldn't worry about that; they're unlikely to press charges. The UK Border Agency doesn't really like drawing negative attention to itself. 'Young woman nicked at detention centre' won't make a very good headline in *The Guardian*." Jonathan's mobile phone began chiming out *Land of Hope and Glory*. Maria used the welcome break to close her eyes again. It was a little like having a hangover, except she had never had the pleasure of getting drunk, but she wallowed all the same in the warm, slightly confusing weariness that surrounded her. She imagined she was in her cosy bedroom, swathed in that glorious pink duvet of which she was so fond. Beneath her door crept the smell of bacon and eggs as her landlady cooked her a hearty breakfast ...

"Change of plan", declared Jonathan like a retired brigadier, causing her to jolt awake. "We'll wait for you here. Dash in and get yourself a change of clothes. Small emergency's cropped up."

"But—but ..."

"It's all right, you're young, you run on adrenaline. I'll stand you breakfast."

The Kaptain's Kabin was the sort of greasy spoon cafe Maria would never normally have been seen dead in, but she would have let her boss lead her unresisting into an opium den for breakfast in the state she was in. It had taken her just five minutes to let herself into her house, rush up the stairs and make herself presentable, a personal record. She had vague memories of tearing her clothes off in the middle of her bedroom, covering herself in anything scented she

23

could find—pineapple and coconut buttermilk, strawberry cream body lotion, tropicana body spray, vanilla and pistachio talcum powder—anything at all to take away the smell of incarceration, then throwing on a clean set of clothes, tidying up her hair and racing back down the stairs in time to collide with her landlady in the hall.

"Where on earth have you been?" she asked, as Maria took a dive for the door like an infantry soldier climbing the parapet.

"I'll explain later", panted Maria from the front porch. "It's complicated."

"You really do smell like a fruit cocktail that's been left in the sun a bit too long", commented Jonathan, taking her firmly by the arm. "You're sleepwalking. Don't worry, you'll feel better in a minute."

The cafe was starting to empty out after the early morning rush of builders and lorry drivers getting their breakfast, and Maria was overcome by the mingling smells of deep fat fryers, bacon, chips and coffee. "What have you brought me here for?" she bleated, as Jonathan sat her down at a corner table near a steamy window.

"I fancy a cooked breakfast. Aha!" Maria looked up to see a middle-aged man in a long winter coat and trilby hat standing in the doorway. He was around Jonathan's age, she thought, but with softer features and old-fashioned steel-rimmed spectacles that gave him the scholarly, reliable air of a country doctor. He was the sort of chap you would immediately trust, which was strange because the sight of him set her ever so slightly on edge, and she was too sleepy to work out why. "Come and sit down, Matthew." He motioned to Maria. "You know Maria, don't you?"

"We've met before", she said, recalling where she had seen him. "I thought I recognised your face. You spoke at the medical ethics conference in Oxford last year ... and at the colloquium on the End of Life Care Bill. Dr Kemble, isn't it?"

"That's right, well remembered", he said, settling himself into the chair opposite her. He had evidently been brought up very properly never to slouch and sat up with his back impeccably straight, though Maria sensed that he was as exhausted as she was. There were the telltale smudges under his eyes of a person who has gone without sleep and is now suffering for it. "Do you work for Jonathan?" he asked.

"Yes, that's right. I was at the Catholic Institute before."

"Excellent. You're training to be a solicitor then?" He looked at her expectantly for an answer, but for some confused reason not even

24

known to Maria, she was finding the small talk impossible to sustain. "I say, are you all right? You seem to be shaking."

Jonathan joined them. "Right, I've ordered us all Olympic breakfasts and plenty of coffee. Sorry if Maria's a bit dopey this morning, Matt, she spent last night in cells. Can't get the staff."

Matthew flinched. "You have my sympathies, my dear."

"Sorry", mumbled Jonathan. "You must be climbing the walls."

"I can't say I'm bearing up as well as I ought. I'm afraid it has all come as rather a shock."

"Don't worry about a thing, Matt, we'll get you out of this." Jonathan turned to Maria, who had pulled herself together admirably. "Matthew and I go back a long way. We were at school together. He rang me on my mobile when we were in the taxi earlier because some cretin has accused him of assault." She giggled. "Is something funny?"

"Sorry." She could feel herself reddening. "No—no offence. It's just you don't exactly look like a lecher."

"Not that sort of assault, you idiot!"

Maria was relieved when an enormous woman in a gingham housecoat appeared with three huge plates of food. "Coffee's coming", she announced, placing the plates in front of them. "Half a mo."

"Don't you ever feed this child?" asked Matthew, watching Maria launch herself at the mound of sausages, bacon, eggs, beans, mushrooms, hash browns and fried bread before her. "Fortunate I'm not a cardiologist really." He glanced down at his own plate with an evident lack of enthusiasm. "Look here, Jon, I feel awful bothering you about this, but I've no idea what to do. Never in twenty-five years have I ever received so much as a mild reprimand. I've never incurred any points on my driving licence; I've never even been late paying a bill. I didn't suspect anything at all when the police arrived at my door. My heart was in my mouth because I thought they were going to tell me a relative had died, not that they needed to ask me a few questions."

"All right, Matthew, can you tell me exactly what happened? Do try to eat something, by the way."

"I'm really not hungry. I'll only see it all again within the hour."

"Come on now, old chap, you're not going to go to pieces on me, are you? You need to tell me what happened on the night in question. What did you actually *do*?"

Matthew sank a little into his chair. It was the second of many times in the coming months that he would be forced to relive the events of a night about which he would otherwise have quickly forgotten. "A girl was brought in after a suicide attempt. The friend who called the ambulance and accompanied her to hospital handed me her living will. I went ahead and treated her."

Matthew had treated so many drug overdoses during his career that the motions of the procedure had been quite mechanical. He had fed a tube down her throat. Since the girl was out cold she did not resist, though he noted that the gag reflex still kicked in when the tube touched the back of her throat, but even so the process of rinsing out her stomach had been the straightforward part of the treatment. She had not made it easy to save her life. In her despair and possibly panic, the woman had simply taken whatever drugs she could lay her hands on. Paracetamol was a commonly abused drug found in most homes, but she had appeared not to have taken very many as she had escaped major liver damage. The sleeping pills must have been prescribed to her, possibly years before and hoarded, or she had obtained them illegally, not at all difficult with so many online traders touting for business. She might even have bought them off a friend who was foolish enough not to realise that it was illegal to sell unused medication. As to the insulin, it was almost too easy a temptation for a depressed diabetic to overdose herself, and it had triggered hypoglycaemia and hypotension, putting her into a coma.

"She's still in the coma", he said, as though this were the worst possible coda to his story.

"Will she come out of it?"

"Oh, yes, no real worry there, though the overdose of sleeping pills might well have left her with temporary brain damage—memory loss, inability to concentrate, that sort of thing—but that will pass in time. Hopefully, she will make a full recovery, get the psychiatric help she needs and rebuild her life."

"And you in the meantime have been charged with assault."

"Not formally charged with anything. I wasn't actually arrested. The police came to the door and said they wanted to talk to me because they said that an allegation had been made by the girl's brother. He said to them that he thought I had treated her unlawfully as she had shown a settled wish not to be treated under such circumstances."

Jonathan brightened up. "You know, they might well decide not to press charges then. In fact, they probably won't. The Boys in Blue have decided to do some sabre rattling, you know, given you a bit of a scare, but the Crown Prosecution Service would be hard pushed to claim that putting a doctor on trial for treating somebody would be in the public interest." He descended into silence for a minute. "Though it would be really quite interesting if they did."

Matthew looked askance at him and for the first time became positively animated. "Are you *mad*?"

"Possibly."

"Have you no notion of what this means to me? If I end up with a criminal conviction, I could face prison, I'll be struck off. I—I have a young family. We'll lose *everything*."

The arrival of the coffee plunged the table into taut silence. "I'm sorry, Matthew, I don't mean it like that. I know what it would mean if you were convicted, but first you would have to be convicted, and you haven't even been charged yet. What I mean is that this could be *big*. I mean a huge test case. You're being accused of assault because you treated a dying woman who had been rushed into Accident and Emergency after a suicide attempt. You did so in the full knowledge that she had a living will and had requested no treatment in such an event. In that single act of following your conscience as a doctor, you defied an unjust law. That's what I mean when I say it could be big."

Matthew looked miserably down at his breakfast. He had picked up a piece of fried bread and proceeded to break it into small morsels. "I wasn't defying anything; I was simply doing what I have done hundreds of times before. The woman was seriously ill. I had the power to save her. It would have been unconscionable to leave her to die; I could never have lived with myself. I don't believe even a government bureaucrat would have been that heartless."

Maria glanced at the man's sad face and thought of Lydia sitting in that detention centre awaiting news of her fate. Through her mind ran images of the interminable little cogs in the hideous bureaucratic machine that kept people like Lydia locked away from the world—the government officials with their colourless jargon and sound bytes; the businessmen whose companies were paid to run the centres; the endless administrators and security guards processing forms, locking and unlocking doors, obeying orders; the men who drove the caged vans; the escorts who marched the failed cases onto planes and dumped them at their final destination; the journalists who papered over the evidence ... She clutched her head, staggering under the weight of a relentless barrage of poker-faced persons, cocooned like grotesque caterpillars by procedures and procedures and procedures and procedures ... "A government bureaucrat *would* be heartless enough to let a woman die," said Maria out loud, "as long as the correct procedures were put in place."

"I say, are you sure you're all right?" asked Matthew, but Maria was miles away. With her breakfast finished, she felt peculiarly hot and drowsy, quite unable to move.

"Sleep deprivation, and it's her own silly fault", declared Jonathan, standing up abruptly. "Matt, why don't you get Maria into a taxi whilst I settle up? I won't be a minute. We've all got work to do."

"Anyone would think I was the drunken tart at the office party", Maria whimpered, but five minutes later, she was in the back of another black cab, dozing off on the arm of a man she barely knew from Adam but who was too much of a gentleman to ask her to move.

4

As soon as Matthew arrived home, he went straight up to his study in search of information. To call it a study was putting it in rather too dignified terms; the room was a converted attic, dingily lit by a small skylight which he seldom got round to cleaning, containing a cheap desk and chair he had bought flat pack from a do-it-yourself store years ago, an Anglepoise lamp and a radio. It was never the right temperature—too cold during the months of the year when the central heating was off, stiflingly hot during the months it was on when the warm air from the entire house wafted up in his direction—not at all like his father's smart little domain at the back of the house where he had grown up, with its creaking antique bureau and treasured oil paintings lining the walls. Like his father himself, that room had had gravitas, and Matthew had entered it as a child only with the greatest trepidation.

This was, however, Matthew's one private space where he could escape the racket of small children squabbling whenever he needed to think. He sat at his desk and from one of the drawers pulled out a file labeled "End of Life Care Bill—GCW". He had never admitted it to anyone, but GCW was his abbreviation for Grumpy Catholic Work because the director of a campaigning organisation with which he had been involved at the time had said that there were certain tasks only a person who was grumpily in love with the Catholic Church could possibly do, and he was one such person.

It had been an ugly campaign, Matthew remembered. The bill had been phrased in sufficiently innocuous terms that it had slipped under the radar of many people who would otherwise have been up in arms; religious groups had remained silent; the Catholic hierarchy, keen as ever to appease the establishment they fondly believed they were influencing, had acquiesced. The bill had been a government bill rather than a private members' bill, meaning that MPs from the governing party had been obliged to support it. To cap it all, some campaigning organisations that might have opposed the bill had been persuaded to support it and campaign only for amendments.

Matthew's folder bulged with the archived history of the campaign, his endless correspondences with MPs and bishops, the tedious standard replies to his concerns that his "views had been carefully noted" but were so obviously wrong. Newspaper cuttings, articles, reports from public meetings, scribbled notes from private ones ...

Matthew flicked through page after page before pulling out a couple of sheets of paper stapled together, entitled "Memorandum: Bishop McEvoy's meeting at Saint Mary Magdalen". That had been the moment, he thought, glancing over the notes, when he had realised without doubt how vulnerable doctors like him would become if the law passed. It was also the reason he remembered Maria's face, because she had been the one who had initiated the argument that had made the meeting so memorable. He sat back in his chair, the notes in front of him, and switched on the radio, which immediately began to resonate with the soft sounds of Debussy. And he cast his mind back to that unremarkable church hall and the moment he had caught a glimpse of the horror that awaited him.

Bishop Luke McEvoy spoke for over an hour before opening the floor to questions. Maurice Allen in the chair ...

Bishop McEvoy always enjoyed public meetings like this. The audience in the parish hall of Saint Mary Magdalen's church was fairly typical of his diocese and typically self-selecting. A sea of grey hair washed across the hall, contaminated in places by a few younger people who had seen the notice in the bulletin and had some interest, perhaps of a professional nature, in the subject of the meeting: "The End of Life Care Bill: The Church's Response". The chairman, a permanent deacon called Maurice, tapped on the microphone to get people's attention and began introducing the Bishop to the background noise of the audience settling down. There was complete silence by the time Bishop McEvoy began speaking.

"Good evening, everyone. It is such a pleasure to be welcomed to your beautiful parish ..." The Bishop had a congenial tone and could not help enjoying the sense that people were warming to him. He was an accomplished speaker with years of experience putting people at ease, and he was following a well-worn format; he made his introductory remarks, told an amusing anecdote about the day his mother had lost her false teeth and he began to realise she was getting a little confused, before moving on to the more pressing business of the meeting. "It is a very good bill", he said, like a secondhand car dealer presenting a cheeky little motor with only three wheels. "One mustn't listen to the emotional lunatics and their nasty little campaigns. Living wills are an excellent idea; they give people the chance to make choices about their end of life care. It's all about putting people in control of their own lives, and what could possibly be wrong with that?"

He strode across the platform in a relaxed fashion. "That reminds me, I really must make my living will." There was an encouraging patter of laughter. "You must all make a living will. It is a very good idea. In fact, I think Catholics should be taking the lead." He looked up and became aware of a young woman, dressed in a crisp trouser suit, shuffling abruptly to her feet. "Yes, my dear?" His tone remained congenial, but a little uncertain now. Interruptions always threw him off course, and he sensed trouble coming. "Do you have a question?"

"If I may, my lord?"

Her formal tone unnerved him even more, and he would have liked nothing better than to tell her to get lost. If she had been the sort of young person with whom he got along, she would have been dressed in jeans and a hoodie, and she would have called him simply "Father". "Certainly", he managed to say. "This is a public meeting, after all. It's all about brainstorming and exchanging ideas." He chuckled nervously. "Don't want to monopolise the platform or anything."

"Thank you. Let me introduce myself. Emotional lunatic who has a problem with this bill, but you might want to listen anyway." A shudder of surprise ran through the audience, that sound of feet shuffling and voices murmuring to one another that punctuates an unexpected turn of events. "I'm a little confused by you supporting living wills when there are very serious concerns about them. You are asking people to make plans for a hypothetical situation they cannot possibly anticipate and to which they may be held. This bill would codify in law a definition of medical treatment as including food and fluids, meaning that people may be left to starve and dehydrate to death."

"That's a rather emotive way of putting it, if I may say so", Bishop McEvoy burst in, sensing an Achilles' heel to the girl's argument. "The whole issue of food and fluids is very complex. There are no easy answers. I certainly do not have an answer when it comes to the withdrawal of food and fluids under certain circumstances."

"That's all right, my lord", she reassured him, when all her tone did was to set his teeth on edge. "The Holy Father seems to have an answer. In the case of persistent vegetative state ..."

"Exactly! I'm so glad you brought that up. PVS is a case in point. No one, least of all me, wants to see a person's death hastened, but with PVS you are pretty much keeping a dead body alive. There are no right and wrong answers here, I have no answers ..."

"It's all right, my lord", she persisted—and even Matthew, who never normally noticed these things, could hear the sarcastic tone creeping in. "As I said, the Holy Father has a few. Perhaps he should have come to address the meeting today."

There was another ripple of laughter throughout the hall, this time less friendly, and Bishop McEvoy felt himself breaking into a sweat. He was a great believer in female emancipation; he just wished they'd go and be emancipated somewhere else, disappear into their gender agenda committee meetings or something. Meditate in circles around a brick about their subjugation by evil male celibates, anything at all other than get in his way. "I think we're on the same side, and—well, I entirely appreciate your concerns." Affirmation and all that. "We are all concerned about the bill and its potential consequences. I—we all realise that there are problems with the bill, but as Catholics we should not be afraid of it or indeed afraid of supporting it."

"But what about the doctors and nurses who will have to carry out the dictates of this bill if it passes into law?" demanded Maria, and she was almost pleading this time. "What if a doctor is told to stand back and leave a person to die because he has a living will that specifies no treatment or his attorney instructs the doctor not to treat him? What if a nurse is forced to withdraw food and fluids from a patient for the same reason and has to watch him slowly dehydrating without having the power to save him? What on earth is a doctor to do in such a situation?"

Bishop McEvoy hesitated and looked down at his feet whilst he pondered his answer. The room was completely silent now, and he knew he could not afford to make a mistake. The fact was that the bill about which he was so enthusiastically speaking might indeed leave doctors in an impossible situation, forced either to withdraw from the case and effectively abandon their patients or to follow instructions that went against the dictates of the Hippocratic Oath. It was a worst-case scenario and one that was unlikely to become common practice, but saying so would hardly help, and he knew he could not simply dismiss the problem now. "I think there are situations where a doctor could make a stand in good conscience, even if it meant facing prosecution."

"And would you stand by such a doctor?"

Something snapped; she was setting a trap for him. "That would depend upon the facts, wouldn't it?" he blustered. "And only a judge would know the facts."

"I take it that's a no, then?"

"I really think we need to move on now", came a new voice to the proceedings, as the chairman appeared at the microphone, and the entire audience realised that they had completely forgotten about him. "No more interventions from the floor until the end of the session, please."

And that has been that, thought Matthew, putting the notes back in the file and opening the drawer where it lived. Abandonment. He had known, as Maria had clearly known, as all the emotional lunatics who had campaigned unsuccessfully against the bill had known, that if the bill passed into law, it would only be a matter of time before some conscientious doctor fell foul of it, and that when they did they would face the consequences alone. Nobody with any power, with any authority to help the man—or woman—concerned would come to his assistance.

Maria, who had finally been permitted to go home and was struggling to sleep, stared up at the ceiling and mused on exactly the same question: Who on earth would consider standing by a doctor accused of assaulting an unconscious patient? She sat bolt upright in her bed. "You are not alone!" she called out to the empty bedroom, like Frodo Baggins at the Council of Elrond. "You are not alone. The lie will not come into the world through me."

5

Matthew had only been home from work for half an hour when the doorbell rang. Thomas, desperate for a diversion from his homework, made a leap for the door. "Don't!" ordered Eva, rushing after him. "I'll get it. Why don't you join the others in the garden?"

Thomas was not stupid and knew that something infinitely exciting must be lurking behind the front door for his mother to suggest that he leave the kitchen table and the complexities of the solar system behind. He scurried towards the back door and hovered awkwardly, one foot in the kitchen, the other in the garden, waiting to see what would happen, whilst Eva braced herself and opened the door. Two police officers were standing on the doorstep. "Mrs Kemble?" asked the older of the two, a man aged, she thought, about thirty-five. "I think we had better come in."

"Oh, my God", Eva whimpered, as they brushed past her. She managed to call, "Darling, there are some people to see you", a second before the policemen stepped into the sitting room, where Matthew had got up from the armchair where he had been reading the paper.

"Don't worry, Evi, I'll deal with this", said Matthew calmly. "Just keep the children in the garden." Eva hesitated, unwilling to leave her husband alone with the force of the law bearing down on him, but he signaled to her that it was all right for her to go, and she slipped out, almost knocking into Thomas as she went.

"For goodness' sake, Tommy!" she shouted, only to feel immediately guilty for taking out her panic on him. He looked up her at with those huge, reproachful brown eyes that had got him out of so many tellings-off in the past. "I'm sorry, Tommy, but you shouldn't have been listening in."

"I didn't hear anything", he said, as though that solved a problem. "Mummy, why are there policemen here?"

"They just need to talk to Daddy for a minute", she said, shoving the child in the direction of the garden, but the others had heard the doorbell and come inside to see what the fuss was about. "We mustn't disturb them. Daddy needs to help them with something, that's all."

Parenthood is full of lies, thought Eva miserably, as she tried desperately to think of a suitable diversion for four curious children. *And they know I am lying.*

Meanwhile, Matthew almost felt relieved. Despite Jonathan's reassurance, he had known from the tone of the police officers' previous questioning that it was only a matter of time before he was formally arrested, and the anticipation had been unbearable. The urge to cut and run, the increasing paranoia he had felt, constantly wondering when they would come for him—at work, as he walked to the news agent's, as he sat having dinner with his family. Then there had been the thinly disguised awkwardness and even hostility from some of his colleagues, who seemed either uncertain as to whether they should associate with him at all or positively to want him to vanish from their lives. Now that the moment had come, he felt as though he had stepped into a d-list police drama and simply needed to go through the paces of a scripted performance.

"As you know, Dr Kemble," said the senior police officer, "some very serious allegations have been made about you."

"One allegation, as far as I am aware", said Matthew. "I know why you have come."

"I am arresting you on a charge of assault and battery." Matthew waited for him to say, "You have the right to remain silent, but anything you say may be recorded and used in evidence against you." Then he remembered that the right to silence had been abolished amid the tidal wave of legislative changes the country had undergone in the past decade. Instead, he heard the rather less reassuring words: "You do not have to say anything. But it might harm your defence if you do not mention when questioned something which you later rely on in court. Anything you do say may be given in evidence."

The younger officer, who looked about twelve years old, took out a set of handcuffs. Matthew shrank back in alarm. "I'm sorry, sir, but it is standard procedure."

"Have you taken leave of your senses?" exclaimed Matthew. "I'm not resisting arrest. You can't march me out of my house in handcuffs in front of my children!"

"Put your jacket on, Dr Kemble", instructed the senior officer, indicating the long, dark coat hanging up on the inside of the door. "We'll be very discreet for the sake of the kids."

35

Matthew put on his coat and suddenly noticed that his hands were shaking; he was going to panic. He almost wished that they had arrested him in some more anonymous location; his own hospital would have been an improvement, even if it had meant being arrested in front of his colleagues and patients. The invasion into his domestic life threw him off balance completely. Never had his children witnessed so much as a family argument before. "How on earth is this discreet?" he asked, holding out his hands. "Just get on with it. This is ludicrous."

Outside the room, the younger children had sensed the menace in the house and were in floods of tears, making it impossible for Matthew so much as to look at them. Eva stepped purposefully forward. "What do you want me to do?" she asked quietly.

"Just phone Jonathan." He kissed her. "Hopefully I will be back soon." He held his nerve and looked at the children. "It's all right. I'm going to help these people solve a case", he said, trying to sound as upbeat as possible, but the younger ones did not understand what he meant, and Thomas and Cecilia knew perfectly well he was a liar. Grownups were hopeless at hiding fear.

Matthew could still hear the sound of his children crying as he stepped outside, and Eva was not quite quick enough closing the door to block Angelina's indignant yell. "Daddy! Come *back*!" They would always remember this, he thought wretchedly, feeling the pressure of the two officers nudging him in the direction of the waiting car. However this ended, it was one of those moments that would haunt them all their lives, even perhaps little Angelina. He settled himself into the back of the car as best he could but found that his hands were still shaking, and this time he was not sure if it was fear or anger. His own father, who had served as a doctor during the war, had said to him once, "Be a man of principle, but if you are going to go to the stake, let it be for something important, because you will never be the only one to suffer."

At that moment, Matthew really was not sure for what he was going to the stake, but he doubted his father would have understood the Britain in which he was living any more than Matthew did. He was adrift.

Having only ever entered a police station once, when he was a student at Cambridge reporting the theft of his bicycle, Matthew was not very sure what to expect when he was escorted into a small room for questioning. It was a pretty indistinct sort of a room, containing a desk and three chairs with what looked like video-recording equipment on the wall. The shackles were removed from his hands, and he was instructed to sit down whilst the two officers settled themselves opposite him. An awkward sense of being in the headmaster's office bothered him, and he noticed his knuckles smarting, but dear Father Cleary's study had been positively homely compared with this, with its bay window overlooking the playing fields and its shelves full of books. And even a Jesuit would not have gone so far as to humiliate him in front of his entire family, lock him up and ruin his life.

"Are you filming this?" asked Matthew vaguely, pointing at the recording equipment. It was no good. He felt flustered and panicky, quite incapable of concentrating. "Would you mind awfully if I took my coat off?"

"Yes, we are filming this," said the senior officer, "and yes, you may remove your coat." Matthew was relieved to have been given something to do. When he sat down again, the officer continued, "We need to ask you a few questions, Dr Kemble."

Matthew's bewildered mind snapped into focus; Jonathan had warned him about this bit. "I'm not prepared to make any comment whatsoever until my solicitor arrives."

"That's all right, sir", said the junior officer. "You're entitled to a phone call."

"I don't think that will be necessary. My wife rang my solicitor when I left the house."

Matthew could not recall ever having been deliberately locked in a room before and found himself quaking in his shoes when he was left alone to await the arrival of Jonathan. *This is pathetic*, he chided himself, sitting with his head in his hands. *Your ancestors were recusants!* He often tried to recall the tribulations of his Elizabethan forefathers to keep his own anxieties in perspective; the crippling fines, the public disgrace, the raids on their houses, the many arrests and imprisonments and in one case a slow death by hanging ... but it did nothing to distract him now. Round and round his head went images of his panic-stricken children, Eva desperately trying to be brave, the endless stream of open questions about what he was going to do if his career came to an end, the prospect of losing everything. If he was forced to leave medicine, he would ever after be known as the disgraced doctor.

He would be financially ruined, and they would almost certainly lose their home. In the silence of the locked room, Matthew let his mind slip along the darkest possible journey, through conviction and public disgrace and bankruptcy and a future in which he would never be able to hold up his head again. His thoughts were punctuated by flashbacks of the night at the hospital, the moment when he had made the decision. He saw himself back home phoning in sick, he saw himself in a broken-down car unable to get to work, he imagined every possible reason why he might not have been on duty when that particular casualty was brought before him. In his cowardice he wished so desperately that he had been anywhere else.

"Well, you were there," said an acerbic voice beside him, "and it was you. Do you usually talk to yourself?"

Matthew looked up wearily. "Jonathan, thank God you're here. I've been arrested."

"Yes, I rather thought you had been. Let's get down to business, shall we?"

Matthew watched Jonathan's precise, cheerful movements as he removed his coat, took a palmtop from his bag and sat down opposite Matthew. "I've no idea what to do in a police interview", he admitted. "Is it anything like the films?"

"Well, they're not going to beat a confession out of you, if that's what you mean", promised Jonathan with a smile. "Pull yourself together, man. You're not alone now. In a few hours this part will all be over, and you will be back home with your family."

"They—they won't keep me here, then?"

Jonathan chuckled. "Oh, no, dear me, no. You're not a serial killer; they have enough of a capacity problem as it is. Just answer the questions. Then you will be let out on bail, and you'll stay out until the trial. Assuming it comes to trial. Now, as to your answers, tell them the truth about what happened that night. Don't bring in any moral arguments; don't make any comments about the legitimacy of the law. Simply make it clear that you were acting in good faith as a doctor and had the best interests of the patient at heart. It's utterly ridiculous that such a case should have gone quite so far already."

"That sounds straightforward enough."

"Don't dither, don't pontificate. Don't feel obliged to give them information they do not need. I would suggest a slight pause before you open your mouth; it helps to ensure the brain is engaged."

38

"Anyone would think", Matthew protested a second before the police reappeared, "that I was some blundering geriatric who needed a minder."

"No comment."

TRANSCRIPT OF POLICE INTERVIEW BETWEEN DETECTIVE CONSTABLES LAWRENCE KERR AND MICHAEL HORNE AND DR MATTHEW KEMBLE

DC: Matthew, please explain your movements on the night of 22 February.

MK: I was on a night shift at the Edith Cavell Hospital.

DC: This was your usual place of work?

MK: Yes, I have been a consultant at that hospital for seven years.

DC: How long have you been qualified?

MK: Over twenty-five years.

DC: Have you ever been the subject of a complaint?

MK: No, certainly not. Never in my entire career has any patient or colleague made a complaint against me. My record is entirely clean.

DC: Back to the night of 22 February. In your own words, describe your movements.

MK: I drove to the hospital.

DC: I meant your movements at the hospital.

MK: I came on duty at eight o'clock. There was handover—you know, the staff going off duty handing over cases.

DC: Is this a lengthy process?

MK: Oh, no, not really. Casualties move in and out of Accident and Emergency quite quickly normally. Once they're seen, they are usually discharged or transferred to a ward. It wasn't a particularly busy evening, the usual flow of patients.

DC: What sort of patients?

MK: Well, you know, people who'd had accidents. There were a few broken bones, if I remember rightly, a suspected heart attack. A couple of cases of alcohol poisoning, concussion ...

DC: Does the name Daisy Havisham mean anything to you?

MK: No comment.

MK's legal representative: It's a question of medical confidentiality, Constable.

DC: I understand the doctor's concern, but he is entitled to disclose information within a police interview. Matthew, did you treat a woman by the name of Daisy Havisham?

MK: I'm afraid—well, it's not very easy to remember names. Well, there are so many of them, and one doesn't tend to retain the information. But I did see a woman that night by the name of Daisy. Would that be who you mean?

DC: In your own words, Matthew, what exactly were your dealings with her?

MK: I was treating another patient when a colleague asked my advice about a situation.

DC: The colleague's name?

MK: Dr Harry Anderson. I went with him and saw the casualty. She was a young woman, unconscious. He told me that she had taken an overdose involving multiple drugs, including insulin, but she had a living will and was not supposed to be treated.

DC: But you did treat her, didn't you?

MK: Yes, I did. It seemed to be the only appropriate thing to do under the circumstances.

DC: You understood clearly that she had a living will?

MK: Yes, her friend showed it to me.

DC: You were in no doubt that she had requested not to be treated in such a situation?

MK: I understood that to be the case, but ...

40

DC: So you treated her in the knowledge that she did not want to be treated?

MK: Look, the girl was dying. Her friend could not even say how long she had been unconscious when she found her. She might have taken the overdose several hours before. If I had wasted time analysing the living will, it might well have been too late. I had to act quickly.

DC: Were you warned that you might face prosecution if you proceeded to treat her against her will?

MK: I am more than aware of the law, sir. I was not prepared to leave her to die.

ENDS

6

Maria loved the grandeur of the High Court: its vast stone arches, its sweeping spiral staircases and the restrained buzz of urgent activity everywhere. One of the things she found most attractive about the legal scene was the sense of it all being so rooted in history. She liked the idea of being a part of this peculiarly English mixture of ancient and modern, the judges in their enormous wigs and robes, the barristers talking frantically into their state-of-the-art mobile phones. Some of the most notorious criminals in English history had been tried in this building; some of the most significant decisions on the future of the country had been determined here. In a few years' time, Jonathan promised her, she would have lost her sense of awe, but for now Maria felt pleasantly overwhelmed by it all.

She knew where to go to for her particular errand and moved purposefully through the building, lingering momentarily in the bear garden, where her footsteps were hushed by the thick pile carpet, and she felt the first sunshine of spring touching her face through the windows. Her client—a Chinese priest in exile in London—was waiting for her when she arrived, shuffling nervously on a bench. He stood up as soon as he saw her coming. "You are from Adamston and Kirkpatrick?"

"That's right", she said. "Maria Hargreaves." They shook hands formally. "I'm sorry I was a little delayed. I hope you've not been waiting long?"

"I have brought the fee", he said, opening his briefcase and passing her a brown envelope. "What do you think the chances are? I did an appeal at the parish, but you know even your small fee is quite hard for us. I'm not sure we can run into any more legal costs, but we don't want to give up on our poor friend either."

Maria discreetly counted the bank notes before stuffing the envelope into her own bag and bringing out a receipt for them both to sign. "It's all right. There won't be any more fees. I will now submit the paperwork to cancel her removal orders and apply for a judicial review. That will give us time to put together a new case based upon her pregnancy, and if we fail there, we can appeal again. If necessary we can try to fight this as far as the European Court of Human Rights, but I think we have to be realistic about her chances. Unfortunately, we are likely to have difficulty persuading the Home Office that she is at genuine risk if she is sent back to China."

"But it is so obvious!" exclaimed the priest. "Anyone who knows about China must realise that? If she returns to China pregnant, certainly she will lose the child. They might be waiting for her at the airport."

"I know that, and you know that," said Maria, "but it is more a case of whether the Home Office wants to know that. They're sending people back to Afghanistan. We'll do everything we can, even if it is just a case of stalling Lydia's removal until after the baby is born, but I hope we can do better than that. In the meantime, is there anybody who can bail her out? She really should not stay in a detention centre in her condition."

"Yes, a local family said they would do that for her. They know her from the parish and have room to put her up."

"Good. I have a list of things they will need to provide me with to set the ball rolling. ID, bank statements, proof of address et cetera."

The priest took the signed receipt and the list she had given him, along with another bundle of paperwork. "What's this for?" he asked. "All this paper!"

"We're very fond of form filling over here, as you have probably gathered by now."

He shook his head incredulously and sat down to look through it whilst she set to work. Twenty minutes later, after she had queued at an office and applied for the removal orders to be canceled, they walked together down to the main entrance of the High Court. "Is there anything else I should be doing?" he asked.

Maria gave a wry smile. "Pray", she said. "I'll be in touch the night before the bail hearing."

As she waved him off, her mobile phone began to ring. "I've met with the client, collected the fee and made the application", she said, before Jonathan could say anything. "I'm booking a bail hearing in anticipation of the orders being canceled."

"Yes, yes, very good", said Jonathan impatiently. "Matthew has been formally charged. Where are you at the moment?"

"Outside the High Court. I'm coming."

"Great."

Maria arrived in Jonathan's office to find a council of war in full swing. "I can't believe the bloody CPS are actually pursuing this!" declared Jonathan, and he was the only person in the room who sounded remotely surprised by the way things were turning out. "You'd think the Crown Prosecution Service had better things to do with its time putting the real crooks behind bars. They're obviously trying to make an example of you."

"How very reassuring."

"I suspected you might end up hauled in front of the General Medical Council to answer a charge of professional misconduct, but this is ridiculous."

"Don't worry, Jon, that'll happen afterwards."

Jonathan turned to Maria. "These idiots have charged Matthew with assault and battery."

"You're not that surprised, are you?" she asked, pulling up a chair.

"I'm not", said Matthew. "I always tend to assume the worst nightmare scenario is going to happen. Can't think why."

Jonathan looked steadily at him. "Might I suggest you discover optimism before this thing comes to court?" he said as lightheartedly as he could. "It really will help a lot."

"Not really in my nature, I'm afraid."

"Now, we will be pleading necessity. You were acting in an emergency situation, you had very little time to make a decision, et cetera, et cetera ... erring on the side of life as you have been trained as a doctor to do. We could also look at the circumstances surrounding your patient drawing up the living will, her state of mind, any undue pressures that might have been placed on her at the time she drew it up. We could, in fact, look into the circumstances surrounding the suicide attempt itself, which might or might not be relevant to the case."

"That all sounds very sensible", said Matthew, a little hesitantly. "There's a catch, isn't there?"

"Not a catch as such but something I think you need to be aware of. There is likely to be quite a bit of publicity, and you just need to be prepared for it, that's all."

"I don't see why there should be." Matthew had begun tearing at a small piece of note paper. "I'm a private person, Jonathan. I've never had to deal with anything like this before. I'm getting a little old to have to start negotiating with journalists."

"I know, Matthew. I'm not trying to turn this into a public spectacle, I assure you", Jonathan promised. "Far from it. But the fact is, this case will attract a great deal of interest. In some quarters you'll be portrayed as a monster, in others a martyr. If you're psychologically prepared for what's coming, you can keep focused and not let it get to you."

"Get to me! Oh, don't worry about me. I shan't mind at all having my good name dragged through the mud! Can't you see what a born crusader I am?"

Jonathan reached over and touched Matthew's arm to stop him scattering fragments of paper all over the desk. "I know you're very cut up about this, Matthew, and I know you're not in much mood for a fight at the moment, but you have no choice. Even if the fight hadn't come to you, just think about it. What if by the time your children have grown up, it is no longer legal for Catholics to train as doctors?"

"I hardly think . . ."

"It's not as fanciful as it sounds. Over the last ten years, you and I—latterly Maria—have watched law after law after law being passed that makes it hard to be a Catholic in public life—hard to act in good *conscience*. They're using the same drip-drip approach they used at the Reformation, slowly and unobtrusively hemming us in with laws and regulations, all in the name of equality. No one is going to turn this into some battle of ideologies. We're here to defend you against an assault charge, but you have to stand firm and fight your corner. A good deal more might hang on the verdict than your liberty."

Matthew sat in silence, looking at his old friend in cold terror. It was no good; his mind simply could not take it all in. He had warned on the campaign circuit, before the law was passed, that it was only a matter of time before a doctor got into trouble as he went about his business—he could hear himself saying as much at seminars around the country—but he had always quietly hoped it would be some other doctor when it came to it. "May you live in interesting times", he said to himself, not realising he was speaking out loud.

"I beg your pardon?"

"I think it's a Chinese curse", said Matthew. "I can't remember. May you live in interesting times." He stood up and draped his coat over one arm. "Listen, Jonathan, my head's reeling. I need to think about this. May we talk later?"

"Of course."

7

Maria allowed the crowd to push her out of the train and up the escalator, then along the jammed concourse, where she dug her heels in and ground to a halt at the ticket barriers to find her Oyster card. Maria had lived in London for some years now, but she had never lost that nagging, unnerving feeling in situations like this that she was losing any sense of identity. She was merely a face in the crowd—she was almost *always* just a face in the crowd—as she went about her business traveling the London Underground network, walking along a busy street, slipping in at the back of some meeting. If it were not for her job and for the little network of friends she had built up over the brief years of campaigning, she wondered in darker moments (of which there were quite a few) how much her life was really worth in the grand scheme of things. If she died suddenly, how long would it take for anybody to notice that she was even missing, and when they did, how long would it be before she had been completely forgotten or just become a wistful memory in the minds of a few people who had known her? If she had been the one rushed to the hospital that night, would there have been anyone to hold her hand in the ambulance? Come to think of it, would there have been anyone to call an ambulance in the first place?

Stop it! called the voice of an invisible spiritual director. *Haven't you got anyone better to think about?* Maria emerged into the glare of an overcast morning in Victoria, greeted by the roar of black cabs and red buses hurtling past her. Near the entrance to the terminus were men handing out free newspapers and souvenir vendors selling miniature Big Bens, Union Jack tea pots, tea towels with the Underground map on them and T-shirts scrawled all over with *my boyfriend went to London and all I got was this lousy T-shirt*. Maria's inner snob always bristled at the thought that a city that had nurtured some of the greatest intellects and literary talents of all time should be symbolised in the minds of so many visitors by tins of sweets shaped like red telephone boxes and plastic dollies dressed as beefeaters. She paused at the busy traffic island whilst the lights changed and began the familiar walk down Victoria Street.

It was another part of London Maria knew well, as it was where the cathedral had been built over a century ago, and the whole area had become something of a Catholic enclave over the years, with various Catholic bookshops and charities based there. Her objectives that morning, however, were of a secular nature and took her down a side street she had never entered before. She carefully followed the grainy map she had downloaded until she found herself outside a very grand, very imposing office block, which triggered a sudden wave of nerves. It was one of those buildings which on the outside resembled a very elegant Lego set, the sort of creation an architect might have designed who had spent his entire childhood making things out of those multicoloured plastic bricks, whereas the lobby resembled a smart, restrainedly chic hotel. She had deliberately arrived at the busiest moment in the office timetable, the beginning of the working day, and men and women in sharp suits clutching cardboard coffee cups rushed past her through the lobby, scanned in their ID cards and slipped through the security barriers as though their lives depended upon arriving at their desks by nine o'clock. Maria went along with them and fumbled extravagantly with her Oyster card before glancing over to the reception desk and making a gesture that indicated her ID card was not working properly.

"Get a move on, love!" snapped someone behind her, as her presence rapidly caused a bottleneck.

"My card's on the blink", she called to the receptionist. Eager to put a stop to the mayhem Maria was causing, the receptionist hurriedly pressed a button, which opened the security barrier and let Maria through without delay. She gave a brief nod of thanks in the direction of the reception desk and rushed out of sight.

Office buildings like these were always a rabbit warren of corridors and staircases, but Maria had a good idea of how such places were laid out and reckoned that any recreation room would have been built downstairs. As long as she looked as though she knew where she was going, she doubted anybody would question her presence, and they didn't as she strode purposely she knew not where. *Thank God I am not doing an office job*, she thought to herself every time she passed a yucca plant adorning some sharp corner or a picture of a yacht sailing on a vast, fictitious ocean, which someone in Human Relations must have thought would break up the institutional feel of the place. *I would really feel devoid of an identity then.* On a hunch, she walked down a flight of stairs until she heard the telltale clink of crockery and glasses being moved and the low level of chatter people make when they are ordering food.

When she entered the canteen, she found it only about a quarter full, containing people stopping for a brief breakfast who had no doubt come in early to deal with overseas conference calls. It was enough to shield her though, and that was all that mattered as she went nonchalantly up to the counter, looking as though she went there every day of her working life for her morning croissant and skinny latte. She paused just long enough to check that people paid in cash here rather than using an account card, then grabbed a tray, helped herself to a Danish pastry and went up to the till to order a drink. "Hot chocolate, please", she said to a friendly looking elderly lady in a red apron.

"Certainly, love", and she called to a younger woman, who answered in a Polish accent and immediately set to work on a machine.

"Miserable weather", ventured Maria, taking as long as possible to get the right change out of her purse. In a moment of inspiration, she yawned expansively.

"Late night last night, love?"

"Yes, horrible. I was at the hospital visiting Daisy. You remember Daisy?"

The woman's manner changed immediately from friendly to uneasy and finally to crestfallen, as though somebody had taken the Cheshire Cat's batteries out. "Of course I remember Daisy, the poor love. How is she doing?"

"They say she'll make a full recovery, but it'll be a while before she's properly conscious again. It's a nice private hospital ward, though; she's certainly being looked after."

"Such an awful thing to happen, and you'd never have guessed it to look at her."

The Polish girl reached out and placed Maria's hot chocolate on the tray next to the Danish pastry. "I'm actually trying to get a message to her ex-housemate", said Maria. "There are some things she needs. The thing is, I haven't been working here very long, and I don't really know people's faces that well."

"Of course, you don't think about people needing things when they're in hospital", said the woman, handing her a receipt. "You must mean Jennifer. Frosty girl, never bothers to say hello." She paused to think. "Have you got a minute? That crowd always come down for a break

48

around now. They're the diehards who always arrive early and leave late. You know the type I mean, the let's-have-a-heart-attack-before-we're-forty brigade."

Maria laughed a little too enthusiastically. "Yes, I know exactly what you mean. I just need to make a few phone calls. Why don't I sit in that corner seat over there, then maybe you could point them out when they come in?"

Maria hid as carefully as possible behind her copy of the *Metro* and tried to concentrate on an article about some D-list celebrity's latest drug-fueled escapade. Having never taken a recreational drug in her entire life, she would normally have taken a certain voyeuristic interest in what happened to people who did even if just to cheer herself up that this was one method of screwing up your life by which she had never been tempted, but today she could scarcely take in the words. Maria had moved on to another story about a primary school teacher who had been sacked for giving a five-year-old a hug after he had fallen in the playground on the grounds that it had broken child protection policies when she heard footsteps moving in her direction and slowly lowered the paper.

Instead of the Hooray Henry brigade she had been expecting, two men in uniform were glaring at her. They both looked like sixth formers, she thought, one of them wiry and not yet grown out of his adolescent acne problem, the other built a little more like a rugby player, with the blank, disengaged look of a kid who has been deprived of his computer console for five minutes. "Excuse me", said the wiry one. "Could I see your ID, please?"

Maria squeezed her feet together under the table. "Is there a problem, gentlemen?"

"Yes", he replied, without missing a beat. "The problem is that you do not appear to work here. May I ask how you got in?"

"Like everybody else", answered Maria tartly. "You didn't think I'd abseiled through the window, did you?"

Mr Wiry leant forward, resting the palms of his hands on the table in a gesture that was clearly intended to intimidate. "Come with us, please. If you come nice and quietly, we don't have to call the police."

Maria felt as if the entire world and his wife were looking at her as she stood up as calmly and cheerfully as possible and was escorted out of the room. She glanced momentarily at the woman behind the till, who smirked in her direction before turning her back on her; the

Polish girl sniggered. The men insisted on standing on either side of her as they walked up the stairs, as though they seriously imagined she was going to cause trouble. This was the moment in films, thought Maria, when she would be led to a soundproof room where nobody could hear her screams, but being the heroine of this particular situation, she would knock both men unconscious in the doorway and make a run for it, escaping down some rickety fire escape.

Instead, Maria found herself being marched unceremoniously out of the front door and just had time to hear the receptionist being shouted at before she made a dash down the street. Her biggest fear, now that she thought about it, had been the horror of Jonathan finding out about her latest misadventure, and she endeavoured not to tell him about it.

Matthew stood in the piazza outside Westminster Cathedral and drew a deep breath. It was a remarkable piece of architecture, ostentatiously Byzantine in design, with a huge dome and tower that must have been even more imposing when it had first been built, among the slums of this most socially divided of cities. Now, like so many once deprived parts of London—Battersea, Clapham, Docklands—Victoria was a fashionable and expensive place to live, a teeming centre of commerce and business enterprise punctuated by fashionable little apartments reserved for an elite few. A number of sightseers gathered in a huddle in the middle of the piazza, taking photographs of the cathedral front, and as Matthew walked up to the door, he passed a homeless man selling magazines.

He stepped inside, dipped his hand in the holy water stoop and crossed himself, then paused for a moment at the back of the central aisle to look at the sumptuous, but unfinished sanctuary before him. The Church had run out of money part of the way through decorating the cathedral, and the exquisite decoration of the side chapels and walls was brutally interrupted in places by black brick, but it somehow seemed quite right that it should be like that. The cathedral was a monument to unfinished business, beauty revealing the harsh reality of what was still a missionary Church struggling for survival in the middle of England's greatest metropolis.

Matthew genuflected and walked across to the side aisle, towards the chapel dedicated to the martyrs of England and Wales. He always came to this particular side chapel when he visited the cathedral and knew it well, with its sarcophagus of Saint John Southworth, the Jacobean priest-martyr, lying in state on the outside of the railings, and the cream-coloured marble walls a little too garishly lit by electric bulbs. A large crucifix dominated the front wall, and around the sides, the names of the dead soldiers from two world wars were engraved on slabs. A tired-looking wreath of poppies had been left beneath one of the slabs the previous November, and nobody had had the heart to remove it yet.

Matthew noticed a hunched figure sitting in one of the pews, a woman whose head was veiled in a white mantilla, and he was just about to sit down when the woman obviously heard a noise and turned to look at him. It was Maria. She nodded uneasily in acknowledgement and turned back to look at the crucifix, leaving him cringing in mortification. He took several backward steps—making yet more noise—before turning around and fleeing the chapel as fast as he could, not stopping until he had reached the refuge of the chapel of the Blessed Sacrament. There was something terribly embarrassing about intruding upon another person's prayers. It might have been simply an English awkwardness about religion in general, the residual sense that piety was so private it should be completely hidden from view or just the feeling that a solitary person praying in silence in a chapel really ought to be left alone.

And Maria was happy to be left alone. She was not a good keeper of anniversaries, but Matthew's case had drawn attention to the losses in her own family. When she had been thrown out of the office building, it had seemed natural to come here, to calm down if nothing else. She liked the anonymity of it, the sense that she had a right to be still and quiet here, so much so that even when she had been recognised, there had been a silent agreement between the two of them that he was not to intrude.

She had died on this day, a woman Maria barely remembered now. She had the confused recollection of a neighbour coming to the school to take her home and of being excited to be able to get off lessons, the sense of being important that she had felt when the school secretary had come into the classroom, whispered in the teacher's ear, and Maria had been summoned to leave.

She remembered eclectic details, the exact style of the grey pinafore dress she had been wearing, with its double row of covered buttons and course texture, the blue-and-white ribbons that had adorned her plaits to match the colours of her school uniform (her mother had been very keen on colour coordination), but she could not recall the name of the neighbour who had picked her up. She just remembered getting into her car and being driven home to find that there was nobody there, and the neighbour had been instructed to let her in and get her some tea. She had kept asking where everyone was, and finally, shortly before it was time for her to go to bed, her father had appeared in the doorway. Or he had resembled her father, but a change in him had occurred, so terrible that he barely looked even human. His barley-coloured hair, always a little wild, looked unkempt like burnt grass, his eyes stared ahead of him as though he could hardly recognise the world around him, and he was breathing so noisily and raspingly that Maria had panicked and hidden under the kitchen table. There had been the sounds of a scuffle as this creature she hardly knew was led into another room to calm down, but even after the room had gone quiet, she had been too frightened to get up in case he returned.

Staring up at the crucifix, Maria tried very hard to conjure up a positive picture of her father. He had been quite a handsome man, as the few remaining photographs revealed, though as a child Maria had never noticed that sort of detail, but she knew that there must have been happy times before everything went wrong. She must have seen him laugh or at least smile; there must have been outings and treats and the sort of happy events people always remember about their child-hood years, but she could not think of anything. Instead, she felt her-self backing into a corner so that the two walls seemed close enough together to crush her. She saw again her father's face, twisted with rage, his eyes bloodshot and terrifying, howling at the top of his voice almost like an animal, "Don't you dare *ever* do that again! You disgust me! I can't do anything right for you, can I?"

Maria blinked, screwed her eyes shut, but the image would not go away. *Say a prayer*, Maria commanded herself. *He needs your prayers too, perhaps more than she does. Have a heart.* But her heart felt as though a cast-iron vise were crushing it to death, and no prayer came. Even in that most evocative of places, with the sight of the dying Christ before her, she felt only an empty sense of betrayal. "I'm sorry", she said out loud. "I'm so sorry." Then she stepped out of the side chapel, paid her respects to Saint John Southworth and walked out of the cathedral with slow, reluctant steps.

She was just taking off her mantilla and wondering what her next plan of action was going to be when she noticed a young man walking resolutely towards her. He was dressed in the uniform of the city: sober suit, not so sober shirt and tie. For a horrible moment she thought he had something to do with her escapade that morning. In fact, she was so absolutely certain he had something to do with it that she did an about turn and began to climb the steps to the sanctuary of the cathedral again. "Wait!" he called, and she felt a hand on her shoulder, which caused her to jump. "Just a moment, please. Don't run off."

8

Maria spun around to face the man, comforting herself that they were in a place so public that they were probably being photographed by Japanese tourists at that very moment. She took a closer look at her assailant and immediately began to relax, noticing that he was clearly not acting in an official capacity. He had the look of a person who had not long been in possession of his own bank account but for whom the transition to the world of work had been a trial. She noticed the thin lines making semicircles under his eyes and the flyaway ginger hair that would not stay in quite the right position. "How may I help you?" she asked.

"Sorry to bother you", he said, still catching his breath, "but you were in the canteen this morning, weren't you?" She could not think of the correct answer, so said nothing. "I thought I heard you talking to that woman about Daisy. I'm right, aren't I?"

"Yes", she said. "I was, as it happens."

"I thought so. You mean Daisy Havisham, don't you? There aren't that many Daisys around; it's quite an unusual name for our generation. I thought it had to be her." Maria nodded. "But you were lying when you said you were at the hospital last night. I was."

"I see." It was no good. She could think of nothing worth saying that would explain why she had lied. "Look, I really ought to be . . ."

His hand was on her shoulder again. "I wonder if we could talk somewhere where we won't be disturbed?"

Maria was of a reckless disposition, but not entirely without common sense. "How about a little walk around the park?" she suggested.

He smiled, sensing her logic. "Perfect."

They walked together down Victoria Street in silence, crossed the road and made their way to the imposing black metal railings at the entrance to Saint James' Park. She had chosen it because it was a public place where there were always plenty of people, including the odd policeman milling around because it was so close to Buckingham Palace and New Scotland Yard, but where it was still quiet enough to have a decent conversation. "Well?"

"I hope this doesn't sound rude, but you're obviously snooping", he said. "I don't know all Daisy's friends, but I'm sure you're not one of them—not really the type, if I may say so."

Maria felt the weight of the enormous chip on her shoulder, built by an expensive education to which she had never felt entitled. "No comment", she said.

"I guess you're not a private detective either, given the hashup you made of your little stakeout this morning, so what are you exactly? I'd just like to know."

Maria let herself be distracted by a grey squirrel scurrying across the path. "I might be more inclined to answer your question if you told me who you are first."

He raised his hands in mock surrender. "Sorry, fair enough. I'm Daisy's boyfriend. Peter Baxter." It was the moment they might have shaken hands, but the occasion for formal introductions had clearly passed. "Now would you please tell me who you are and what you think you are doing?"

"One more question, please, if you don't mind. I know it was her family—her brother, in fact—who reported the doctor to the police and who wants to see him sent down for treating her. Where do you stand on all of this?"

He turned sharply to look at her. "Look, I'm glad she's alive. Who wouldn't want the person they love to live? For what it's worth, I'm glad the doctor intervened, but I'm not getting involved in all of this. And I want to know why you are involved. Are you a journalist or a lawyer?"

"I work for a legal firm", she said. "Does that help?" She reached into her pocket and pulled out a card. "I assure you I'm not snooping for the sake of it. Now can we talk?"

He indicated a park bench near the pelican enclosure. "I suppose so. What do you want to know?"

"Thanks", said Maria, sitting down. "I do appreciate this. What I'm wondering is, did you have any idea that Daisy was suicidal?"

Peter shook his head. "Everyone's asking that. No, of course I didn't, or I would have tried to stop her. It came as a complete shock. I'd guessed that something was wrong, but not that wrong."

"She hadn't spoken to you about any particular problem?"

"No, she wasn't like that. She was quite a private person really, nervous of opening up, even to me." He sighed wretchedly. "I knew

55

that something was wrong though. She started behaving strangely, getting very listless and withdrawn, you know what I mean. But she just wouldn't tell me what was going on. She'd always been prone to getting a bit depressed, and I guess I thought it was just a phase she was going through."

"Had she ever received any medical help?"

"No, not so far as I know, though she probably should have done. She's not the sort of person who would go running to a doctor."

"A strong person, then?" asked Maria, getting into her stride as an interviewer. "Someone who liked to be in control?"

Peter gave Maria a withering sideways glance. "This has to be a windup", he said. "Of course she wasn't strong. I don't think she'd ever been in control of her own life for a single second, even when she was trying to end it! Look, we haven't been going out that long, but I'd already worked out that she was quite a contradictory person in a way. She had a reputation for being ... well, a little pushy, I suppose ... but that wasn't her at all. People used to manipulate her, particularly her emotions. Her family were the really strong ones."

"Oh? In what way?"

"Look them up in *Who's* bloody *Who*!" He was getting angry, thought Maria, which might or might not be to her advantage. Either he would tell her a lot more than he had intended because it let his guard down, or he would lose his temper and storm off before she had all the information she wanted. "I mean they're arrogant toffs. They're the sort of people who are used to getting their own way. She had the kind of education where you never ever *ever* admit to a weakness, not even if it's killing you. She could have been bipolar, and she would never have seen anyone about it."

"Was she close to her family?"

"Oh, to look at them, you'd think they were happy families personified." He pressed his fists together and looked fixedly down at his bony knuckles. Maria suspected she was hearing snatches of a conversation he had held in his head over and over again. "As far as I could make out, they kind of doted as much as they controlled, if that makes any sense. Daisy's father loved her. On the one occasion I ever had a conversation with the man, he made it pretty obvious that he thought far more of her than her brother. Thought she was the sensible child of the family. But they stifled any ability Daisy had to make a decision of her own. By the time she finally made a break for it, it was too late. She didn't know how to do anything for herself. They'd always made the decisions for her."

"She made a break for it?"

"Oh, yes, she hadn't been on speaking terms with her mother for months. They didn't have a row or anything, you understand. Daisy was incapable of it. She just walked away. You know, just found excuses not to go home any more. Didn't answer her phone when their number flashed up on the screen. That sort of thing. She did stay close to her brother, I suppose, even though he was worse than the lot of them."

"He's the one who made the complaint to the police", said Maria without thinking.

Peter sprang to his feet immediately. "Look, I've already said I did not want to get involved. I'm glad she's alive, that's all. I'm glad she's going to recover and there's a chance we might be able to make some sort of a life together, but if you think I want anything to do with anybody's nasty little campaign, I don't."

Maria got up. "If you're glad she's alive, wouldn't you at least be prepared to say so?"

"I'm glad she's alive. What do you want me to say, I wish she was in the ground?" His pale face was blotched red with the effort of controlling his temper, but Maria was too accustomed to being on the receiving end of rage to care. "It might seem a little strange to someone like you, but I also believe people have the right to do what they want—dying included—without busybodies getting in the way. I can't stand Daisy's family because they are control freaks. I felt the same about some of her friends running rings round her. The same, for that matter, goes for people like you. When I followed you down Victoria Street, I could have come into the cathedral to talk to you, but I wouldn't be seen dead in a church. Don't think I don't know what your agenda is too."

"Would you have stopped her committing suicide?" asked Maria, but he pushed past her and walked off, blazing temper with every footstep. Maria began to follow, but was already struggling to catch up with him when her loathsome mobile phone went off, and she was forced to stop to answer it, knowing that it might be something important. It was Jonathan.

"Maria, where are you?"

"Saint James' Park, but I've got a perfectly reasonable explanation."

"Yeah, yeah, whatever. Can you travel to Birmingham tonight?"

"Why?"

"I need you to go with Robyn to Birmingham for Lydia's bail hearing. The orders were canceled when she arrived at Heathrow Airport, so we need to get her out. The hearing is at nine o'clock tomorrow morning."

"There's something I need to tell you about Matthew's case", said Maria. "I've just had a rather interesting conversation with ..."

"Maria, I told you not to bother yourself with Matthew's case just at the moment. It could be months before it comes to trial."

"I have a funny feeling about it", Maria put in. "I think they're going to try to rush it through."

"I'm not remotely interested in your funny feelings", came the response she had known he would make. "Just get yourself back to the office PDQ and stop gallivanting around London making a nuisance of yourself. I need you in Birmingham tonight."

There was a click on the line, and she realised he had hung up.

It was midafternoon before Jonathan came back from court to find Maria sitting at the computer with an open copy of *Who's Who* in front of her. She looked up defensively. "It's all right, I've done everything you needed. I've booked rooms at a travel lodge for Robyn and me, and I've spoken with the couple who are going to stand surety for Lydia. They know what they've got to bring, and Robyn is going to brief them about the sort of questions they might be asked. They're very nervous, of course, but it should be all right."

"Good."

"Case going all right?"

"Might have been better", answered Jonathan, throwing down his files and papers. "My client was only obliging enough to get himself arrested again whilst on parole."

"Oh, dear."

"Shoplifted from a Leonard Cheshire shop. Can you believe that? Pinching secondhand clothes from a *charity* shop?"

"Oh, *dear.*"

"And just to make your day, Maria, I got a call as I was leaving court to say that Matthew's first hearing has been scheduled for next week. Your funny feelings might be going somewhere after all."

"Do you want me to go along?"

"No, no, it's only a technicality at this point. The important thing is to stop Matthew having a nervous breakdown. What were you up to this morning, anyway?"

"I met up with Daisy Havisham's boyfriend", she replied, praying he would not ask how. "He said Daisy's family are very wealthy— 'toffs', he called them—so I looked them up in *Who's Who* and did a little search of the Internet. It turns out they've been big donors to Death Wish in the past. The thing is he also said they were very controlling, so much so that he thought they had deprived Daisy of any ability to make decisions of her own."

"Good, good. Would he be willing to stand as a witness?"

Maria shook her head. "No. I'm afraid he was rather hostile. Doesn't want to get involved."

"How useful of him."

"He said he thought she was a bit prone to getting depressed", she continued, desperate to have come across something that was worth knowing. "Particularly recently, he said she'd been acting very strangely. Sad and withdrawn, I think were his words. We could argue that she is a person who is very easily controlled, who might perhaps have been talked into making a living will. Coercion, undue pressure, domineering family, you know. If she was suffering from depression at the time she drew up the living will . . ."

"Had she seen a doctor? Had she been diagnosed as a depressive?"

"No, he said she was the sort of person who would never have gone to a doctor." He made an irritating huffy noise and turned away. "Look, it's not my fault! There must be thousands of undiagnosed depression cases in this country! Smiling depression, I believe they call it. Plenty of people don't want to admit that something's wrong when mental illness carries such a stigma. If we could provide evidence that she was at least exhibiting signs of depression . . . She did try to commit suicide, after all."

"Yes, yes, thank you. Looks like we need an expert witness to talk about depression. As well as that, a close associate who could vouch for her behaviour would help the case enormously. Would you print out those webpages you've been looking at? Perhaps you could put together a summary of what you found out today. That will make it easier for me to get my head round it all."

"Just by a strange coincidence," said Maria cautiously, "I couldn't help noticing in *Who's Who* that Daisy's family home is not very far from Birmingham. I could get a taxi out there quite easily."

"Absolutely out of the question", Jonathan retorted, wearing his very best ex-military expression. "The purpose of your going to

59

Birmingham is to get Lydia out of the clink. You will then return to London. You will return *directly* to London." She smiled her sweetest, most appealing smile. "I mean it. Robyn will be under strict instructions to see you get back on that train. By force of violence if necessary."

9

The hearing was a perfunctory affair, as such events always were. Robyn questioned the couple as gently as possible about their financial situation to prove to the judge that they stood to lose a significant amount of money if Lydia absconded and therefore had a vested interest in keeping an eye on her whereabouts. The whole point of letting asylum seekers out of detention on bail, as far as Maria could make out, was basically to get ordinary members of the public to do the police's work for them. If Lydia was granted bail, it would be the job of the softly spoken couple who knew her from church to ensure that she returned to their home every evening. If she failed to do so and they did not report her absence to the police, they would lose their life savings.

The solicitor from the Home Office made every possible effort to question the couple's ability to perform this law enforcement role until the judge instructed her very courteously to shut her mouth and stop delaying matters needlessly. Throughout the whole hearing, Lydia's pensive face could be seen staring out of a screen which linked her to the courtroom from a room in the detention centre. "I am not impressed with your case, young lady", said Judge Piowski, whose own parents had come to Britain as immigrants half a century before. "A cynic would say that having failed in your first attempt at claiming asylum, you deliberately got yourself pregnant to give yourself another reason to make a claim."

Maria felt herself getting hot under the collar, but it was Lydia, her voice tinny through the video link, who spoke. "No, sir, I really didn't . . ."

"Be quiet and listen", continued Judge Piowski, with the air of a man who is used to deference. "As I said, I am unimpressed with your immigration history, but whether or not you are to be given the right to remain in this country is for another jurisdiction to determine. I am, however, impressed by the Christian witness I have seen in this courtroom this morning. It seems to me that your friends are sincere witnesses to the truth, and I find it heartening to see that, in this day and age, there are still people who care so much about the fate of others. I can therefore see no good reason to keep you in detention, young lady, particularly in your current condition. I am therefore releasing you forthwith." He glanced over to Robyn. "She will need to be removed from the detention centre today. Is there someone who can pick her up?"

"Yes, sir. Arrangements have been made. I just need to make a telephone call."

"Well, that went nice and smoothly", said Robyn, as they stood in the crowded waiting room, which was full of sad, nervous families who sat in huddles waiting to be called. She was a sharp, energetic woman who was reaching the stage of her career in which minor victories failed to elicit much enthusiasm. She nodded to the couple and handed them back the dossier of bank statements, identification documents, proof of address and mortgage information the courts had demanded of them. "Thank you very much, Mr and Mrs Taylor. Will you be taking the train back to London?"

"No, we drove up early this morning", said Mr Taylor. "We'll get a nice cup of tea, then head back down south. We'll need to be home in time for Lydia's arrival."

"Excellent. Maria and I had better make a dash for the station." Robyn looked around. "Maria?"

But Maria had vanished, apparently into thin air.

Maria was not sure what passersby must have thought when they saw her racing out of the court as fast as her little legs would carry her and jumping into the back of the nearest taxi, but she did not greatly care. The idea of being mistaken for an escaped convict was mildly appealing. "Could you drop me off in the middle of the city, please?" she puffed to an astonished taxi driver in a turban. "Somewhere nice and near the shops."

Maria had planned things quite carefully, and as soon as she got out of the taxi she found her way to the nearest public convenience and changed into the casual clothes she had brought for the purpose, stuffing her trouser suit into her backpack. She had done one or two other things the afternoon before about which she had not deigned to tell Jonathan, including looking up the Havisham family's house online, finding out its precise location and looking at the best possible way to get there. A tourist information site had been kind enough to inform her that there was a regular bus service out into the village and the house was a short walk from there.

In fact, the tourist site had told her many things about Satis House; for example, it was one of the few stately homes (admittedly of a very modest size compared to some) that was still in private hands. It was also open to the public, the family living in a small section of the house, with the rest providing a fascinating insight into the history of England's minor aristocracy. The two-hundred-year-old Flemish porcelain laid out in the dining room was particularly worth a look.

Maria had decided that for this little excursion she was going to be a slightly overeager history student. To complete her disguise, as the bus clattered through the morning traffic out of the ugliness of the city and into the surrounding countryside, Maria took off her daily disposable contact lenses and put on her glasses, thinking it made her look a little more studious. Then she tried to relax, banishing Jonathan's apoplectic face from her thoughts as she looked out at the lush green hills and trees she so rarely ever glimpsed in the thick of London's concrete jungle. "There's some corner of a foreign field that is forever England", she quoted to herself softly, but it was no good. Even the beauty of the natural world around her could not steady her nerves completely. She was not entirely sure what she was even looking for, but had some sense that there must be a clue hidden in the house if she could only take a look. And then there was going to be Jonathan to contend with. *Oh, dear me, Jonathan . . .*

Contrary to the promise made on the website, the bus stop turned out to be a good two miles from the house, and she felt like something of an impostor walking down the endlessly long driveway to the house, which traced its lazy way through acres of woods and farmland. It would be hard to imagine from her rooms in London that anybody lived like this any longer, so perfectly secluded from the ugliness and turmoil of life as it was experienced by millions of people. She slowed her pace, partly because the brisk walk had made her hot and partly out of habit, as she always tended to slow down when she was deep in thought. Of course, the seclusion was not real; there were no hiding places from modern life apart perhaps from the few contemplative convents and monasteries that still dotted themselves about the country. As the house came into view in all its antiquated splendour, she spared a thought for the family who lived there and the trauma they must be going through worrying about their sick daughter lying in a London hospital bed.

Maria saw what looked like a ticket booth ahead of her, which somewhat spoilt the Jeeves and Wooster look of the place. "House, gardens or both?" enquired an elderly anchorite in a cloth cap, poking his head out to greet her.

"House, please."

"That'll be £3.60 then." He tore off what looked like a raffle ticket and gestured in the direction of the Elizabethan pile directly ahead of them. "That way. You can't miss it."

"Thanks."

Tudor manor houses were the kind of places schoolchildren got taken on trips they were supposed to enjoy, armed with worksheets and terrible packed lunches consisting of sandwiches curling at the edges, windfall apples and a tiny chocolate bar risibly named "fun size". Maria had been on several such excursions as a child, but had usually found the experience quite enjoyable. It had offered an escape from the claustrophobia of school for a start and an opportunity to daydream about life in a bygone age when ladies wore dresses with farthingales and gazed out of leaded windows, awaiting the arrival of knights in shining armour. This house looked very much like any other of its kind. Maria climbed a flight of steps into an impressive hall replete with marble floors, oak paneling and a vast wooden staircase framed by ornate bannisters. Portraits of men in ruffs and floppy hats grimaced at the people in her group as they waited for the tour guide to arrive.

A small, timorous lady, who had obviously taken on the job as a retirement hobby, scurried into the room armed with several glossy brochures. "Would anybody like to buy a guidebook?" she asked in the glorious accent of 1930s BBC airwaves. None of the assembled group stirred, which she seemed to find disappointing. "Oh, well, my name is Violet, and I will be taking you around the house. This house has been in the family for over five hundred years. It was acquired after the dissolution of the monasteries . . ."

That means it was pinched from the Catholic Church, thought Maria, wondering where the remains of the priory were and precisely which religious order had been kicked out to line the pockets of Henry VIII's friends. Maria followed the little group up the stairs and began to look out for information. She was still not really sure what she imagined she would find among the spooky suits of armour and French furniture pilfered (or was that rescued?) after the Revolution, but there had to be some reason why her instincts had brought her here.

They entered a long drawing room dominated by a central corridor where early Victorian ladies would have walked up and down very slowly taking what they imagined to be useful exercise. To one side there was a large fireplace surrounded by beautifully upholstered chairs in red and gold velvet, and in one corner was a mahogany bureau, set out to look as though the master of the house might sit down to peruse his accounts at any moment.

Maria hung back and glanced over the study area. A number of old photographs were hung up on the walls and propped up on the bureau. They caught her eye the way human faces always did. It showed members of the family—captured forever in monochrome—in the company of famous people from the interwar period, the last great era for that class. She recognised a number of faces—George Bernard Shaw, Virginia Woolf—but there were others she did not recognise at all but who seemed to belong to the same sort of circle. She quietly took out her digital camera and photographed the photographs. Spread out on the bureau were a series of old letters, which she also photographed as closely as possible so that the writing would be legible.

"Oh, my dear, you can't take photographs in here!" squeaked Violet, who had finished her account of the various art objects young men of the family had brought back from Italy after the Grand Tour and noticed what Maria was doing. "I'm terribly sorry. It's because of security. We have had thefts before, I'm afraid."

"Hey, that's too bad", said a tourist, which gave Maria time to put the camera away and walk nonchalantly back to the group. "Lose anything valuable?"

"Madam, am I right in thinking the family had links with the Nazis during the 1930s?" asked Maria, fiddling with her glasses in a nervous student sort of a way.

Violet blushed noticeably. "Well—well, that would be putting it a little strongly. That is—unfortunately, a good many people sympathised with the Nazis during the 1930s, but that was before the war. They had no idea how dangerous the Nazis were, or they certainly would have had nothing to do with them."

"Of course. Of course."

"Well, I think we should be moving on. Let me show you the dining hall. It was here that the family entertained William and Mary, shortly after their arrival in England ..."

As they moved along the landing, Maria could not help noticing that they were passing a wing that was roped off. "What's in there?"

"That's private", said Violet. "Nothing particularly exciting, but the family still live in the house and occupy that part of it. That's why it is closed to the public."

Maria let the group get a little ahead and slipped into an alcove whilst Violet was pointing out a rather fetching portrait of a young lady about town by some long-forgotten artist. Then, like the heroine of a Gothic horror novel who knows the body must be hidden in the secret wing of the house, she deftly stepped over the rope that hung across the doorway and into forbidden territory.

She knew the family had had Nazi links and that it went well beyond sympathising. She had also suspected, and her suspicions had been confirmed by what she had found in the study, that they had been connected with the eugenics movement that had poisoned British politics in the run-up to the Second World War. As Violet had said, that was of course before the war and before Josef Mengele's hideous experiments in the concentration camps had been revealed; it was long before Britain's liberal intelligentsia had been forced to cover their tracks.

She put her hand on a doorknob and was about to open it when she heard footsteps behind her and turned around. "May I help you, madam?"

Maria was facing an elderly man, impeccably dressed in a three-piece suit with a watch chain swinging from one pocket, who had clearly emerged from the opposite room. "I'm terribly sorry; I appear to be lost", she said airily, giving him a sheepish smile. Well, he was a man after all, and only charm could possibly work in a situation like this. "I was just looking around the house. I have a ticket."

"This area is private and quite clearly cordoned off", he answered tonelessly, and Maria was uncomfortably reminded of the ghost of Jacob Marley. She wondered whether his head would stay on if he removed his starched collar.

"Silly me. I'm afraid I am as blind as a bat."

"Then I'm surprised you did not trip over the rope, madam."

"Does the family live here then? I thought all these houses were owned by the National Trust these days."

"This house has been in private hands for hundreds of years, and you are trespassing."

"Are they here at the moment?" she asked eagerly, as though she really wanted their autographs. "You see, I'm very interested in ..."

"The family are not here, for your information. They are attending to business in London. I repeat; you are trespassing."

"Terribly sorry, once again." She began walking towards the entrance through which she had so rudely entered, but that meant getting past the ghost of Jacob Marley, and he was blocking her exit. "So sorry to have disturbed you. I'll be going now."

"I'm afraid not, madam."

10

"Well, I suppose we have to be grateful for the common sense of the police force," remarked Jonathan, as they sat on the train to London, "which is more than I can say for you."

Maria sat in silence and looked out at the blur of distant lights that punctuated the grim darkness around them. They were on the last train from Birmingham to London, and Maria had given up looking at her watch half an hour ago. She had some notion that it was nearly midnight and that Jonathan might turn into an enormous ogre at any moment. The worst part of being marched out of the stately home in handcuffs had been the ghastly thought of what on earth Jonathan would say when he found out that she had been arrested again. This time she could not even blame it on youthful passion or provocation—she had been caught trespassing in a clearly cordoned off area, and, as Jonathan would no doubt remind her again in a moment or two, she had had no business going anywhere near that stately home in the first place. The evidence of casual clothes and digital camera made any defence involving impulsive action impossible to sustain. "It did seem a little disproportionate", she tried, but that was the wrong response as well.

"I distinctly remember telling you to come straight back to London from Birmingham as soon as the hearing was over", Jonathan reminded her. "Robyn was supposed to make sure you got on the train. If you think giving her the slip was funny, it wasn't. She was terribly worried. Then you take a little bus ride—or was it a taxi ride?—out to a private house and get nicked."

"Hardly a private house. I'd paid my ticket to go in."

"The police were happy to be convinced that it was all an innocent mistake. Dopey female academic type wanders off whilst on a guided tour, gets carried away looking at stained-glass windows or something and ends up in the wrong place. Your 'little girl lost in the wilderness act' doesn't work on me, however. I know perfectly well what you were up to. You and the word innocence just don't get on."

"I'm not sure I like the implication of that", said Maria. "I'm a respectable girl."

"It's not funny, Maria!" Jonathan had evidently realised that there was virtually no one else in the carriage or simply did not care who heard him. "You will shortly qualify as a solicitor. If you are seriously thinking about having a future in law, you had better buck up your ideas a touch. If you end up with a criminal conviction or even a caution as a result of one of your idiotic escapades, that could very well be the end of it. What you did today was completely selfish and irresponsible. I don't suppose it occurs to you that an employer has the right to be taken seriously? Or perhaps you're just too arrogant to consider that someone else might know better than you."

Maria, who had spent most of her life having various sections of the Riot Act read out to her, stared down at her knuckles and tried hard to listen. One of the difficulties of growing up in the certain knowledge of being perpetually in the wrong was that when she really was in the wrong, she found it quite difficult to take the situation seriously. But the fact was that she liked Jonathan in spite of everything and knew that he had been very good to her, so she listened and slowly began to feel the beginnings of regret. "I'm sorry", she said.

"You've got to learn to get your brain into gear before you act, or you're going to end up in very serious trouble. I mean it. One day you won't fall into the hands of a couple of benign police officers you can flutter your eyelashes at. And there won't always be someone to bail you out."

"I know."

There was a lengthy silence. Maria started to look out of the window again, whilst Jonathan spied the refreshments trolley coming down the aisle and bought some Cornish pasties. "I'm sorry I've wasted so much of your time today", she said. "I honestly didn't bank on getting into trouble."

"I'm not sure you ever do. I don't suppose it's worth me asking why you are taking this case quite so personally, is it?"

"I feel angry about it, that's all. It's just such an injustice. Of course I feel personally about it."

"That tells me a lot."

"If it helps at all, my visit was not entirely wasted. I'd heard a rumour that the family of Daisy Havisham had old links to the eugenics movement."

"A lot of that class did", said Jonathan with a shrug. "Marie Stopes sent racist love letters to Adolf Hitler lamenting the curse of Jews and

Catholics. The problem is proving it now. Try finding any reference to Marie Stopes' views on forcible sterilisation of social undesirables on the official website, or her appearance at a conference in Nazi Germany, for that matter."

"I found these photos and letters", she said. "They were on public display. They weren't even trying to hide them, which made me think that the family probably don't care about their eugenicist past. Look." She handed him the camera, and he began to play back the photographs. "That's George Bernard Shaw. Now they could just say there was a literary interest or something, I suppose, but ..."

"You recognise all these people?"

"Some of them."

"That portrait is of Nietzsche. Ever read him?"

Maria giggled. "We had a Jewish lecturer who said once that Nietzsche lost his faith in God but never in his PhD."

"That sums him up quite nicely. German philosopher, horror of illness and frailty. Described the incapacitated as 'parasites' who should be treated to a daily dose of disgust. Nice idol to have hanging up on your wall. Where did you find these letters?"

"I told you, they were all spread out on the bureau, you know, a kind of reconstruction of the gentleman's study. No one ever looks at the things. It's possible that whoever put them out didn't even look or else didn't care."

"Do you recognise the signature on this letter?"

"No, but I noticed the symbols on the letterhead, so I guessed it was someone involved with the Nazis. Swastikas are a bit of a giveaway."

"The man who wrote this letter was one of the doctors executed after the Nuremberg trials. Rather ironic under the circumstances."

"I didn't realise doctors had been tried at Nuremberg."

"Oh, yes, the famous Medical Trial. Plenty of doctors got their hands dirty, not just Dr Mengele, and that swine escaped to Argentina."

"I knew about him. He became an abortionist in Argentina ..." It was no good. She was tired and was losing the battle to keep her eyes open. "The court papers were—were released ..."

"Well, I have to hand it to you. This is a goldmine of historical information. The question is how we use it."

"When a doctor kills, he becomes the most dangerous man in the state", murmured Maria dreamily. "Who said that? Was it Poirot or Sherlock Holmes?"

"Sherlock Holmes, I believe. The episode with the poisonous snake. Personally, I think all doctors are the most dangerous people in the state. They know how to kill and to kill more subtly than any serial killer. Think about what happened to Harold Shipman—all those people he killed, mostly elderly women, before the police caught up with him, and his patients protesting that he was a wonderful doctor who wouldn't hurt a fly."

"I know."

"When people go on about doctors not moralising, I'm not sure what they'd prefer. A world where doctors are not guided by morality is a country heading for the gas chambers."

Jonathan glanced up at Maria and realised that his pontificating had had the predictable effect of sending her to sleep, but he suspected he had given her this lecture before. Her head was turned a little to one side, and she was shivering, though it was not at all cold in the carriage. He pulled down her coat from the overhead luggage rack and covered her as best he could, but it made no difference.

Maria was in one of her least favourite places—a hospital—but she could not remember how she had come to be there in the first place. She was lying on a stretcher, covered by those familiar crisp white hospital sheets and a green coverlet, which disguised spilt blood so well, being propeled with restrained haste into a sterile labyrinth of stark lights and white, cold corridors. She could feel herself panicking, that appalling tightening of the chest, the hammering sensation in the neck and that terrifying, choking struggle to breathe. She grasped the metal bars at the sides of the stretcher and tried to sit up a little to relieve the pressure on her lungs, but her breath came out in a long, wheezing gasp.

A hand came down on her shoulder, causing her to hold her breath completely. As a child, Maria had become used to just one response to any display of distress or panic. A middle-aged woman, her face lined by years of resentment and frustration, would glare at her with palpable hatred and shout "CUT IT *OUTTTTT!*" If she timed it properly, she would manage to spit on the final T, and Maria would be reduced to shocked silence, too terrified to make a single sound, whilst the woman she had offended by her initial unhappiness turned her back abruptly and stalked off out of sight.

"Lie still, love", said a nurse with a calm, pensive face. "It's all going to be all right."

"Why am I here?" demanded Maria, but even being greeted with a gentle response could not stop her panic. The tight feeling over her chest was spreading to her throat; she could barely speak. "This is a mistake. I shouldn't be here!"

She had to get off the trolley; she had to get out of the hospital. Something horrible, beyond her most macabre nightmares, was taking her over, and she could not escape. In the midst of her confusion and dread, she had some sense that she had brought herself here and ought to know why, but all she was certain about was that she had to get out. The trolley was gaining speed; she could feel herself being rushed faster and faster down a corridor that seemed to be without end. "Leave me alone", she murmured, but the paralysis was creeping over her mouth. "Please leave me in peace. I—I don't want to be here!"

Something demonic was awaiting her; she knew she could not reach the end of the corridor. "This is your own silly fault", came a pre-dictably venomous voice, from the wizened, trouser-suit-clad figure struggling to keep up with them. Maria did not need to be able to see her to know what sort of a look she was getting. There had been a time when her guardian had become so angry with her that her eyes had gone bloodshot, and the whites had disappeared altogether. "Take it like a big girl, if you can!"

"Please ... please ..." It was too late; they had reached the end of the corridor. She had been swallowed by a room and brought her hand up to her eyes to shield them—dear God, why so much light? Why so much searing, piercing, blinding *light*? "Please ..."

Maria heard the sound of male footsteps approaching her, and her hand was carefully removed from her face. "It's all right, my dear. You're going to be all right." She squinted to see who was talking to her, but the man's face was cast into shadow by the overhead lights. "Try to remain calm; we're going to have to rinse you out."

Maria's hands went to her face again. She could hear the sound of nurses moving about in the background and began shaking uncon-trollably. "Leave me alone! Leave me ... I'm dying ... leave ..."

"You are not alone," said the calm but quite determined reply, "and you are not going to die."

She felt her hands being drawn away from her face again. "Please don't, I'll choke. *Don't!*"

"You won't choke; it's all going to be all right." She felt the cold, unyielding end of a tube snaking its way into her mouth. In a last act of desperation, she grasped the man's sleeve, but the room was lurching and spinning. She felt herself falling ...

"I wonder if I am pushing you too hard", said Jonathan, when he had finally given in and woken Maria from her nightmare. "It's preying on your mind too much, the whole thing."

"It was just a dream", she said. "Don't read anything into it. I've always had nightmares. I suppose I have been thinking about it rather a lot."

Jonathan opened the miniature bottle of brandy he had bought in the buffet car earlier and handed it to her. "I wonder if you need a break. Couple of days off or something. You could do with getting out of London."

"Like Matthew can get out of the case, like Lydia can get out of Brookwood."

Jonathan groaned. "That is precisely your problem, Maria. You just don't know how to distance yourself, and you're going to have to if this is going to be your career. Lydia is out of detention for the time being ..."

"Pending a fresh application."

"Which we will get on with. That's my point exactly. You're the sort of person who takes everything completely personally, and you just can't carry on like that. There is such a thing as being overcommitted, you know. You need to develop a ... a certain emotional detachment."

Maria took a swig of the brandy. It was a little rough, and she felt as though fumes of pure alcohol were drifting up her nose. "It makes my tongue feel like a carpet", she said thickly.

"I thought your generation were supposed to be the ladettes generation, hardened drinkers by the age of twelve or something."

"Not me. I was far too scared of losing my dignity."

"Dignity?" he chuckled. "You seemed happy enough to dispense with it at the police stations I've followed you to in recent months."

"Not the same thing at all", she answered, a little sulkily. "Some of my friends got into really ghastly situations when they were drunk. They never realised how vulnerable they were." She handed back the bottle. "Are you really that emotionally detached from all this? He's an old friend of yours. You surely can't treat it like just another case?"

Jonathan smiled. "All right, it is different in this case. I want to win because I don't want to see a dear friend's life destroyed. But I won't do him much good if I act rashly, now will I? And I want you to take a break. Just a long weekend. Take Friday and Monday off and come back to work on Tuesday. All right?"

A polite voice over the intercom enunciated, "This train will shortly arrive at London Euston, its final destination. All change, please. This train will shortly arrive ..."

Maria got up and gathered her things together. It was difficult to explain to a man with a wife and a home of his own that taking a holiday could be more stressful and depressing than working, but she also knew when she was not welcome and suspected that Jonathan desperately wanted a holiday from her for a few days.

11

"Don't go getting into a state", said Jonathan, as he and Matthew approached the building. "It's just a first appointment. Think of it as a technicality. You just go in there, confirm your name, and that's pretty much all there is to it today."

If Jonathan had not known better, he would have thought that Matthew was deliberately walking very slowly, like a child afraid to go to school on the morning he has not finished his homework. "I could develop quite a bad allergy to courtrooms by the end of this", said Matthew. "I've never liked being put on the spot."

"Think of it as an adventure. Have you never fantasised about being the hero of some thriller or action film? We've all done it."

"No."

"Oh, come on, have you never imagined yourself making a stand against injustice, being the little guy fighting Goliath?"

"No", answered Matthew emphatically. "Never in my entire life have I ever had the desire to be a hero. Remember, I'm a boring Englishman. I'm the benign, grey-haired doctor of children's nursery rhymes—and I've never had any imagination whatsoever." Matthew jumped at the sight of a few protesters clustering round a large banner near the front entrance of the court. There were only about five of them, he noticed, a couple of old ladies he suspected had been frequent visitors to Greenham Common once, since one of them was sporting a Ban the Bomb sweatshirt. Then there were a man about his age handing out leaflets and two young women holding the banner, which read "RIGHT TO DIE".

"Just ignore them", instructed Jonathan, as Matthew blenched. "They're just opportunists looking for an excuse to get some cheap publicity."

It was all right for Jonathan to say that, though; he was not the one being glared at. It was amazing, thought Matthew miserably, as he turned to look at the protesters and the two girls holding the banner glowered at him, how much hate could be conveyed by a pair of narrowed eyes and pursed lips. "There'll be more of them before long", he said, as they stepped indoors. "Mark my words."

As Jonathan had promised, it was all quite an anticlimax. The whole procedure lasted minutes, and Matthew felt an odd sense of liberation at the thought that the whole grisly judicial process had begun, a little as he had when he had been arrested. He suspected it was rather as a patient might feel who has been waiting in fear and trembling for months for a major operation, when he finally finds himself in the anaesthetics room with a mask over his face. Perhaps it was simply the feeling of there being no going back.

As they stepped out of the building, Matthew could hear chanting. The small gaggle of protesters had been joined by a few more now, and they were spouting something incomprehensible. He could just about make out shouted words like "doctor" and "patriarchy", but he got the message. "You don't even need to look at them", said Jonathan. "Don't give them the benefit of a reaction." He was about to change position so that he was standing between Matthew and the protesters when he heard Matthew make a strangled cry and turned round in time to see him stagger sideways, almost losing his balance. "Move!"

To the sound of peels of scornful laughter, Matthew felt himself being bundled into a car. "It was an egg, wasn't it?" asked Jonathan as soon as he had got into the car himself. The egg had broken against Matthew's neck, causing the contents to slop all over the lapel of his jacket and the collar of his white shirt. Matthew, meanwhile, had broken into a cold sweat. "Okay, let's get you home. Think of the martyrs or something."

"I'm thinking of what I'll tell Eva", he replied. "When I said I thought there would be more of them, I didn't expect it to be quite that quick."

But when Matthew unlocked his front door and fell into his wife's arms, he did not need to tell her anything. She held him silently until she sensed that he was calming down before helping him upstairs. "Where are the children?" he asked as he took off his soiled jacket, tie and shirt. He looked in the mirror and noticed a small graze on his neck where the egg had cracked open and thought what a ridiculous fuss he was making about something so small. His ancestors would have been pelted with eggs and stones as they were paraded through the streets on their way to the *scaffold*. No, it was no good; he still felt wretched, and there was no getting around it.

"Thomas and Cecilia are at school, Dominic is at nursery and I have just put Angelina down for her nap."

"I see. Sorry, of course they are. I've lost track of time." He sat on the edge of the bed to untie his laces and listened to Eva in the en suite bathroom, running him a bath. "There were protesters outside the courtroom", he said.

"Evidently." Eva knew about the protesters as she had known that her husband had had an egg thrown at him, because there had been a short report on the local radio station about it, but she decided not to tell him. She poked her head around the adjoining door and gestured for him to follow her. "Come and have a soak in a nice warm bath. Just forget anything happened."

As he slipped into the bath and felt the warm, scented water overwhelming him, he felt the delicious sense of being protected. It was a long time now since he had felt so safe, and he luxuriated in the joy of being looked after. With his eyes closed, he lay still whilst Eva rubbed shampoo in her palms and began massaging his head. He felt her delicate fingers weaving through his hair, caressing his scalp, and he gave a long, contented sigh. "I do love you, Eva", he whispered. "I'm not sure I tell you often enough."

"Ssh. I know." She cupped the warm water in her hands and poured it over his head, watching the tiny soap bubbles sliding back into the water. His hair looked so much darker when it was wet, the colour it had been when she had first met him. "You don't have to tell me anything." She pressed the back of her hand against his face, so that he instinctively nuzzled up against it, kissing her fingertips. "Whatever happens, I'm here."

"Thank you." Matthew was aware of every muscle in his body relaxing and the soft cloud of perfume lingering in the room as his wife stepped quietly back into the bedroom. He could hear the sounds of Eva pottering about, singing to herself before he heard her retreating footsteps down the stairs. Not so far away, an infant slept peacefully, curled up under her pink duvet, innocently unaware of the world of courtrooms and hospitals and police stations. When adults hankered after childhood, it was the security of innocence for which they were searching, the desire for everything, even fear to be uncomplicated. Children feared all sorts of things—monsters

77

under the bed, the horror of the lights being switched off—but for frightened adults anticipating every possible catastrophe, childhood fears at least seemed straightforward, easily dealt with, easy to comfort.

Nothing in adult life was ever straightforward.

Matthew could smell coffee when he stepped into the kitchen, comfortably and casually dressed almost in defiance of the formality of the courtroom, and he sat at the pine table watching Eva opening a packet of biscuits. She really was a beautiful woman, he thought, nearly ten years younger than him with not a trace of grey in her black hair yet or a single hard line on her face. He had always felt so proud of her at social events, cutting an elegant but curiously mischievous figure at his side. She had always had a plump, rounded face, not fat but enough that she still had dimples in both cheeks when she smiled, which had made her look quite childlike in spite of the passing years. When she turned around to look at him with the sunlight of the afternoon slanting across her body, he could not help noticing that she looked quite drawn.

"You look thin, my darling", he said, reaching out to take her hand. "You must try not to let this get to you. You'll get ill."

"I'm all right", she said, sitting down beside him. "It's you I'm worried about. There will be a break now before the trial, perhaps for months. Maybe we should try to get away."

"I do hope it won't be that long. It's the anticipation that gets to me the most. Whatever the end result, we just have to live with it. It's the uncertainty I can't live with."

"I know." She stroked his damp hair, then traced her hand lightly along the sunken contours of his cheek. He fell slowly forward and nestled his head on her shoulder, listening to the gentle, regular pulse beating in her neck. He was aware of her vital, physical presence surrounding him, the aromatic scent of her flesh; the subtle, almost teasing touch of her hands caressing his head. "I know."

"Evi, I'm scared", he whispered. "I'm terrified of what I'm doing. What I've done."

Eva grasped his head between her hands and looked him directly in the eye. "You did your job", she said. "That's all you did. It's not your fault if the world's gone mad."

"I know, I know, it's just . . ."

"You know you would never have left the poor girl to die. It would have haunted you for the rest of your life. I wouldn't have left the girl to die either."

"I'm just scared of what I'm doing to you. God knows what this could mean for the children."

"We'll manage", she said in a tone that should have ended any argument. "Whatever happens, we'll manage. I want the children to grow up knowing that some things are worth making sacrifices for, worth *suffering* for." He was on the verge of tears, she thought, and threw her arms around his neck because she could not think of any other possible response. "Darling, you've always been so protective of me. Now you must let me look after you a little."

"Possessive, I've been possessive!" he cried. "I've taken you for granted as though—as though you were made to be at my side when you had a life of your own once!"

"Don't be silly."

"They had to call me patriarchal, didn't they? They could have called me anything else!"

"Stop that. They always say those things. It's a cliché—patriarchal, paternalistic. It doesn't mean anything." She rocked him to and fro very gently, as though trying to send a feverish infant to sleep. "You talk as though I was forced to marry you, you silly man. I made a choice, and so did you. And I do have a life of my own."

"You deserved better than this. You deserved better than me."

She kissed his forehead. "Stop it, I mean it. I'm very proud of you. I always have been, and the children will be proud of you when they're old enough to understand. I know they will."

"I'm not sure they should be", Matthew choked. "I'm a terrible coward. You know what frightens me the most about all of this? It's the tiny part of me that wonders, if I had known how terrible the consequences would be, would I have made the same decision that night? Or might I perhaps have walked away and washed my hands of the whole affair, found some excuse not to act? That's what really scares me. Would I have passed the test if I had thought through precisely what it would mean?"

Eva shook her head slowly and smiled. "Perhaps it's a blessing that we don't always know how things will turn out, or we would all be cowards. And I'm not sure that you really didn't know. You and your friends who campaigned could see where it might end. That was why you fought. I don't believe for a single second that you would ever leave a patient to die, even if your life depended upon it."

"I hope not", he said. He rested, exhausted in his wife's welcoming arms, unable to think or move. But for a brief, blessed moment he did not have to do either.

12

Maria woke up to the pleasing sound of human activity not far away from her. After fretting away part of the Thursday night wondering what on earth she was going to do with herself for the next four days, Maria had remembered that there was someone she could go to outside London who would be pleased to see her. She had got out of bed, fired off a quick email to her friends and taken a sleeping pill, waking up with that delightfully relaxed, warm feeling of having rested deeply in a drug-induced sleep. When she switched on her mobile phone, she found a voicemail message waiting for her in her old friend's dulcet tones: "My dear, it would be simply wonderful to see you again; it's been far too long. Hop on a train as soon as ever you can, and I'll make sure the attic room is all made up for you. See you shortly."

The Herons were a family she had met at the chaplaincy when she was a student. They had lived at the time in central Oxford in a rambling house she remembered as being filled with books and intelligent conversation, where the dining room table perpetually heaved with food. Paul and Elizabeth Heron were academics, one long established in the English department, where he specialised in Anglo-Saxon poetry, whilst the female half of the marriage was a philosopher who had written books about Wittgenstein about which Maria was still too frightened to ask.

In the few years since Maria had graduated from Oxford, the Herons had retired, and the youngest of their six children had gone to university himself, giving them a reason to sell the big house in Oxford and establish themselves in an eighteenth-century terraced cottage in the nearby town of Abingdon. Fortunately, it was still full of books and intelligent conversation, and Maria could hardly contain her excitement as she fought her way through the rush hour crowds on tube, train and bus, knowing that as soon as she knocked on that red wooden door, she would be greeted by the unchanging vision of Elizabeth Heron, artistically swathed in floral print. There had to be some ever-fixed marks in every person's life, even someone as turbulent as Maria. The Herons, who had not so much as changed their hairstyles over the past twenty years, were Maria's living proof that there was such a thing beyond time and space as the Eternal Present.

She arrived just in time to find Paul, Elizabeth and their eldest daughter, Christina, having a late morning brunch. "Aah, good morning", Paul greeted her, standing up when she stepped into the breakfast room as though Maria dropped in for scrambled eggs on toast every day of the week. "We were a bit worried about you when we saw what time you wrote that email. Christy found it when she woke up for her early morning run. Did you get any sleep in the end?"

"Oh, yes, thank you, I had—erm, a rather long day. Had to go up to Birmingham for a hearing." Maria sat down and caught sight of the copy of the *Daily Gazette*, half buried by the loaded toast rack and the scattered remnants of the morning post.

"Did you win?" asked Elizabeth.

Maria put on an air of supreme self-assurance. "Naturally."

"Good. Help yourself to toast—I don't suppose you've had any breakfast this morning? The eggs are in that covered dish. I was just going to make some tea."

Maria somehow managed to spread butter over a slice of toast and exchange niceties with Christina as she scanned the article tucked discreetly into the right corner of the front page with the headline "Doctor in Right to Die case formally charged". The article began:

Dr Matthew Kemble, the doctor embroiled in a controversial right-to-die case, has been formally charged with assault and battery. Kemble, pictured, was reported to police after he ignored a living will and treated a suicidal patient who had expressed a direct wish to be spared medical intervention. The Crown Prosecution Service made the decision to bring the case following a complaint by the victim's brother and extensive investigations by police. If convicted, Kemble faces a custodial sentence and being struck off the medical register. As he left the hearing, he was greeted by angry protesters and pelted with eggs.

"Poor chap", said Paul, indicating the black-and-white photograph that accompanied the article, showing Matthew looking characteristically bewildered outside the courtroom. "I never thought I'd live to see the day when a doctor had to defend himself in court for saving somebody's life. It's like a scenario from Mein Kampf."

"Would you excuse me a moment?" asked Maria, springing to her feet. She rushed out of the room and dialed Jonathan's number.

"I should have refused to answer when I saw your number on the screen", said Jonathan. "I'm in the middle of a meeting. What do you want?"

"The papers are saying Matthew was pelted with eggs. Is he all right?"

"It was just the one egg, and he's fine. I saw that article too and all the others in all the other papers. You're supposed to be on holiday."

"I could hardly help reading a newspaper."

"Okay, I'm not answering your calls again. A holiday means a holiday." With that, he hung up.

Paul followed her into the room. "We were just thinking it might be nice to take the bus into Oxford this morning. Maria, would you like to join us? Don't worry if you'd rather stay back and rest, but we thought we might take a picnic to Christ's Meadows if the weather holds out. Anne's working at Saint Philip's bookshop at the moment and might be able to join us."

"That sounds perfect", she said. "I'd love to come." The phone rang again. "Sorry, I'll switch it off after this." Paul discreetly stepped outside again. "Hello?"

"Hi there, is that Maria? It's Mike from Westminster Radio."

"Hi, Mike, haven't heard from you for a while." Mike was the presenter of a popular prime-time news show and had built up quite a following among ladies of a certain age who were attracted by his cheeky Cockney style. He had established a professional friendship with Maria over the past year and often called on her to comment on issues surrounding ethics or Catholicism. Maria fancied that in his personal telephone directory she was the entry for Rent-a-Catholic-Nutter, but she couldn't say she really minded. "What's up?"

"Well, it's this right-to-die case that's appeared in the papers. Know anything about it?"

"Know anything? I'm up to my eyeballs in it!"

"Cooly cool, I just thought you might be. Fancy coming in to the studio to talk about it?"

"Mike, I can't possibly talk about a case if it's ongoing ..."

"Nah, I don't mean the actual case; that'll be in the news bulletin. We thought we'd follow it with a right-to-die debate. I'll have you up against some git from—what's it called? *Drop Dead* or something."

Maria hesitated. She knew Jonathan would absolutely not approve in this instance, though he had often encouraged her to go on the radio in the past. Added to that, she had got on his nerves once too often in the past couple of months and could not risk pushing her luck with him any further, but she found it almost impossible to resist a media request. It appealed to her vanity or her sense of duty, she was never sure which. "Could I do the debate over the telephone?" she asked. "It's just that I'm in Oxfordshire for the next few days on holiday."

"Course you can if you'd rather."

"And I just need to ask someone about it first, if you don't mind. I have to be a little bit careful because I'm involved in the case."

"Okey-dokey. Tell you what, darlin', give me a call in the next ten minutes, and I'll get a technician to touch base with you in time for the late-morning news."

"Thanks."

Maria rang Jonathan's number, then remembered that he was in a meeting and had probably switched his phone off. In any case, he had said emphatically that he would not be answering her calls for the rest of the weekend. She let herself imagine him on a really good day, after some big legal victory, with a gin and tonic in one hand and a grateful client thanking him profusely (they were never that profuse), then thought of him not minding. She dialed Mike's extension.

Matthew had spent the night in that excruciating state of being exhausted but quite unable to sleep—exhausted in every sense of the word; his joints ached as though he were going down with flu, and he felt so mentally tired that he would be halfway through indulging some morbid thought about the future when he would suddenly realise that he could not remember exactly what he had been thinking and where the thought had been going. At some point during the still watches of the night, Angelina had woken up crying with night terrors, causing Eva to wake up with a start, but he had told her to go back to sleep since he was already wide awake and might as well deal with it himself.

He had a vague recollection of carrying Angelina's stiff, hot little body into the bathroom and cooling her temples before bringing her into bed with him to try and settle her. Her hair felt hot and damp, and she shivered in his arms as she cooled down. He felt a little uncertain about how best to soothe her, since it was usually Eva who got up to console the children in the night, and it occurred to him that perhaps he ought to sing to her.

Now there was another link with the past. He had never been very good at nursery rhymes, but he had been a chorister once, years ago when he was a student, making him the most knowledgeable Catholic boy on the subject of Anglican worship in his year. He could still envisage the oak-paneled chapel at Magdalene College, Cambridge and the ranks of students in gowns blinking in the candlelight, looking every bit like time travelers staring into a world to which they did not belong and could not frankly understand but which nevertheless compeled them. *Oh, God, save the Queen . . .*

There had been plenty of secular concerts too, smart events in civic centres and concert halls where the men had dressed in DJs and gowns and the girls had decked themselves out in shimmering masterpieces, but they were harder events to remember because they had always been slightly drunk before they had even started. He tried to think of something from that vast library of repertoire suitable to sing to a fretful toddler.

> *Summertime, and the living is easy.*
> *Fish are jumping, and the cotton is high.*
> *O your daddy's rich, and your momma's good-looking . . .*

It sounded a little absurd, those Deep South lyrics intoned by a long-retired English choirboy, but Angelina's head rested peacefully against his chest, comforted by the deep rumble of his voice and the murmur of her mother's gentle breathing close by.

> *One of these mornings, you're gonna rise up singing*
> *Then you'll spread your wings, and you'll take the sky.*
> *But till that morning, there's a-nothing can harm you*
> *With daddy and mommy standing by . . .*

It was the strain. He could blame everything that was happening to him that he did not understand on the strain, but he could feel tears running down his face and the juddering spasm in his throat that made it impossible to sing any more. He lay down with Angelina fast asleep in his arms and stifled his own sobs for fear of waking his wife or daughter. Not for the first time, he was petrified by the sense that he was out of control. He had not cried since he was at primary school. The sensation felt bizarre, but he could not help himself and was amazed to discover that it gave him a dark feeling of release. He heard the soft sounds of Eva and Angelina breathing in the darkness and felt the warmth of Angelina's head beneath his hand, but no sooner had he begun to think how infinitely blessed he was to have them when he began to imagine losing them along with everything else, and he wept all the more.

Matthew must have slept, though he could not remember dozing off, because when he opened his eyes again he was cold, and Eva had evidently got up and put Angelina back in her bed whilst he rested. He felt the queasiness of having slept deeply for a very short time and knew he would never get back to sleep again, drifting instead in and out of consciousness as the sky lightened through the slats of the Venetian blind and the children began to stir. He felt Eva reach over and kiss him before she slipped out of bed. "Stay where you are", she said, when he made a halfhearted attempt to rise. "I know you didn't sleep. Come down when you're ready."

Matthew slumped gratefully into the mound of crumbled bed-clothes, yearning for oblivion to return.

The older children had already been safely dispatched to school and Eva was clearing away the breakfast things by the time Matthew limped down the stairs. There was something conspicuously missing from the table. "Any sign of the morning paper?" he asked.

"Would you feel up to taking the children to the park this morning?" asked Eva. "I really need to do some shopping, and it's much easier without the little ones running around."

Matthew sighed. "What is it you don't want me to see?"

Eva looked a little sheepish. "It was really nothing, just a report of the hearing. I didn't think you particularly needed to see it."

"All right, what did it say?"

"Nothing, really nothing at all important. I didn't think you would want to see your name in print, that's all."

"I think I'd better take a look at it", he said grimly. "You don't have to protect me from the paparazzi."

Eva felt her shoulders drooping. "What's the point?" she said quietly, looking down at the floor. "You'll only upset yourself, and you're enough of a bundle of nerves as it is. What does it matter what a lot of journalists have to say? It's the trial that is important."

"If they're dragging my name through the mud, I need to know what they're saying. I'm a grownup. I promise I can take it."

Five minutes after Eva had been persuaded to hand over the newspaper, Matthew was on the phone to Jonathan, enunciating into his voicemail recorder. "What does it mean I could face a custodial sentence? I thought that was supposed to be highly unlikely?"

He was interrupted by the sound of two small children fighting in the playroom, forcing him to hang up the phone and rush over to see what they were doing. Dominic was struggling to push Angelina off a small bench, which he had evidently decided was a car, and she was squealing and protesting. "Dominic . . ." Matthew began, but before he could break them apart, Angelina had sunk her teeth into Dominic's arm.

"Bite me!" he shrieked, bursting into tears. Angelina, who had more than recovered from her night terrors, gave a triumphant grin. "Bite my arm!"

Matthew stifled an almost unbearable desire to laugh. It was his young son's first lesson on the perils of failing to take an angry female seriously. "You mustn't bite, Angelina. It's very bad."

"I not bad!" *Oh, no*, he thought, *wrong word. Very definitely the wrong word.* "I not bad! I not BAAAAD!"

He was beginning to sympathise. A small part of him felt like doing exactly that—throwing himself on the floor, rolling around and shouting at the top of his voice: "I not bad! I NOT BAAAAAD!" It was almost a pity to have to pretend to be a mature adult.

"Stop it!" he said, as sharply as he could manage, but she was already calming down. "Now, kiss and make up and play nicely." Angelina and Dominic glared at one another as she finished the process of returning to normal, then looked up at their father before evidently deciding it was better to get on with it and give one another a perfunctory hug. Matthew kept a watchful eye on them until they had settled down to playing with the train set before stepping back into the kitchen and switching on the radio.

"It is a scandal in this day and age, in a supposedly civilised society, that we do not have the right to die with dignity. Doctors should accept it as part of their job to help patients who are suffering unbearably. Public opinion is on our side in this matter. What this doctor has done is to highlight the heartless, outdated attitudes of a dogmatic minority who would rather see a patient suffer than do the compassionate thing and let him slip away."

Matthew felt the tediously familiar lightheadedness overtaking him, and he sat down. Never in his life had he read about himself in the newspaper, never had he switched on the radio to hear himself being discussed on a live news debate. Never, for that matter, had he been cast as the villain in so much as a playground dispute. His head swam with the weirdness of it all.

"Thanks, Leslie", said the presenter. "Back to Maria. How would you respond to that?"

Matthew actually squeaked with indignation. What on earth was she doing on the programme? Jonathan might have had the decency to tell him this was happening. "I would begin", she said, in a calmer tone than he would normally have associated with her, "as I begin any conversation about euthanasia, by pointing out that it can never be a doctor's duty to kill, no matter how compassionate the motive might appear. The first command of the Hippocratic Oath is do no harm. A doctor cannot in good conscience use his medical knowledge to kill a patient. To do so would be to cross a moral barrier so fundamental that the consequences for society and for that individual would be horrific. Even if that were not the case, euthanasia groups have never been able to explain persuasively how they would prevent abuses being carried out."

"This is an old argument. You only have to look at the case of the Netherlands . . ."

"Excuse me, I haven't finished yet . . ."

"The Hippocratic Oath has not been obligatory for doctors to take for years, because right-minded people know perfectly well that it's outdated and irrelevant to modern society. In any case, living wills don't ask doctors to kill anyone, simply to mind their own business. Can't you people get your head around that?"

"Morally speaking, there is very little difference between actively killing somebody and deliberately leaving them to die. We should be proud of doctors who care about their patients enough to put their welfare first."

"Proud? They should be struck off! What Dr Kemble did was assault, nothing more, nothing less. He's a criminal."

"Thanks, I'm afraid that's all we've got time for", said the presenter. "Our phone lines are now open if any of you have any comments."

Matthew seized hold of the corner of the oilcloth in front of him and wrung it until it threatened to tear, whilst the radio emitted a low clicking sound and a lady called Maureen from Bristol came on the line. "I think it's disgusting! That poor girl just wanted to die. Why do men always have to interfere? They always think they know best. If I had my way I'd lock him up and throw away the key ..."

"The woman had a living will, which clearly stated she did not want to be treated under such circumstances." This time it was a solicitor from Tunbridge Wells. "However regrettable the situation, the doctor concerned must have realised he was acting unlawfully. Doctors who act on impulse and emotion rather than in accordance with the law should not be permitted to practice."

"What sort of a patriarchal, paternalistic cretin ignores the clear wishes of some poor, vulnerable woman?" This was Susan from Peterborough, whom Matthew could almost see, forty years previously, standing on some picket line outside the Lambeth Conference in her dungarees. "Why can't people take patients seriously? If you have the right to life, it follows that you have the right to die, and no one has any business interfering with that, particularly not a *doctor*." She said the word "doctor" as though she had really meant paedophile.

"Let's face it", said Barry from Northampton. "Some people are better off dead. A woman as messed up as that will probably keep making suicide attempts until she finally succeeds. It costs a fortune to keep people like that alive, and what's the point? And what about the strain on her family? If it was a dog, you'd put it down humanely, and no one would make a fuss."

"I think Dr Kemble is a hero", said Judy from Surbiton, and for the first time Matthew felt his little heart warming inside him. He had begun to wonder whether anyone on the entire planet was going to phone in on his side. "And God will reward him. The end times are coming. We are living in the last days, and God will smite the evildoers, the secularists, the nihilists, the abortionists ..." Matthew's heart sank like a dead haddock. He took a deep breath and reached for the phone.

"Dr Matthew Kemble", he said when he was put through. "An awful lot of comment has been made about my actions, and I seem to be the only person whose opinion has not been asked." He could hear the sound of his voice being picked up by the radio's transmission equipment and relayed to thousands of homes around the country, but for once he sounded and felt entirely calm. "I would simply ask the question: What sort of a society do you want to live in? What sort of medical establishment do you want to serve you? Do you want to see a society where the weak are simply chiseled away like so much dead wood and where human life is denied any inherent value at all? I have heard people speaking about putting dogs to sleep—is that really the way you see yourselves? No different from a dumb animal? Please consider the lessons of history before you state so casually that doctors should be forced to become killers. As Maria has already said, to do so would be to cross a moral boundary, the consequences of which might be more terrible than anything you could envisage."

He put the phone down and gathered up the children's outdoor shoes. By the time they had reached the park, it was all beginning to feel reassuringly far away again.

13

"I really do wonder whether I should just lock the pair of you up in some dungeon somewhere with duct tape over your mouths until after the trial!" roared Jonathan down the phone as soon as he had heard Matthew's radio performance.

"Look, I was getting desperate!" yelped Matthew. "Have you any idea what it feels like to have every Tom, Dick and Harry discussing your motives without having a clue what actually happened? When that nutty woman got started about the end times, it was the last straw. Why are the barking mad people always on *our* side?"

"Save the eloquent speeches for court, Matthew. You really don't need exposure like this just at the moment."

"I'm getting exposure whether I like it or not . . ."

"Just ignore it or rise above it, Matthew. I don't want to hear your dulcet tones on the radio again—is that clear? I do not expect to see you quoted in the papers. The same goes for Maria. I could wring her little neck. She was supposed to be on holiday."

"Don't go getting angry with Maria. It was very brave of her to go on live radio. I'm extremely grateful."

"Matthew, have you any idea how close the pair of you came to getting into serious trouble? If either of you had started discussing the case, you could both have found yourselves facing a contempt charge. It's not worth the risk to spend a couple of minutes getting your point across."

"Neither of us discussed the case. I wouldn't have done . . ."

"I'm very glad to hear it! But just in case you didn't hear me the first time, there will be no more of this. Do you understand? The best thing you can do to help your case is to keep your head down. I shall be saying the same to the female Dogtanian I seem to have employed."

"The who?"

"Children's cartoon my nephews used to watch, *Dogtanian and the Three Muskahounds*. Not important."

Jonathan indulged in a girly giggle after he had put the phone down, partly inspired by nerves. It did not occur to Matthew—and probably not to Maria either, though it should have—that he had driven away from his meeting with the radio interview in full swing, sweating with fear that Maria and then Matthew would let something slip. He knew already that Maria's first line of defence would be that she had said nothing incriminating and had never had any intention of saying anything she oughtn't, not appreciating in her missionary zeal that one false move from her could have had such devastating consequences.

One for all and all for one ... It had never occurred to him to call her the female Dogtanian before, but it was an apt description, and he had a feeling the nickname might stick. Dogtanian was the impulsive, spirited puppy dog of the story, whose courage was always praised after he had been beaten unconscious by a gang of dastardly alley cats with cudgels. "He fought well for one so young—mwah ha ha ha!" Jonathan slapped himself in the face. Heavens above, the strain was beginning to get to him too.

Late on Monday evening, Jonathan was not surprised to see Maria burst through his doorway, brandishing papers. "Thank goodness!" she gasped. "I was afraid I'd missed you."

"Highly likely, with my nine-to-five job", smirked Jonathan. "Found something earth-shattering then?"

"Well, it's not exactly a smoking gun," she began, anticipating that—as usual—he would not be as enthusiastic as she was, "but it does call into question his motives."

"Well? What is it?"

She passed him the file that she had been gathering together. "Well, you see, I thought you might be a bit unimpressed with me going on that radio programme ..."

"Deeply unimpressed."

"You see, my friend Mike rang me up and asked if I wanted to do it, and I couldn't get through to your phone to ask."

"I think you could have guessed the answer would have been no."

"Well ..."

"Familiar with the expression 'contempt of court', are we?"

"I told him I wouldn't discuss the case, and I didn't!" she exploded, giving her desk an unladylike kick. "The callers talked about it, but I didn't! I just talked about the legal problems with euthanasia and—and ..."

"I know, I heard the whole thing", he said, in the same cool tone he had used to needle her. "No harm done, as it happens, but don't ever sail that close to the wind again. If you'd been momentarily distracted and let a detail slip, it could have had consequences I don't need to describe to you. And there's no need to raise your voice."

"I'm sorry", she almost whispered. "I hadn't realised I was shouting."

"It's all right, but that's most of the problem, really, isn't it?" He glanced in the direction of the papers she had unsettled by jolting the table; she took in a sharp breath, aware of the tension she had created in the room, and dropped onto one knee to gather up the mess. "Just as long as you understand it's 'no' from now on."

Maria felt herself reddening with the humiliation of having put herself in the wrong yet again and wondered miserably what the secret was that every single person she knew seemed to possess of being able to remain calm when she never could. What peculiar energy enabled others to control that ever-present torrent of inner rage or even go through life without such a roaring inferno to power them? She glared out of the window, half expecting the glass to melt, until she felt calm enough to take up the threads of the conversation again. "There was something I thought you might want to know."

"Yes?"

"You know that really offensive caller on the radio programme?"

"They all sounded pretty offensive to me. Who did you have in mind?"

"Barry. I couldn't help thinking that the caller was really rather well spoken for a Barry."

"Oh, really, Maria, you are a proper snob!"

The bantering insult had the desired effect; Maria gave him a wry look and let her face relax into a smile. "I'm sorry, but it just felt wrong. I mean, the name didn't match the voice somehow. It was just a hunch. Anyway, I asked Mike about it afterwards, and he took a look for me. Sure enough, when they looked at the number Barry had called from, the code wasn't Northampton. He had rung from just outside Birmingham. Now, they weren't supposed to do this, but I was able to get hold of the number, and I gave it a ring."

"Maria, you should have just given it to me."

"Guess which nice little family pile I got through to? I can't prove it was her brother, but it does seem a little bit of a coincidence, doesn't it?"

Jonathan was starting to fidget. "And the significance of her brother is what exactly?"

"Wait. Mike said he'd send me a recording of that comment, but I didn't think it would be enough in court, so I did a little more work. It turns out it was her brother who went with her to make the living will. Nothing wrong with that in particular, but it might put a rather different spin on things that he believes some people are better off dead, particularly for the sake of their families. Self-interest and all that."

"Could you speak a little slower, please?"

"Sorry, sorry. Yes, self-interest. I also double checked that he is a member of the euthanasia-campaigning organisation Death Wish. Again, nothing particularly wrong with that either, except that you could argue he might have had other reasons for reporting Dr Kemble to the police than that he thought his sister had been the victim of an assault."

Jonathan shrugged. "He'll just say that he feels passionately that nobody should have his life prolonged against his will and that this tragedy occurring to his own sister only hardened his resolve to seek justice. I think the first point is more important."

"There's more." Maria sat down in a chair; she was going to impress him if it killed her. "I didn't think it could be a financial motive because Daisy did not have a will, and when I looked she had very few assets."

"This was your idea of a holiday, was it?"

"Sssh. She had very few assets. An insubstantial sum in the bank, no savings, no capital. But we know she was from a very wealthy family, and upon the death of her father she was due to inherit a considerable sum."

"Does she have other siblings besides her brother?"

"No, just her brother, and according to the terms of her father's will, she would have been the principal beneficiary. She was older, and the father seems to regard her as being the more sensible."

"Who told you that?"

"It was mentioned to me, shall we say", she answered mysteriously.

"You mean you've been hanging around her friends listening to gossip."

"The important thing", she continued a little tetchily, "is that if she died before her father, her brother would inherit everything. That

94

hardly makes her brother a murderer. The suicide attempt appears to have been genuine, but it does give him a reason to want her dead beyond mere ideology."

"It certainly does." Jonathan opened the file and glanced over the contents. "The details are all in here?"

"Yes."

"Excellent." They were both distracted by the irregular tread of a set of footsteps coming up the stairs towards them. "And that, if I'm not very much mistaken, is the faltering sound of a limping warrior."

"Poor man", said Maria. "He must be going through hell. I can't imagine anything like it."

"I'm sure you can", said Jonathan gently, then, in a more business-like tone: "Anyway, that's what we're here for. To get him out of hell—or keep him out."

Matthew poked his head round the door. "Evening, Jonathan", he said in an apologetic tone Maria was getting used to hearing. "Sorry to be such a pest, but I just happened to be in the area, and I thought I'd check up on how things were going."

"Don't worry, Matthew", said Jonathan, glancing momentarily at Maria. They both knew perfectly well that Matthew had been nowhere near the area; there was no reason why he should have been. "Maria here has been digging out some excellent evidence. Why don't you take a seat for five minutes, and we can talk."

"Do you mind if I head off?" asked Maria, moving towards the door. "There's somewhere I'm supposed to be this evening."

"Anything nice?" asked Jonathan. "Theatre? Cinema? Romantic dinner for two?"

"Actually, there's a talk about Pius XII at the Brompton Oratory I wanted to go to."

"Sounds scintillating. Well, we can't have you missing that; see you tomorrow."

As Maria sat on the Piccadilly line train to South Kensington, she looked at her reflection in the murky opposite window and told herself that it was not the same. What Matthew was going through was like nothing she had ever known, in spite of what Jonathan had hinted. When things just happened to you, particularly when you were very young, they simply had to be endured, but he had made a choice. It was not at all the same thing as living with somebody else's choice.

95

The train ground to a halt at her station, and she stood up to the sound of that decades-old male voice warning politely "mind the gap". And what made her feel even guiltier was the knowledge that she could step away from Matthew Kemble's crisis in a way that even Jonathan could not completely. For the space of an evening it would not be her problem. She would sit at the back of a warm, elegant meeting room in a fashionable part of London, and her attention would be absorbed by a speaker taking her through the details of an entirely different subject. There would be a discussion, there would be chatter, there might even be a trip to the pub with a few friends afterwards. It was an odd means of escape, but it was still an escape.

"Matthew, you don't look at all well", commented Jonathan. Matthew had waited patiently for half an hour for his friend to finish working, and by the time Jonathan had been able to give him his full attention, Matthew was so distracted that there had been little point in talking about the case. Jonathan had thought it a perfectly splendid idea on the spur of the moment to take Matthew to one of his favourite pubs and cheer him up—a quiet drink never failed to lift his own spirits, after all—and this was no ordinary public house either. The White Hart was one of the oldest pubs in London, and its clientele were primarily lawyers and other professionals who descended upon its oak-paneled inner sanctuary every lunchtime and evening, gasping for refreshment. They sat together at a small creaking table in one of the many small alcoves adorned with framed old newspaper cuttings and wartime propaganda posters, staring unenthusiastically into pints of warm beer.

"I'm not so bad really", Matthew ventured. "It's quite strange having so much time for the family. I took the little ones to the park today. Angelina loves the swings, giggled away like anything whilst I pushed her. It was quite nice doing all that rushing around in the fresh air." He paused, waiting for Jonathan to interrupt, but he said nothing. "I think the children must imagine I'm on some kind of extended holiday. Eva and I were thinking of taking them all for an outing on Saturday to a theme park or something."

"Good idea. Keep yourself busy, make the most of the time." Jonathan took a huge swig of beer and sat back in his chair. It had been a long day, and just sitting down in a nonwork environment was making him feel a little woozy. "After all, before you know it, the case will be over, and you will be back at work. Then you will look back at all this leisure time and wonder what you did with it."

"Or of course I could be in jail."

"You're not going to jail, Matt."

"The paper said I faced a custodial sentence."

"You don't want to believe everything you read in the papers."

"Or I suppose I could be permanently on leave." Matthew glanced up at one of the old newspaper cuttings on the wall opposite him. He could not read the date, but the photograph was notorious and appeared in every modern history textbook—Neville Chamberlain waving a piece of paper beneath a massive headline "Peace in our Time". "Do you know something, Jon? I'm beginning to wonder whether it would really matter in the long run if I get struck off. Life would have to change, but it might not be a complete catastrophe in the long run. I'd—I'd get used to it."

"Matthew . . ."

"I heard of another doctor who was struck off—indecent images on his laptop, I think it was—and he got a job in adult education teaching at a night school." He looked fixedly downwards, aware of Jonathan's wholly unconvinced presence bearing down on him. "He—he ended up setting up his own business. There would be more time for the family, not so much stress . . . I could—well, I could just learn to live with it all . . ."

"Don't be ridiculous, Matthew", snapped Jonathan, giving him a wary glance. "You're going into defeat mode, and none of my clients are allowed to do that."

"I'm just trying to be philosophical . . ."

"Well, don't." Jonathan sat up straight so that the two men were at eye level across the table. "I'm not remotely interested in your fake optimism."

"It's not fake."

"It's like my friend Father Holloway used to say. There are two types of optimism, real optimism and fake, cowardly optimism. Real optimism sees the Valley of Dry Bones and says, 'These bones will rise!' Fake, cowardly optimism says, 'I like these bones. Dry bones are so very artistic to look at.' We're not going down the second road, are we now, Matt?" He watched Matthew sitting in dejected silence. He had never been any kind of an optimist, Jonathan remembered, but in the past it had hardly mattered. "It's all right, Maria found some excellent information today. I feel a lot more positive about the whole case."

"Oh, yes?"

"Yes, Maria has been going after the girl's brother. Obviously, he will be a key witness for the prosecution because he was the one who first reported you and seems to be the driving force behind this case, so we'll be going for him—in a civilised fashion. Maria has been ferreting about, getting herself arrested and all sorts ..."

"Oh, dear, again? I really don't want her to get into any trouble on my account."

"It's all right, Matthew, it was entirely her fault as usual, and she loves it. There's a certain kind of person who just enjoys making a nuisance of himself."

Jonathan and Matthew sank into silence, each occupied with his own thoughts. Jonathan mulled over the details of what Maria had told him earlier, whilst Matthew allowed his attention to wander to the strains of an Andrew Lloyd-Webber song ringing out from one of the loudspeakers. He recognised it as something from *Phantom of the Opera*. "How do you know her?" asked Matthew, finally. "Maria, I mean."

"I met her at a conference when she was in her first year at university", said Jonathan. "She might even have been one of the organisers— can't remember now. Anyway, Freya and I went along. I was giving one of the talks, and we got chatting afterwards. She and Freya became friends, and after she graduated, she called me up and asked if there was a job going."

"I see."

"She wasn't sure exactly what she wanted to do initially, so I found her a job with the Catholic Institute as a researcher. As I suspected she would, she ended up enrolling on a law conversion course."

"And she's completing her legal training with you."

"You must have come across her on the campaigning circuit?"

"Oh, yes, her name was familiar, but our paths never really crossed much before. It's just ... well, nothing, I suppose. I just find her quite hard to make out."

Now there's a surprise, thought Jonathan a little cruelly, because his friend had always come across as the sort for whom women and the younger generation were almost infinitely mysterious. "Not much mystery there, really", he said instead. "She's fairly typical of that John

Paul generation of London Catholic. You know the type: orthodox, highly strung, highly educated, take themselves *far* too seriously, but we can forgive them that. The future of the Church we all hoped for when our own friends were making tie-dye skirts and smoking pot."

Matthew gave a halfhearted laugh. "You know something, Jonathan? I don't know what your misspent youth was like, but I was never once even *offered* a drug. Maybe I was just so busy trying to pass exams that I missed the trendy season." He smiled to himself, and Jonathan noticed how much the change of subject was relaxing him. "You weren't a rebel, were you?"

"Had a few regrettable haircuts, if that's what you mean." He hesitated. "Matthew, what's bothering you? It's not the case this time, is it?"

Matthew held up his hands in mock surrender. "I'm sorry, nothing. I'm always seeing problems where there are none."

"And?"

"Not sure what I'm really going on about, really. I suppose it's just that—well—when a young woman is so driven, I can't help wondering what brought her to that. I'm not saying there's anything wrong with being a campaigner, you understand, it's a laudable thing to do, but it's a bit like choosing to be a professional troublemaker. I'm always interested in people who do that."

"Maria is quite alone in the world", said Jonathan, cautiously. "I suppose that's why Freya and I feel so protective of her. She lost her parents when she was five years old."

"That's awful! What was it, a car crash?"

"Her mother was killed in a car accident on her way home from work. Her father couldn't come to terms with it, and six months later he stepped in front of a train."

Matthew looked up at him in silent disbelief. "Suicide? Look here, I'm not sure she should be involved in this case at all. I'd no idea!"

"It's all right."

"But it must be *torture* for her hearing about suicide all the time. Talk about a sensitive subject!"

"No, no, I think it's quite good for her. Please don't worry."

"Good for her?" he blustered. "How can it possibly be good for her?"

"It's what you picked up on", explained Jonathan steadily. "She's a fighter because she's always had to be a fighter, and I don't think she'll ever be able to stop now. I just need to make sure she's always fighting for a good cause."

"And I'm a good cause?"

Jonathan looked a little uncomfortable for the first time. "Matt, I'm not exactly a shrink, but I'd say she's fighting your corner because she wishes that there had been someone to stop her father all those years ago."

"Hmm" was the only response Matthew could manage.

"Look, she knows, like anyone who's lost a relative to suicide, that it isn't just about personal autonomy. She has had to live with the consequences of that choice all her life."

"That explains everything."

"Including her attitude to men, I suspect", said Jonathan with a smirk. "I don't think she honestly believes any man's worthy of her trust."

"No young man on the scene?"

"Absolutely not, never has been. Well, would you have had the guts to ask her out?"

Matthew slumped back into his chair. "You know, I wouldn't want to judge anyone, Jonathan, but I just can't imagine doing that to a child. I won't pretend that I'm not pretty close to the edge at the moment, but even in the darkest moments I know my children need me."

"That's because you're still capable of thinking rationally."

"I'm not sure about that," he said, "but if nothing else mattered to me, the idea of leaving my children alone would be unconscionable. The sense of betrayal doesn't bear thinking about."

"Quite", said Jonathan. "She's never spoken of it, but I suppose that no matter how much she can convince herself her father was mentally unbalanced and didn't really know what he was doing, part of her will always feel—well, abandoned, I suppose."

Matthew sat in silence, drinking with interminable slowness before answering. "I wondered why she was so on edge with me at that horrible cafe, right at the start. Well, at least it all makes sense now." Another silence; Jonathan drained his glass. "What injuries people do carry with them! In my profession I come across so many terrible situations, but it still never ceases to amaze me what people have to bear."

"Indeed."

14

"What the hell do you want?" snarled the voice at the end of the phone.

Maria drew in a sharp breath. She had not been expecting a particularly friendly reception and had prepared herself for a response like that, but hostility was never easy to bear all the same. "Peter, I know you said you didn't want anything to do with this, but I was just wondering ..."

"I made it abundantly obvious I didn't want anything to do with you and your ilk again. I wish I'd never made contact with you in the first place. I've regretted it ever since. How did you get hold of my number?"

"There's this thing called directory enquiries."

"I'm warning you, get out of my life. You really don't want to get in my way."

"Is that a threat?" But a click followed by the discreet buzz of the dial tone made it clear that he was no longer there to answer the question.

Maria was sitting at her desk in Jonathan's office, surfing a social networking site when her employer came in. "What are you doing messing around with that rubbish during working hours?" he demanded, throwing his briefcase onto the desk with an impolite thud. "I'll have that site blocked. You're supposed to be working on Lydia's case."

"It's all there", she said, pointing in the direction of his desk, "under the case you've just lobbed at it. I'll go down to the High Court in a minute and deal with canceling Lydia's removal orders."

Lydia's fresh asylum claim had been turned down on the grounds that China was relaxing its family planning laws. There was no evidence on the ground to back up such a claim, but Maria had long grown out of the notion that the UK Border Agency was living on planet Earth and had not been especially surprised to read the reasons for Lydia being refused asylum. This was, after all, the institution which had allegedly once turned down an asylum claim on the grounds that "guerrillas" were not commonly found in the claimant's country and, like most primates, seldom attacked humans unless their habitat was disturbed.

The dismissive expression "totally without merit" had jarred horribly, but Maria had tried not to let it rankle as she began the next part of the rescue process. "I've got quite a good dossier together if I say so myself", said Maria, as Jonathan dragged the file out from under his case and began to leaf through the pages. "I telephoned a campaigning organisation, and they gave me a whole list of contacts. Lord Clandon wrote me a submission, a senator in the United States ..."

"That'll be Senator Ashfield, bless him."

"Yes. An Australian parliamentarian and the directors of an international pressure group. I've also included reams of information on the current situation in China for women who have unauthorised pregnancies. Doubt if they'll bother looking at it, but it's there. Of course, if she was sleeping with her caseworker ..."

"I know, I know. Don't let's get bitter. You know she's back in Brookwood again?"

"Yes, I received a phone call from her in a state when she arrived. Said she was locked in the back of a van so long she wet herself and everyone laughed at her. I'd like to punch their lights out!"

"Professional detachment, Maria ..."

"Sorry. At least the pregnancy is a little better established by now, but she still shouldn't be in a place like that. I'll book another bail hearing when I make the application to cancel her removal orders."

"Good." Jonathan grimaced at Maria's computer screen.

"It's not my profile page I'm looking at", said Maria, by way of self-justification. "It's Daisy Havisham's."

"Eh?"

"Well, it occurred to me that with so many people of my generation using social networking sites, it was likely Daisy must be. I've been through them all—MyPlace, SNAP, and I've found her on Friendbook. Fortunately, she's a bit lax about her privacy settings, and there's a great long list of her friends here for me to look through. Don't know why I didn't think of it before."

Jonathan sat down, frowning. "I don't know. It all feels a bit sneaky somehow."

"Oh, I'm very, very sneaky", admitted Maria. "I've done worse."

"Yes, I know. I suppose this is legal at least."

"Interestingly enough," said Maria, "the woman who accompanied her to the hospital—Jennifer Little—isn't listed among her friends. But then, she might well be one of those people who hasn't signed up yet. There are lots of Jennifer Littles, so it's difficult to know."

"Good heavens, the loser!" cried Jonathan. "Not on a social networking site? Whatever could the girl be thinking?"

"Yeah, yeah, all right."

Daisy's privacy settings were so low that her entire profile was on public display, something she might not have realised was the case, and there were a huge number of messages from friends on her wall, ranging from "Get Well Soon xxx" to lengthy expressions of disbelief. "You can learn a lot from people's profiles", said Maria out loud. "She's a member of all sorts of groups, but no euthanasia lobby groups, surprisingly. And she's posted on a prolife discussion board."

"Oh, yes?"

"It's dated about a fortnight before she made the suicide attempt. Listen to this: 'I wish you'd stop going on about the sanctity of life, it's just arrogance. Do any of you honestly believe your lives are that important? If I died tomorrow, the world would hardly grind to a halt, only a handful of people would even notice and in a few years' time it would be as though I had never lived. Life isn't precious, it isn't sacred. You just pretend it is to forward your own agendas.' "

"It's all about issues and agendas with your generation, isn't it?" mused Jonathan. "Can you make a printout of that before someone deletes it?"

"Certainly." Two clicks later, the printer roared into life. "The problem with finding out who her friends are is that there are so many of them. She has just over two hundred Friendbook friends, which isn't even very many by some standards, and many of them will be little more than acquaintances."

Jonathan stood behind her and peered at the screen. "How exactly does this thing work?" he asked. "I mean, can anyone become your friend?"

"No, you send a friend request to a person, and they have to confirm it. Now, some people are quite scrupulous and security conscious, so they would only add or confirm as friends people they know very well, but most are a little more slack, so they'll include pretty much anyone—people they've met very briefly through other people, people they've only ever come across on the Internet. Sometimes they'll confirm friend requests of people they don't even remember, so it's quite a smorgasbord."

"Sounds absolutely crazy if you ask me. All the public fuss there is about government databases and thousands of young people putting up their personal details on the Internet for the world and his wife to see. Are you on sites like this?"

"Oh, yeah."

"Crazy."

"You run a blog, don't you?"

"That's different. It's anonymous."

Maria smirked and typed his name into a search engine. A few of the links that came up referred to a different man of the same man—an architect from New York by the looks of things—then there were some mundane links to legal directories. Six or seven links down the page was a link to a popular political blog. The excerpt read, "Jonathan Kirkpatrick, who writes under the quirky title of 'Horace Rumpole', puts it succinctly when he writes ..." "Very anonymous, Rumpole. Cloak and dagger stuff if ever I saw it."

Maria left Jonathan to nurse his hurt middle-aged pride and went back to the task at hand, printing off a list of Daisy's friends so that she could cross off the unlikely candidates. It was a process of elimination, a question of working out slowly but surely who her close circle of friends was likely to be. There were various factors she could consider— the frequency and tone of wall posts, the precise network to which the friend belonged. Old school friends might know her well but probably did not have the close contact with her in adult life that they had had once. Extended family such as cousins could be useful, but Daisy's family relationships had been such that Maria was loath to trust any of them. University friends offered the best possibilities as they tended to be the sort of friendships that were completely freely chosen and lasted into early adult life ... but then again, which university friends?

"You have remembered we're meeting with counsel this afternoon, haven't you?" asked Jonathan. "And we'll be discussing witnesses, amongst other things."

"I've remembered."

"We need a close friend of hers to talk about her state of mind. If the boyfriend still won't play ball ..."

"He definitely won't", she winced. "What about the friend who discovered her and accompanied her to the hospital?"

"She's appearing for the prosecution."

"Oh. That is a pity. I wonder if I could ..."

"No, whatever it was."

"What about Daisy herself?"

"Out of the question. She won't be appearing in court at all."

"Is she really too weak at this stage?"

"Yes, disastrously so. She was in a coma for weeks, thanks to the insulin overdose, and she's apparently suffered minor brain damage— memory loss, which is most convenient from our point of view. I gather she is expected to make a full recovery, but it could take months, so for the moment she's tucked up in hospital in far too fragile a condition to be involved in a trial."

"If I didn't know better", mused Maria, "I'd think that the trial was being rushed through as quickly as possible to make absolutely sure that a certain person could not take part."

"No conspiracy theories, please. Things are sinister enough as they stand, thank you very much."

Maria gave him a withering look that Jonathan would have dismissed as "making lazy eyes" if he had happened to be looking in her direction when she did it. "Strange, though, isn't it? To think that whilst all this is going on, the only person who knows nothing about it is the woman who unwittingly started the whole thing."

Jonathan opened his mouth to make a sardonic retort, but he realised that Maria was the one looking inexplicably fragile, and he rapidly changed tack. "See who you can find. Just be careful."

"Cross my heart and hope to ... whatever." Maria went back to work, ticking off names and faces, demolishing as she went the many interconnecting circles that make up a person's identity— school, university, work, the sharers of hobbies, music, sport, reading, political or religious interests. She struck them all down one by one like a trained marksman until only two faces peered at her in black and white from the printed sheet. Melanie Lewis and Rebekah Walter.

She tried to calculate, simply by looking at them, which was the most likely woman to be close to Daisy, then decided to email them both.

I wonder whether I could speak with you in the strictest confidence about your friend Daisy Havisham? I assure you that my interests are entirely professional. My number, should you be willing to get in touch, is at the end of this email.

Yours,
Maria Hargreaves

She had one predictable reply within the hour. "Who the f*** are you?" screamed a hysterical voice when she ecstatically answered the phone.

"I work for a firm of solicitors ..." Maria almost stammered.

"How nice for you. What d'you think you're playing at getting in touch with me? What do you want with Daisy?"

"I was just wondering whether we could talk. I—I would be interested in finding out ..."

"Well, we can't. Mind your own bloody business and leave me alone. I just happen to be a friend, that's all."

"Yes, I thought you were", said Maria desperately. "That's why ..."

"You've been hassling other people, haven't you? As if her boyfriend doesn't have enough to worry about without people like you on his back."

"As a matter of fact, he ..."

"Just back off! Which bit of 'back off' don't you get? Come after me or any of her friends, and I promise you'll wish you hadn't."

Maria grasped the edge of her desk. "Listen, there's no need to threaten me ..." but the increasingly typical sound of a phone hanging up arrested her midsentence. In what Jonathan might mistakenly have believed to be the beginnings of professional detachment, she stood up as calmly as she could manage, picked up Lydia's file and headed towards the High Court. For once, she was quite looking forward to spending an hour negotiating her way around the hypnotically familiar labyrinth of procedures and protocols.

When Maria left the High Court, she discovered that she had acquired an appendage by the name of Rick with whom she had got chatting in the queue to make her application. He was not an unattractive appendage, she had to admit, and would probably cut quite a dashing figure in gown and bands. Unlike some of the arrogant, patronising little specimens she remembered from the law faculty at university (come to think of it, they had almost all been like that, particularly the men), he had come across as amiably self-deprecating as they chatted about immigration law and its pitfalls.

"The worst thing about it", he had said as they walked through the imposing building together, "is how much of a game it is, which box they tick—deport, don't deport. If you're happy to play the system as a game, it doesn't much matter, but if you really care about what you're doing ..."

"I do care", she cut in. "It a pretty shabby game when the tokens are people, isn't it?"

"I know you care. It does rather show." She blushed alarmingly. "Oh, please don't be embarrassed, that wasn't supposed to be a put-down. I think lawyers *should* care. We're all so cynical, then we wonder why people think we're a bunch of heartless ambulance chasers."

Outside, in the melee of the real world, Maria ground to a halt, and Rick stopped with her, both of them wondering what the next move was, if there was to be one. "I tell you what", said Rick, after a judicious pause showed him that she was reluctant to leave his company. "I'm rather enjoying this conversation. How about a coffee?"

Maria was about to answer that she would love a coffee as long as it was quick when her wretched, wretched, *wretched* phone rang. It was like an emotionally charged moment in a film being ruined by an unexpected power cut. "Would you excuse me for just two minutes?" she pleaded, looking at the display screen and realising she did not recognise the number.

"Of course. Answer your call."

Rick made halfhearted attempts at avoiding overhearing her conversation, but found himself picking up enough snatches of it to wonder what on earth she was involved in. "Is everything all right?" he asked, when she slipped the phone back in her pocket, visibly shaking.

"Certainly", she replied, clearing her throat. "It was a—a client." She felt desperately awkward. "Look, I'm afraid I'm going to have to go. Here." She handed him her business card. "Maybe we could have that coffee some other time?"

"Why not?" he said, giving her a polite nod.

Maria walked away in the gloomy realisation that a moment had passed. They would not have that coffee, she thought. He would never dial her number.

15

Angus Wetherby QC had always fascinated Maria in a way that all members of an older generation who represented some lost art intrigued her. In Angus Wetherby's case, it was his ability to appear every part the dear old duffer, obsessed with wine-soaked dinners organised by the British Heraldic Society, whilst being one of the most brilliant minds she had ever encountered. He came from a long line of lawyers, and several of his long-dead relatives had been judges, which had shocked Maria when she had first met him.

"You mean your forefathers sentenced people to death?" she had asked in undisguised indignation.

"Of course they did, my dear", he had answered, without apparently noticing her tone. "My own father dispatched a few quite famous villains."

"But how could they live with themselves?"

Angus had shrugged his vast shoulders in a gesture that reminded Maria of an enormous raven preening its feathers, before answering. "Well, whatever did you expect? A judge must act within the law. You cannot remember a time when the state reserved the right to hang murderers, so you find it morally repulsive. As it happens, I am inclined to agree with you, but for centuries nobody in particular questioned the practice."

"You agree with me?"

"Yes, as a matter of fact. Does that surprise you? I daresay you think I'm Attila the Hun."

It had crossed my mind, thought Maria. "Why?"

"Why am I not Attila the Hun? Well, as a matter of fact, I'm more than aware that the British justice system, like any other, is flawed and sometimes makes mistakes. It's distressing enough when an innocent person goes down for years for a crime he did not commit, but capital punishment is somewhat terminal. What would your reasoning be?"

But Maria had blushed and heaved a sigh of relief as Jonathan had interrupted to get the meeting under way, because she would have been too embarrassed to admit to a man hardened by years of legal battles that the reason deep down why she hated capital punishment was because she did not want anyone to go to hell and thought that if a person had time—years even—to contemplate what they had done, they might regret it before it was too late. But it sounded so absurdly sentimental that she could almost hear the guffaws of laughter she would surely provoke.

The three of them—Jonathan, Maria and Matthew—sat in the waiting room whilst Angus Wetherby's clerk informed him of their arrival. "You'll get on with Angus", Jonathan promised Matthew, who was glancing around at the crimson wallpaper, trying to decide whether it felt more like waiting to see the dentist or being back at school again. School came into his thoughts quite a lot at the moment, mostly because of the feeling of being in disgrace that had dogged him since the complaint was first made. "As much as anyone gets on with Angus, of course. I've worked with him many times over the years, and he is an excellent barrister, just the chap you want on your side in a tight spot."

"I hope you're right", said Matthew.

"Don't be put off by the whole process. It'll be a relatively informal meeting, but he'll need all the nitty-gritty detail if he's going to advise us properly."

"Wonderful."

"Oh, do cheer up, Matt; you'll feel much more reassured after this, I promise you."

Andrew, Angus Wetherby's clerk, stepped into the waiting room. "He's ready to see you now", he said.

They trooped into a slightly musty meeting room, where Angus Wetherby, as large as life, was sitting at a heavy polished table. He stood up to usher them in. "Come in, come in, Jonathan. Good to see you again. Dr Kemble, I presume?"

No, I'm Old Mother Hubbard, Matthew almost responded, but he took the man's proffered hand cheerfully enough, and they all sat down. "Well, Dr Kemble, I've taken a look at your case, and you've certainly got yourself into a rather sticky situation, if I may say so, but not irretrievable."

Matthew flinched. "I assure you I didn't see it that way at the time", he said. "I rather thought saving lives went with the job."

"Don't get me wrong; it's a preposterous case", replied Angus, in a placatory manner. "I'm amazed the CPS took the trouble to take it on in the first place, which leads me to think that someone wants to make an example of you."

"Splendid. That's what Jonathan said."

"Has Jonathan told you what to expect?"

"Yes", Jonathan interrupted. "He knows you're going to ask him some questions and why."

"Good. Perhaps, in your own words, Dr Kemble, you could tell me exactly what happened on the night the incident happened?"

Matthew's shoulders drooped as though crippled with a sudden weight. "I've had to tell this so many times . . ."

"If you wouldn't mind?"

"I went on duty—I was on a night shift. I saw various casualties, the sort of cases you'd expect to find in A+E at that time of night. Then a junior doctor asked for my opinion on a difficult case."

"I see. Go on."

"I couldn't understand at first what the problem was. It was a suicide attempt, a drug overdose, and we get plenty of those. But then the doctor told me that she had a living will . . ."

Angus had the habit of listening to clients accounting for their actions with his eyes closed, so as to concentrate as precisely as possible on the actual words being spoken. He would open his eyes every so often to take down a note or two or when he wanted the client to stop talking momentarily, when he would make eye contact with them and raise one hand as though hailing a taxi. He had to stop Matthew relatively frequently as he tended to digress or become preoccupied with a minor detail, or Angus would have to ask him to explain a medical term he had casually dropped into the narrative. It did not help the flow that every time Angus closed his eyes, Matthew thought he was nodding off and paused to ask if he was still awake.

"Hmm", was Angus' verdict, when he had finished putting Matthew through his paces and Matthew was sitting back in his chair, exhausted and somewhat deflated. "There do seem to be one or two fairly serious gaps in the evidence. Where are the medical notes?"

"The prosecution have been very cagey about letting us see them", Jonathan explained. "We are in the process of applying to the court for them, but that shouldn't be a problem."

"I see. Your list of witnesses is a trifle thin. Very thin, in fact."

"Yes, well, there are rather more people willing to line up to condemn a doctor in a situation like this than stand by him. Professor

Nigel Reid, consultant psychiatrist at Saint Luke's, is our expert witness on depression. If we can make the point that the woman might well have been suffering from depression, whether or not she had been diagnosed, it would cast doubt on . . ."

"Yes, yes, yes, I can see the direction your case tends. What about this Dr Harry Whatshisname? Is he sympathetic?"

"Yes, he's finally agreed to give evidence for the defence, but he'll need a lot of direction. He's . . ."

"A spineless airhead", Matthew chimed in. "A charming spineless airhead, you understand, but he'll dither his little white coat off in the witness box."

"That's funny", commented Angus. "I've only ever heard the word 'airhead' used in connection with women before."

"Not sure why it should be", Maria returned, suddenly aware of being the token oestrogen presence in the room. "I can think of plenty of men who fit the bill. It's like Bimbo."

"Thank you for your contribution, Maria", said Jonathan, like the chairman of a contentious debate when the loopy woman in the big hat stands up to make a point. "Matthew, of course, will have to have his turn in the witness box."

"Yeeees." The moment the defendant stepped into the witness box was every defence team's worst nightmare. The trial could be going along perfectly nicely, thank you very much, only for the defendant to open his mouth and paint himself into such a ridiculous corner the Archangel Gabriel would be unable to find a way of getting him out. "You need a witness close to Miss Havisham, a relative, a friend perhaps, who could cast doubt on her capacity to draw up a living will in the first place."

"We've tried her boyfriend", said Jonathan.

"And?"

"He'd make an excellent witness", Maria came in. "He basically said that she was completely controlled by her family. He didn't think she was capable of making a firm decision on anything, but he won't budge."

"Any chance he could be persuaded?"

"Absolutely not. He's rather conflicted about the whole thing and thinks we're a bunch of reactionaries peddling an antichoice campaign."

Angus sighed. "I see."

"Unfortunately, the girl who found her is appearing for the prosecution," added Jonathan, "and the other girl she shared a house with has completely melted away into the background. We haven't been able to trace her."

"Well, you need to find somebody to fill that gap. If the family are lined up against you, it will have to be a friend, but you must find somebody." Angus pressed his hands against the table in front of him and stretched. "Well, aside of that gap, it seems to me that you have a good case, and you should enter a plea of not guilty. The case will hinge upon whether or not Miss Havisham made that living will freely and in full possession of her mental faculties and upon whether Dr Kemble here acted out of necessity in ignoring the living will, given the shortage of time to consider the implications of such a document. However, it will be almost impossible to fight this case without calling into question the prosecution's view of the policy behind the law itself."

Matthew glanced up at him in alarm. "I understood that it would not be necessary to challenge the understanding of the actual law. Surely it will only weaken my chances of acquittal?"

"It might not weaken your chances, though of course it raises the stakes considerably. The fact is, if living wills and third-party attorneys had not been codified into law by the End of Life Care Act, you would not be in this situation, Dr Kemble. You would have made a legitimate medical decision on that evening, similar to many others you have made in the past, and that would have been an end to it. It would never have come anywhere near the courts. What we will need to do, I suggest, is to persuade the court that Parliament did not intend by this act to diminish or overthrow good medical practice or to allow deliberate killing or, worse, inhuman or degrading treatment, such as a slow death by dehydration. If the court is not with us on that, then we might have to argue that such a view of it makes it incompatible with Articles 2, 3, 8, 9 and 14 of the European Convention." He turned to Jonathan and Maria. "We need that witness."

"I'm working on it, Mr Wetherby", promised Maria, but her heart sank. She wondered how many more obscene phone calls and vague threats of retribution she would have to endure before someone crawled out of the woodwork to save the day. "There must be somebody she knew who's glad she's alive and isn't afraid of saying it."

"There you are, don't you feel rallied for the fight?" demanded Jonathan as they walked through the maze of narrow, quiet lanes back to the noisy main road. "You should feel confident with a man like Angus on your side."

"Of course", said Matthew, with the tone of a child thanking his spinster aunt for an unwanted Christmas present.

Maria swore audibly. "Really, Maria!" exclaimed Jonathan. "I didn't know a nice girl like you even *knew* the expression."

"I've got a missed call from a withheld number, and they didn't have the decency to leave a voicemail message. I'll never be able to get back to them now." She began trying to access her emails but found it impossible to keep pace with her colleagues and fiddle with her mobile at the same time. "Can't we just stop a minute?" she begged. "This might be important."

"Can't you wait five minutes and check your emails back at the office?" came the wearyingly reasonable response.

The Leningrad Symphony erupted into life, causing the three of them to jump. "You wouldn't be feeling a little paranoid, by any chance?" asked Jonathan, as Maria put the phone to her ear, silencing the ominous rumblings of Nazi jackboots immediately.

"Hello?"

"Hi", said a quiet voice. "Is this Maria Hargreaves?"

"Speaking."

"Hi. I'm Rebekah. You sent me a message." There was the sound of her clearing her throat. "I'd like to know what's going on, please."

"Of course. Are you based in London?" Maria stopped in her tracks, causing a woman speed walking behind her to swerve dangerously, shouting a mouthful of abuse in her direction as she stalked away. Jonathan and Matthew stopped to look back at her. "Good. Not today? OK, how about tomorrow afternoon then? Could you manage that? Great. Why don't I give you the postcode? It's very easy to find. Great. Bye for now."

"Who were you talking to?" asked Jonathan, when Maria had caught up to them.

"The missing link, I hope", she said.

16

Jonathan scrutinised Maria's latest find with the scepticism of a man who has watched witnesses go to pieces in court once too often and is dogmatically determined not to go through such a humiliation again. Rebekah Walter did not come across as an especially promising specimen; he noted her eyes darting nervously around the room from behind bottle-top spectacles and her starchy appearance, pie-crust collar poking out from beneath a buttoned-up cardigan embroidered with clematis flowers. "I thought I was meeting with a woman called Maria", she said, in a stronger tone than he had anticipated.

"I'm sorry about that", said Jonathan, sitting at the desk opposite her. "I'm afraid Maria has been called away to deal with an emergency—an asylum case we're dealing with has taken a turn for the worse. I hope you won't mind talking to me instead."

"I suppose not. I would like to help."

"Good. Are you comfortable with the details of the case?"

"Oh, yes, I think so. To be honest, when I heard what had happened, I couldn't really believe it. It never occurred to me that anyone would have a problem with what the doctor did. It seemed to me to be the natural thing to do."

"I see." Jonathan took the lid off his fountain pen. "Do you mind if I take some notes whilst you're talking? It's just so that I don't forget anything important. You can take a look at them afterwards if you want."

She smiled awkwardly. "It's all right. You know, I do hope I'm not wasting your time."

"I'm sure you're not. Now, could you tell me again how well you knew Daisy?"

"Oh, very well, as far as anyone did."

"What do you mean by that?"

She stopped to consider. "I mean that she was really quite a private person, though it was not always obvious. She could come across as quite open, but then you'd realise that actually you knew very little about her, she hadn't revealed anything to you at all."

"Would you have put her down as a strong person?"

"Oh, yes, to begin with, but as I've just said, nothing was ever quite as it seemed with her. I discovered by chance she was really quite emotionally fragile."

"Indeed?" Jonathan's ears pricked up. "In what way?"

"Well", Rebekah shuffled in her chair. "I do feel terribly as though I'm gossiping, you know."

He smiled encouragingly. "Please don't worry. You're not indulging in idle gossip, I promise. I need to know what she's like for the sake of the case. We're not prying for the sake of it. When did you make this discovery?"

"Perhaps emotionally fragile is a little strong. Easily hurt, maybe. Well, it was quite a trivial thing really, but there was this time when a group of us were sitting round the table having dinner together, and we got talking about school and things we wished we hadn't done. You know the kind of conversation ..." She looked up at him for reassurance. "You know—a practical joke that went wrong, that sort of thing—and Daisy said that she had once reduced a teacher to tears. She said afterwards that they had been halfway through an RE lesson on the Crucifixion, and the teacher had said that Mary and John were at the foot of the Cross; she wasn't sure which John, probably John the Baptist. And Daisy had burst out laughing and said it couldn't be, because John the Baptist had his head chopped off. The teacher was quite newly qualified, I think, and was maybe a bit stressed, but she apparently felt completely humiliated and fled the room. Later on, Daisy was summoned before some prefect or other and told that she had to apologise to Miss for ruining her class and making her cry. Anyway, that's not really the story, because she never had the chance to explain how she had reduced a teacher to tears. As soon as she said it, this other girl sitting opposite her gave her this horrible death stare and said, 'That must have made you proud.'"

"This upset her, did it?"

"Not visibly, but afterwards she was so cut up about it. She wouldn't stop talking about it. Kept saying that she must be such a contemptible b ..." She choked on the word. "A contemptible—well you know—if anyone thought she'd be proud of hurting someone's feelings like that. It was awful. The girl was just being sarcastic for the sake of it. She'd always made it quite obvious she didn't like Daisy very much, and she was just taking the opportunity to put a boot in." Rebekah looked across at Jonathan almost pleadingly. "There was no reason for her to be so upset. It was just a pointless comment by some girl who was always coming up with things like that. If it had been me I would have brushed it off and forgotten all about it. I thought Daisy would do the same, but she was devastated that anyone would think so badly of her. I kept wondering afterwards why it mattered and what sort of low opinion Daisy had of herself to call herself something like that. It was horrible."

Jonathan put down his pen and leant back in his chair. "This is all very interesting."

"Is it?"

"Immensely so. Perhaps more than you realise. Did you know she had a living will?"

"No, but there's no reason why I should."

"Were you surprised to discover she had had one?"

Rebekah rocked her head from one side to the other in a gesture that irritated Jonathan rather. "A bit, I suppose. It just seemed a little morbid for people our age to be thinking about, but I suppose others would say she was only being prudent. It can happen any time and all that … but in her case, it just would have seemed morbid."

"Why?"

She hesitated, as though trying to find the kindest way of phrasing an awkward point. "Because she used to get down", she said. "Not massively so, you understand, not enough that you'd worry about it, but—well, you know—you might just think 'why is a healthy twenty-something worrying about this?' Does that make sense?"

"Absolutely. Am I to assume from what you've said that Daisy's suicide attempt came as a complete surprise?"

"Of course it did!" There was a tone of indignation creeping in now, which Jonathan found quite encouraging. "It came completely out of the blue. I said she got down, but there's quite a gap between that and taking an overdose!"

"Had anything happened that might have provoked it?"

"No, absolutely not!"

"Please think." Jonathan leaned across the table. "There's always a straw that breaks the camel's back. Even if it was something really quite minor. You say she was emotionally fragile, easily hurt. The story you've told me makes that very obvious. Did something happen, anything at all, that might have tipped the balance?"

Rebekah got up abruptly and turned to face the window. "What if I'm wrong?"

"About what?"

"You can never be sure what the final straw was. Only Daisy could tell you that, and even she might be muddled about precisely what it was that pushed her over the edge."

"Why don't you tell me your suspicions? Then we can make a judgement."

"What if it's wrong though?"

"Then it's wrong, isn't it?"

"It's just, there was—there was a falling out", she said quietly, her back still turned. "It happens. She was sharing a house with a couple of friends. There was a falling out with one of them, and she decided to move out, joined by the other girl."

"Meaning Daisy was left alone?"

"Yes." Rebekah turned to face Jonathan. "But these things happen. Women fall out with one another all the time, particularly when they're living together."

"But someone like Daisy might have taken it very badly?"

"Well, yes, of course she would. It's not exactly a nice thing to happen to a person. She must have been terribly upset about it, perhaps rather humiliated, but as far as I know it was settled amicably enough."

"Would she have been hurt financially at all?"

"No, I don't think so. Jenny's a very decent sort. She would have made sure that they parted on good terms."

"This would be Jennifer Little, the woman who accompanied Daisy to the hospital?"

"Yes. That was why she found her. She was in the process of moving out and had gone to pick up a few things."

"You said that they'd fallen out, and yet she appears to have been a close friend of Daisy's by the way she behaved in the hospital?"

Rebekah hesitated. "I know how weird it sounds, but it's like I said. Women fall out; they get fed up with one another's company. It doesn't mean they stop being friends. I got the impression from Jen that she just felt enough was enough and it was time to move on. Maybe there'd been one row too many or something, and they both felt that it was better for their friendship that way."

"Are you sure they remained friends?"

"Oh, yes, they'd known one another for years, and I'm sure Jenny wasn't the sort of person who'd just cast someone off like that. She made it very clear to the rest of us that there were no hard feelings or anything."

"Did Daisy talk about the situation to you?"

Rebekah thought for a moment, then shook her head. "Now that I think about it, she didn't, but she wouldn't have done. Whatever you could say about her, she wasn't a gossip. It wouldn't have been like her to talk about a person if he weren't in the room to give his side of the story. She would have thought it shabby." She frowned. "Unlike me."

"You're not gossiping", said Jonathan. "Why don't you sit down?" Rebekah sat down glumly and stared down at her hands. She evidently felt cheap for talking so much, but Jonathan was delighted and scribbled away quietly for several minutes. "Right, let me check that I've got the basic picture. You state that Daisy was emotionally fragile and prone to getting down?"

"Yes."

"Would you be prepared to state this in court?"

"If it was necessary", said Rebekah miserably.

"You were surprised by her taking out a living will and thought it a bad sign in her case, because of her mental state?"

"Yes."

"You had no reason to believe that she would take her own life."

"No, no reason at all."

"A recent falling out had upset Daisy and might or might not have played a part in her suicide attempt." Rebekah attempted to interrupt. "However, you are reasonably certain that Daisy and her friend Jennifer parted on good terms and that there were no other aggravating circumstances such as sudden financial hardship which might have contributed to Daisy's decision to end her life?"

Rebekah nodded. "Poor Jenny. It's just occurred to me how awful it must have all been for her. You'd blame yourself even if it wasn't your fault. I suppose that's why she wanted to fight for her friend so much. It's like writing someone a loving obituary because you don't think you did enough for him when he was alive."

Jonathan had just shaken Rebekah's hand and seen her out when Maria limped into the room. "You genius!" he called to her, closing the door behind him. "The missing link, the vital witness. She's absolutely perfect. She's prepared to give evidence about Daisy's mental state, which will be invaluable in trying to convince the jury ..." Maria looked up at him, and he noted, with customary male terror, that she was ashen faced, and her eyes were red and swollen. "What is it? Didn't you manage to stop Lydia's removal orders?" Maria did not answer. "Don't tell me she's on that flight to Beijing?"

"She's dead", whispered Maria, turning to face the wall like a child in disgrace. Jonathan flinched at the sound of convulsive sobs and backed away, letting an agonising silence descend on the room. He watched from as far away as possible as Maria's shoulders heaved, and she twisted her hair in her hands, too shocked by the turn of events to contemplate taking control of the situation. Only when she showed signs of calming down did he pluck up the courage to tap her on the shoulder and encourage her to turn around and look at him.

"What on earth happened?" he asked.

Maria took a handkerchief out of her pocket and blew her nose. "They refused to cancel Lydia's removal orders", she hiccupped. "I received another telephone call from her as she was being transferred in the back of a van to the airport, then another when she arrived."

"But what *happened*?"

Maria clutched her throbbing head. It was years since she had felt such a terrible combination of rage, grief, guilt and exhaustion; she felt so hot it seemed as though her head would simply explode if she could not calm herself down. And in such a state, she somehow had to find the energy to tell Jonathan about the phone call she had received as she took the express train to Heathrow Airport. "They've locked me in a room!" Lydia had wailed, "until it's time for my flight. The escorts kept telling me what a beautiful country China is and aren't I happy to go back home? When I told them it was nonsense, my father is in prison and I'm not allowed to be pregnant, they got really nasty. They say if I won't get on the plane quietly like a good little girl, they'll put me in chains and shame me in front of everyone. I keep telling them what will happen to the baby, but they won't listen. One of them said, 'Well, perhaps this isn't a good time for you to be having a baby anyway.' "

"Lydia, tell them you'll do what they want", Maria instructed her. "Then they won't restrain you. I'm on my way. I'll be another ten minutes at the most."

But so much can change in ten minutes. As it happened, there was an unexpected delay, and Maria was stranded on the train, spitting with rage and frustration whilst an apology was repeated over and over again on the intercom. When the train finally arrived and the doors opened, she ran as fast as she could up into the terminal building, only to notice a commotion directly outside. Instinctively, she found herself moving towards the huddle of people, but she knew, with the terrible intuition of a woman who has seen death before, that Lydia had been the cause of it.

Directly outside a set of double doors, the pavement was swarming with police and curious onlookers. Maria could see the telltale plastic tape stretched around the accident scene, which included a section of road and a coach with "Woking" painted across the side. A grossly overweight driver with lank, grey hair touching his shoulders was still protesting his innocence to a police officer. "She just run out in front of me! I couldn't've stopped even if I'd wanted to!"

After an infuriating struggle to find someone she could talk to, she was taken into a private room—not unlike the room in which Lydia must have been incarcerated, she thought—and told by a woman police officer what had happened. Immediately after her telephone conversation with Maria, Lydia had asked to be taken to the toilet and been marched out of the room by a female escort, whom she had succeeded in distracting long enough to make a break for it. She had run through the double doors, but as she was heavily pregnant, she could not move as quickly as she thought and was hit by a coach as she attempted to rush across the road.

Paramedics had arrived shortly afterwards, and Lydia was pronounced dead on the scene, before being carried into an ambulance as there was an outside chance the baby could still be saved. With that, the police officer handed Maria the details of the hospital to which Lydia's body had been taken and made some token sympathetic comment she barely registered. As Maria left the room, she almost collided with a woman who had a familiar logo embroidered on her breast pocket. She was one of the escorts employed to drag failed asylum seekers to the airport and force them onto planes. "I was just doing my job", said the woman, returning Maria's glare. "It wasn't my problem she didn't have permission to stay."

Maria continued to look at her and felt such complete revulsion overtaking her that she had an almost irresistible urge to spit in her face. "It must be quite an achievement to be incapable of being moved", she said finally and walked away. Jonathan, if he had witnessed the moment, might have said that she had almost grown up.

"If the train hadn't been late," she whimpered, "if she had kept her head a couple more minutes ..."

"Maria, go home", said Jonathan.

"I'd rather you gave me something to do."

"I mean it, go home. The story will be all over the papers in the morning. Do you know which hospital the ambulance was headed for?"

"The policewoman wrote everything down for me." Maria was slipping into the listless stage of shock and took the paper out of her handbag mechanically, without looking down at what she was doing. "How do they live with themselves?"

"Like all the criminals we come across, they live a lie", declared Jonathan, glancing at the scribbled address. "The worse the evil, the bigger the lie they construct around themselves. I can assure you that the people who were complicit in little Lydia's death will sleep much more soundly in their beds tonight than you will. Just as the people hounding Matthew Kemble sleep soundly in their beds whilst he tosses and turns, agonising over the future."

And just as Jonathan had predicted, as Maria lay in her bed that night, having given up on even trying to nod off to sleep, she heard Lydia's plaintive voice over and over again during their last conversation and imagined everything turning out differently. The train arriving on time, Lydia waiting for her before taking things into her own hands, the bus swerving to miss her ... all the many variables in the story that could have worked out differently but had not done so. As the first light of dawn began to intrude upon her room, Maria finally fell asleep and found herself on that hospital trolley again, being hurried down a sterile corridor with its customary sense of menace, to the room at the end, where a man she recognised as Dr Kemble this time stood over her, explaining why she needed to be rinsed out.

"Don't!" She pushed herself as far back into the bed as she could, as though she seriously imagined the whole stretcher would collapse under her weight if she tried hard enough. "Please don't!"

"Don't be scared, it's all right."

121

"Leave me alone! Please ... please ..."

"It's all right, it's all right. Stop fighting me. You're going to be all right."

Panic. She gagged at the touch of the tube at the back of her throat. Choking panic ...

Maria woke up weeping and trembling, with the ghostly nightmare visions all around her of a young woman driven by some unknown misery to poison herself and another whose rash act to save her life and that of her child had left her dead on a cold concrete road. *Oh, God, so much death*, she thought, *so many wasted lives*. But even as she buried her head under her pillow, she found herself choking again on an imaginary tube that forced its serpentine way down her own resisting throat.

17

Chaos reigned. It usually did at this time of the day where young children were concerned, but bedtime was always a little more frantic when the evenings were light, and Matthew consoled himself that there were restless children running rings around their parents in households up and down the country. The clocks had moved forward by one hour, and they were in what was comically described as British summertime. It had poured with rain on and off for the past five days, and their central heating was doing overtime. Whilst environmental organisations rattled tins in the high street to tackle global warming, they were heading for the coldest, wettest summer on record, but the one small consolation was that the sun did not set at four o'clock in the afternoon, and it was sometimes warm, dry and light enough to sit in the garden briefly with a glass of Pimms or a gin and tonic and pretend that they did not have a care in the world. And it was always possible to predict that the children would feel cheated when it came to bedtime, believing that they were being put to sleep in the middle of the afternoon.

Matthew had got the hang of nursery rhymes over the past few months of his apprenticeship as a child minder and was attempting to calm Dominic and Angelina with a few songs. They were naturally musical and bounced up and down on the bed, singing at the tops of their little voices:

> *Miss Polly had a dolly who was sick sick sick.*
> *She called for the doctor to come quick quick quick.*
> *The doctor came with his bag and his hat*
> *And he knocked on the door with a rat-a-tat-tat.*

What they of course did not know was that the nursery rhyme they were so cheerfully singing was apparently a protest song against doctors and their exorbitant fees prior to the establishment of the National Health Service just after the war. Matthew, who was in the mood to take virtually everything personally, decided to try them on something else. "How about 'Oranges and lemons say the bells of Saint

Clements ...'" but then he remembered that that song was about capital punishment, and he felt the uncomfortable prickling sensation around his neck of an invisible noose. In any case, the children were not listening and carried on with their own song:

> *He looked at the dolly, and he shook his head.*
> *He said, Miss Polly, put her straight to bed ...*

"How about 'Goosy Goosy Gander'?"

"You do realise that's an attack on the Jesuits, don't you?" Eva chimed in, poking her head around the door. "Would you mind helping Tommy out? He's struggling with his project. I'll get the little ones sorted."

"I'm still not sure if Pluto is a planet", Matthew confessed. "The question didn't come up very much during my clinical studies. Now, when he starts biology ..."

"He finished the solar system months ago. He's doing a class project on the Vikings."

"The Vikings? I think we covered them at school as well. Chaps in helmets with horns?"

"No, that was Wagner's idea. I think he has to draw a longboat or something. Do give him a hand."

Matthew sighed and lumbered down the stairs, images floating through his head of Porky Pig in one of the aforementioned helmets, singing, "Kill the wabbit, kill the wabbit, kill the WAAAAbbit" to the tune of *Ride of the Valkyries*. Thomas was colouring in a stripy red-and-white sail. "What do you think?" he asked, looking up as Matthew stepped into the room. "Have I drawn enough shields?"

"Looks good to me", said Matthew. "I'd be scared to death if I saw that thing sailing towards me full of angry Vikings."

Thomas grinned. "Oh, yeah. They had axes and things."

"Well, I'm glad we don't have to worry about that any more. My Danish friends are rather charming, and they'd ..."

There was the sound of an explosion all around them, and the room dissolved in a flurry of shattered glass. All Matthew remembered afterwards was instinctively grabbing hold of Thomas and pushing him under the table before dropping to his knees to shelter himself. Then he thought he heard the sound of retreating footsteps, seconds before a scream rang out above their heads. "Dad, what's happening?" whimpered Thomas. He curled up in his father's arms and buried his face in the fibres of his sweater. "What was that?"

"It's all right", panted Matthew, his head reeling. "It's all right. Whatever it is, it's gone."

Eva rushed down the stairs and pulled Thomas out from under the table. "What happened?" she shouted. "They've smashed the window! Tommy, are you hurt?"

"Get the children upstairs and call the police!" ordered Matthew, clambering to his feet. There was a film of shattered glass everywhere, and what looked like a brick had landed on the floor, having first hit and damaged the middle of the table where they had been sitting. No wonder it sounded as though all hell had broken loose.

He looked at Eva, who was as white as a sheet, holding a sobbing, shaking child in her arms. "Did it hit him?" she asked.

"If it had hit him, he'd be ..." Matthew could not bring himself to finish the sentence. It had taken a split second for the brick to break through the window and strike the table. If Thomas had been sitting there alone, he would almost certainly have failed to get out of the way in time, and as it was they had had the narrowest escape possible. "Just take the children upstairs and call the police. I'll ring Jonathan."

By the time Jonathan arrived at the scene, the police had been and gone, taking the brick with them as evidence. An elderly neighbour who had heard the noise and come round with offers of help was sweeping up the glass. "Come upstairs, Jon", said Eva, taking his hand. "Thank you for coming round. I know how busy you are."

"What exactly happened?"

"Someone threw a brick through the window", she said. Her voice was quite calm, but he could tell that she was still overwhelmed with the shock. "The police are saying it was just vandals, but I really don't believe it. Why would anyone throw a brick through our window for the sake of it? This is a respectable neighbourhood. Things like this simply don't happen."

Eva and Matthew had tucked up the four children in their own double bed, and Matthew seemed to be trying to convince the children that it was all a big adventure. He nodded in acknowledgement as Jonathan stepped through the door. "Someone broke our window", declared Thomas, who had got over his initial terror and appeared moderately excited by the whole ordeal. "A great big brick came in."

Jonathan smiled before turning to Eva. "Is there anywhere you can go with the children tonight?" he asked. "I really don't think you can stay here for the moment."

"There's my parents' house down in Wiltshire", she said. "If we set off now it would be a couple of hours' drive."

"Then I think you should go. Immediately."

"What about my husband?" Eva demanded, taking Matthew's hand. "He needs me. He's about to go on trial!"

"Matthew can come and stay with me", said Jonathan. "The trial is all under control. It seems to me that it's far more important that you and the children are somewhere safe. What do you say, Matt?"

Matthew squeezed his wife's hand. He had a horribly selfish desire to beg her to stay with him. More than at any other stage in their married lives, he felt terrified by the prospect of being separated from her, partly because he knew that if he was convicted they might be apart for so long it was impossible to bear thinking about. "I'll stay if you want me to stay", she said, making his agony all the deeper.

"You must go", he said feebly, sliding his arms around her neck. "I wouldn't be easy in my mind if I wasn't sure you were all safe. I'll join you when it's all over."

Eva disengaged from him and hurried out of the room before she could break down in front of the children, and Matthew heard the sound of her heaving an empty suitcase out from under the stairs so that she could begin packing. "Are we going to Grandma's house tonight?" asked Thomas incredulously.

"Yes", said Matthew, with enforced cheerfulness. "No school for you for a little while."

"Cool!" cried Thomas, jumping out of bed. "Can I help Mummy?"

"Why not?"

His excitement infected the others, who began clambering out to help. By the time Eva had filled a couple of suitcases, the younger members of the family at least had almost forgotten the shock of earlier that evening and positively relished the experience of getting into the car in their pyjamas and dressing gowns whilst the grownups rushed to and fro with bags and provisions.

"I hate to think of you driving all that way at this time of night", said Matthew, as they stood alone in the hall of the house with Jonathan keeping an eye on the children in the car. "Will you be all right?"

"We'll all be fine", she said. "The roads will be nice and clear at this hour, and I've always got my phone on me if there's a problem." She looked suddenly desperate. "Promise me you won't let this distract you, will you?"

He lifted a hand to his eyes, unsure whether he was going to laugh or cry. "I can't pretend bricks through windows don't rather stick in the mind ..."

"You know what I mean! This wasn't vandals. We both know that. Just focus your attention on the trial."

"I know. I just wish ..." He looked into her eyes and let himself become distracted. "I—I so wish this hadn't happened."

Eva laughed lightly and reached up on tiptoe to kiss his face. "Of course you do, you silly man!"

"I mean, I wish none of it had happened."

"Don't talk about it now. The children are waiting."

He leant down and pressed his cheek against hers. "You must go. Let me know when you get there."

Matthew waited until Eva had slipped discreetly out of the front door before sitting down heavily on the stairs and burying his head in his arms. He was still taking deep breaths when Jonathan stepped back into the house. "Matthew, I think you'd better pack your own things and come and stay with me."

Matthew sat up and stared blankly at Jonathan. "We're not being paranoid, are we? It wasn't vandals."

"No, of course it wasn't."

"They could have killed my son, Jonathan! A little boy sitting at the table doing his homework!"

"I know. It's likely they didn't think there would be anyone in the way. They just wanted to give you a scare." Matthew was angry so seldom that Jonathan was always a little thrown when it happened. "It's in the hands of the police now, whatever they imagine the motive to have been. Though I should warn you that they almost certainly won't find them."

Matthew glared at him. "You say that as though it didn't matter."

"Matthew, they were professionals. If they'd been a couple of yobs who fancied throwing a brick through a random window, they'd be easy enough to find. But if, as we know, it was premeditated, the culprits would have been rather more careful about covering their tracks."

"This is why people take things into their own hands."

"Don't even think about going there, Matthew; you've enough on your plate just at the moment as it is. Go upstairs and pack. I'll find something to board up this broken window with, and we'll call a glazier in the morning. You can't stay here."

Jonathan lived with his wife, Freya, in a one-bedroom flat deep in the jungle of suburban London. It was the ground floor of what had once been the respectable out-of-town residence of a well-to-do Victorian family, now divided between three couples. Having married very late, Jonathan and Freya had never had children, so a small but conveniently placed flat near to all the amenities and a five-minute stroll to the railway station suited Freya and Jonathan very well indeed. "Make yourself at home, Matt", volunteered Jonathan, gesturing to an armchair in the warmest part of the room. "Let me take your coat." In spite of the time of year, there had still been a faint chill in the air outside, and ground floor flats always had a tendency to be cold.

Matthew sat down and stared into the spiky blue-and-yellow flames of the gas fire. He had never visited Jonathan and Freya at home before, in spite of the long years he had known Jonathan. They had always managed to meet in central London after work or at Matthew's house, which had felt the more natural meeting place, with its spacious dining room and the omnipresent sound of children racing about. Children always changed the social focus somehow, and for the last five years or so, friends had gravitated towards them rather than expecting them to drag their huge family about. Not that Matthew had ever thought of four children as a large family, but the socially enforced two-child family policy of the South of England was yet another current of contemporary British life he did not understand.

Looking around, Matthew could not help thinking that this was exactly the sort of home he had imagined Jonathan and Freya would have made for themselves over the years. The front room in which they were sitting was lined with heaving bookshelves boasting volumes on legal history, philosophy, popular piety and the array of classics from Dickens to Thackeray that one would expect in the home of an educated couple.

On the cluttered mantelpiece were various objects: a small silver trophy of some kind, a few trinkets collected over the years and an obviously treasured but very much faded tea caddy with a picture of

Prince Charles and Princess Diana on the front, no doubt produced to commemorate their wedding day. It stood there like a tragically defiant monument to the enthusiasm of the 1980s and a world that already seemed so very different from their own. *The past is a foreign country* . . . Matthew remembered it as a time when the country had seemed to be on the up, where everything for a few years had been big, dreams big, fashions big. Matthew had still been young then in a London populated by garish girls with huge perms and masses of eye makeup, emitting waves of terrifying self-confidence, and yuppies brandishing briefcases and mobile phones the size of bricks.

On the sitting room walls, decorated years ago in floral wallpaper, hung pictures and certificates, an oil painting of a scene from the Lake District, a wedding photograph, a black-and-white print of one or the other set of parents as a young couple. The woman had the characteristic look of a mid-twentieth century housewife settling down after the war—sausage curls pulled primly away from her face with pins, a floral print frock which she had probably made herself, giving the camera a charming smile. But it was her face that gave away the era to which she belonged, that impossibly young, contented face which nevertheless bore the look of a woman who had recently known the privations and anxieties of wartime and almost certainly the loss of somebody she loved. Next to her, like something out of a 1950s film about dashingly courageous Englishmen, stood her husband: straight backed, serious and still a little uncomfortable in civilian clothing.

Freya appeared at Matthew's side, liberally swathed in a frilly pinafore. She was obviously halfway through making dinner, he thought, as she looked flushed with warmth and a little flustered, but then she was always a little flustered. "Matthew, how wonderful to see you", she said, as he staggered to his feet to greet her. She gave him an affectionate embrace before hustling him back into his chair. "I'm so sorry about your spot of bother, Matthew. We're all behind you, of course."

About fifty miles behind me, thought Matthew, remembering a line from a comedy about the First World War he had once found amusing, and then cursed himself for being so ungrateful. Whatever could be said about Freya, she was never fifty miles behind anything. She was the sort of person who, since her teenage years, had been in the thick of every campaign from distributing antipornography petitions to addressing public meetings. Now that he thought about it, it had been Freya who had first introduced him to Eva years ago at a Miles Jesu conference she had chivvied him into attending. "I'm dreadfully sorry to intrude like this", said Matthew. "Hopefully it won't be for very long."

"Don't worry about a thing, Matthew", she instructed him, moving swiftly back towards the kitchen, where he was sure he could smell something burning but was too polite to say anything. "How about a nice coffee?"

"That would be splendid, thank you."

"Forget coffee, darling", said Jonathan, stepping back into the room. "This man needs a whiskey. Come to think of it, I think we all need a whiskey." Jonathan went over to the drinks cabinet in the far corner of the room and brought out a decanter and glasses. Matthew's eyes wandered back to the monochrome photograph on the wall. "That's Freya's parents, just after the war," said Jonathan, "not long after her father was demobbed, I should think. He was in the D-Day landings, though you'd never catch him talking about it. God rest his soul."

"My father was an army doctor", said Matthew, looking from the photograph back into the flames of the gas fire. "He was in the Far East when the Allies came across the POW camps, you know, those delightful places where British prisoners had been enjoying Japanese hospitality for years."

"I don't think you ever told me that."

"He never talked about it much either. Somehow being a doctor never sounded quite as heroic as being a combatant, but I'm not sure how I would have coped. He looked after a lot of the men and women they liberated, all terribly ill, malnourished. Traumatised, though of course they would never have called it that. Well, you know what they'd all been through."

"I know."

"I don't think he ever really got over what he saw. He could never bear to watch documentaries about it, it was all so fresh in his mind. But you see he also treated the Japanese prisoners the Allies took. It didn't matter to him whom he treated. As far as he was concerned that was none of his business. He pleaded for the Japanese prisoners to be properly treated and hydrated, when after all the horrors that were emerging, no one would have cared if they had all died of thirst. And he succeeded and saved them." He stopped in his tracks as a thought emerged that hardly bore repeating. "The strange thing is, I felt when this bill was being debated that I was pleading for vulnerable people to be properly hydrated, and I failed. They were my own people, and they had done nothing wrong. And I failed."

Jonathan pressed a glass of whiskey into Matthew's trembling hand. "I know."

"The thing is, Jonathan," continued Matthew, "I'm rather glad my father never lived to see all of this. He simply would not recognise the Britain we are living in, all those values and principles so many people died for, just frittered away. I'm not sure even I belong in Britain today."

"Matthew, it's your country too. Please don't forget that."

Matthew took a long gulp of whiskey, which had the paradoxical effect of bringing him back down to earth. "I'm worried about my family, Jonathan. I never thought I'd put them in so much danger."

"They're perfectly safe; you don't need to worry any more. Eva's taking them deep into the Wiltshire countryside, where they'll be well out of it."

"Evacuees."

"In a sense", said Jonathan. "Well, think about it. When was the last time something exciting happened in that boring little village?"

Matthew smiled. "I think an oak tree fell down about twenty years ago and put all the lights out for a couple of days." He put down his glass with a despondent thud. "Is it because I'm fighting this?" he asked, staring down at his lap. "If I changed my plea, would it make any difference? I mean, the trial would be a formality then ..."

"No, Matthew."

"If I had just pleaded guilty at the start, I would have got a slap on the wrist, left medicine and that would have been the end of it. It wouldn't have turned into some epic battle of ideologies splashed all over the newspapers. No one would have picked on my family."

"Matthew, no!" shouted Jonathan. "Are you mad? You'd have lost everything! Remember what you yourself said right at the start? Your career, your good name, your home ..."

"I'm going to lose it all anyway, Jonathan", he said quietly. "We're going to lose the case, aren't we? You're not going to admit it to me, but I know that's what you're thinking."

Jonathan looked at Matthew's anguished face as calmly as he could, desperately concealing his own anxiety. A nervous defendant was the worst possible kind, so very likely to break down or act unpredictably in the heat of the moment, and he knew, as Matthew did not appear to realise, just how much of the case rested on Matthew's ability to keep his head. "You have got to keep your wits about you. Angus knows what he's doing. He's been doing combat in court for decades, and if he thinks you have to fight, then you have to fight. I promise you he would not have advised you as he did if he had seriously believed you were going to lose. Your children will thank you one day for standing your ground."

Matthew let the sharp, regular flames hypnotise him again. He thought of his father facing the hordes of survivors, women and children, emaciated, broken, who had paid the price for being utterly defenceless in a war that saw so many millions tortured and murdered when they offered no palpable threat to anyone. He saw his father silently accepting the duty he had been given—no preparation, no counseling afterwards—just a vocation to fulfil at a moment of history he would never have chosen to witness. And Matthew wondered, just for a moment, whether he was not only relieved that his father had never lived to see the twenty-first century and all its confusion, but that he had never lived to see his son standing in miserable defiance of it all, reluctant and desperately afraid. "I am trying, Jon. Really I am."

"Your family were not the targets this evening. You were. It was just a cheap trick to throw you off balance before the start of the trial. I don't think it was their intention to hurt anyone. The children are going to be all right now, and you're going to be all right."

"If they failed this time, they'll try again."

"No they won't. Even with the police not giving a damn, it would be too risky. Whoever was responsible for throwing that brick through your window got away with it once. They might not get away with it again, and they know that much."

"I do hope you're right."

18

Matthew was not woken up by his alarm clock on the first morning of his trial. He got up long before anyone else in the household had stirred, having barely slept a wink all night. At one in the morning, he had given in to temptation and telephoned Eva, who had also been lying awake, and she had dutifully kept him talking in the vain hope of calming him down sufficiently to allow him to sleep. Matthew hung on to her every word as she talked about the children and the little activities they had enjoyed, as she assured him over and over again that it was all going to be all right. He could sense the fear in her own voice and suspected she had not slept much over the past few days either, but he hid himself in the pretended normality of a man and his wife talking about family affairs, as though there were nothing strange about having such a conversation over the phone in the middle of the night and he was not about to face the most terrifying, earth-shattering ordeal of his entire life.

For the rest of the night, Matthew found his mind wandering to the trial; he saw himself in the witness box being cross-examined over and over again, stumbling on difficult questions. The prosecution became progressively more aggressive as the night wore relentlessly on until the prosecuting barrister took on an almost demonic persona and loomed over Matthew like some horrendous Dantesque fiend, poised to strike him down with a fiery trident at his first faltering mistake.

In the end, trembling and sweating with anxiety, Matthew got up and ran himself a bath, but even as he wallowed in Invigorating Ice Blue bubble bath, his mind kept sliding back to the courtroom and the horrors that awaited him. By the time he had struggled out of the bathroom, swathed in a worn dressing gown borrowed from Jonathan, Freya was up and cooking breakfast, filling the flat with the aroma of frying bacon. It should have been an inviting smell, but instead he felt his guts knotting up and rushed back into the bathroom, just in time to vomit repeatedly.

"Anyone would think they were going to hang, draw and quarter you", remarked Jonathan, when Matthew finally emerged in suit and tie, looking as haggard and wan as a corpse on an undertaker's slab after it has been dressed up for the wake. "You really will feel better after you've had some breakfast."

"They won't need to sentence me to death", said Matthew, sitting down at the dining table, where Freya presented him with a plate of bacon and eggs. "If I don't end up in clink, they'll probably lynch me on my way out. You know, a nice public demonstration of the right to die."

"Lynching isn't really the British style though, is it?" said Jonathan cheerfully, glancing at the morning paper. "Heartless and Wrong— why Britain's laws on dying belong in the Dark Ages, p. 19", read one of the titles listed at the top of the paper. It was evidently some strident journalist's opinion piece on why doctors like Matthew ought to be lynched or at least struck off. He folded it in half and dropped it by his feet. "Common sense is a great British virtue. Just keep thinking of the good sense of your average British jury."

Matthew tried hard to think of it. He was still trying as Jonathan drove him to the court. When they stepped out to clicking cameras and a growing bevy of protesters chanting, "Right to die!" he gave up on positive thoughts altogether. The photographs of him that graced London's evening papers showed a man looking serious but calm, offering no clue to readers that as Matthew had walked into court, his head had been filled with *Escape from Alcatraz* images of metal doors slamming shut, metal railings, metal staircases, men marching about in faded tracksuits, the rattle of keys, the clanging of bells . . .

"This way, Matt", said Jonathan, nudging him in the right direction when he stopped dead in his tracks. "Inside."

"Jonathan, I was surfing the Internet last night", Matthew began, as they were ushered into the court. "I looked up the case on a search engine, and almost all the links were to articles and blog posts saying I was an evil patriarch."

"I'm not sure you had any business going on the Internet at all. It's like a form of masochism. Why didn't you just watch my *Lord of the Rings* DVD instead?"

"I wish the ring had never come to me. I wish none of this had ever happened . . ."

"Matthew. Remember David and Goliath."

"Yes", said Matthew, but he had a nasty feeling that if he had been the young David, he would have missed.

The court was a grand affair compared with the poky little room in which Matthew had been formally charged, just as he had imagined it would be. He sat down in a chair behind Angus, who was hunched over his papers like Coleridge's albatross. In front of him, currently vacant, was the judge's seat, regally elevated beneath the royal coat of arms emblazoned on the wall. He tried not to look across at the counsel for the prosecution, whom he could hear assembling. *It is all very well for them*, he thought. *Whatever the outcome, it's just a case. They will leave the court and get on with their lives, sink their teeth into new cases. They have no reason to worry about anything.*

"All rise."

Matthew felt his knees knocking as he stood up and watched the judge entering, exchanging a formal bow with the barristers and taking his place. He would have liked to have guessed how sympathetic the judge might be, but his face was completely inscrutable, hardened by years of sitting in judgement on behalf of Her Majesty the Queen, and the wig that framed his face made him look completely generic, which Matthew assumed was the point of that particular object. The jury, in contrast, were not so attired, and when they filed in, Matthew found it impossible not to wonder how easily they might be persuaded. The twelve were evenly split male and female and seemed to consist of mostly either retired people or students, which Matthew found a little unnerving, as though he were to be judged by a combination of disapproving mothers-in-law and anarchic middle-class kids with guilt complexes and red Che Guavara T-shirts. When they came to be sworn in, most swore on the Bible, one old dear in a tie-dye skirt made a promise holding what looked like a sprig of parsley and two young men made an atheist affirmation.

Matthew had not realised how slow court proceedings were to begin. Films only ever re-created the dramatic bits, the climactic clash of personalities in some juicy cross-examination, the denouement, the Churchillian speech by the defence, not the endless fidgetworthy preliminaries, which he was paranoid enough by now to think were done with the specific intention of sending the defendant into a blind panic. He glanced occasionally at Angus' back, noting that the man looked more relaxed in a courtroom than Matthew felt sitting in front of the television. He couldn't bring himself to look sideways at Jonathan in case he inadvertently caught sight of the press gathered in the sidelines like hyenas ... or worse, turn his head round to the heaving public gallery and possibly get marked down by the judge for appearing not to be concentrating. By the time George Ian Dudley QC, prosecuting barrister, got up to start the ball rolling, Matthew had begun fingering the rosary beads in his jacket pocket to steady his nerves.

"This is a clear case of assault," he said, in ringing tones, "a betrayal of trust by a member of the medical profession whom the public have a right to believe should be above reproach ..." Matthew squeezed the beads until he felt the four points of the crucifix pressing into the palm of his hand. He could already see the headlines emblazoned on billboards around the country: "... living will which clearly stated ..." "act of unimaginable arrogance and cruelty ..." "reminiscent of the bad old days of ..."

Matthew wondered, as Dudley's dramatic monologue wound down, whether the political establishment seriously believed that there had been no decent doctors before the 1960s, none at all who had cared about their patients and devoted their lives to tending the sick and dying, whether it really was the received wisdom that doctors like his father had lorded their superior knowledge and education over everyone, particularly women. He thought of the colleague of his father who had been stationed in Malta when the Nazis were laying siege to the island, who had personally dragged casualties out from beneath the rubble after air raids in his desperation to save their lives. There had been one time, oral history had related, when he had had to be physically restrained from running into a burning bus to search for survivors because he had not seemed to realise or even care that the whole vehicle was about to explode ...

"Mr William Havisham", Matthew heard a semiofficial voice calling. A young man, impeccably dressed, stepped into the court and walked purposefully into the witness box. He was rather handsome if a little portly for his age and had the quiet self-assurance of a man used to getting his own way. He placed his hand on the Bible and intoned the words of the oath: "I swear by Almighty God that the evidence I shall give shall be the truth, the whole truth and nothing but the truth."

"Mr Havisham," began Dudley, "please tell the court your full name and address."

"William Thomas Havisham, Satis House, Bratton, West Midlands."

"You are Daisy Havisham's brother, is that correct?"

"I am, yes."

"And it was you who reported Dr Kemble to the police in the first instance, is it not?"

"Yes, it was."

"Please, could you tell the court in your own words why you chose to do that?"

William Havisham looked across the room above the heads of all the people. "I did so because it seemed quite clear to me that a criminal act had been carried out. My sister had an advance directive—a living will—that indicated quite clearly she did not want to be treated. When I discovered through a friend of hers that the doctor had disregarded her wishes, I felt duty-bound to inform the appropriate authorities."

"Are you familiar with your sister's living will?"

"Very much so. I accompanied her to the solicitor when she drew it up."

"Why did you do that?"

"She asked me to come with her", he said, giving a faint smile for the first time, which gave the impression that he was letting the court share in an intimate family moment. "It's not an easy thing to do, of course. Planning how you might want your own death to be managed. I assumed she simply wanted some moral support."

"You are very close?"

"Yes, we have always been very close. We are quite close in age."

"To your knowledge, were you satisfied that Daisy was aware of the full implications of making a living will?"

"Absolutely. She is an intelligent woman, and she knows her own mind. She would never have done anything so serious as to draw up a living will if she had not done her homework first. I am absolutely sure she acted in full knowledge of what she was doing."

"And was there any possibility that she could have been coerced in some way?"

"Certainly not." There was an edge to his voice now, thought Matthew. *Methinks the gentleman protesteth too much.* "As I have already said, Daisy knows her own mind. She would never have allowed herself to be manipulated in the way you seem to be suggesting."

"Are you sure?"

"She knew what she was doing. I was there. I know that living will was perfectly legally valid, drawn up in the presence of a qualified solicitor. I don't believe for a single second that the doctor

137

really doubted the legality of that living will. My feeling is that he was just trying to prove a point, and he used my sister to do so. It seems to me that ..."

"Thank you", said the judge, startling everyone, including William Havisham. "I think the point here is whether or not Dr Kemble acted unlawfully. Mr Havisham, your opinion as to his motives for doing so are not likely to be helpful or even relevant. Please confine yourself to answering the question."

William nodded politely without showing any signs of embarrassment. "Of course, Your Honour. I do apologise. This whole incident has been very distressing for us all."

"Thank you, Mr Havisham. Would you please wait? There might be some further questions", said Dudley.

Matthew watched as Angus took Dudley's place. "Mr Havisham, how long have you been a member of the euthanasia-campaigning organisation Death Wish?"

William Havisham did not so much as flinch. "I became a student member when I was eighteen years old."

"And you feel very strongly that the laws in this country should be changed to allow assisted suicide?"

"My entire family feel strongly on the subject. As far as I know, it is no crime for an Englishman to feel strongly about a controversial subject."

"Indeed not, Mr Havisham", Angus reassured him, though the witness appeared to be dangerously unflappable. "In fact, it would be true to say that your family has a long history of feeling strongly about this subject, would it not? The Havisham family's association with the eugenics movement goes back many decades."

"I fail to see what that has to do with it", answered William, frowning lightly, but the question had clearly confused him, and he hesitated before answering. "What if we did? Many—many intellectuals took an interest in that particular movement before the war."

"Indeed, Mr Havisham. Doubtless inviting Nazi doctors to garden parties during the 1930s was regarded then as a civilised and progressive thing to do."

"Mr Wetherby", the judge's voice rang out again, just as Matthew suspected Angus was getting somewhere. "I fail to see the purpose of your line of questioning. What the Havisham family was up to during the 1930s is hardly the concern of this court."

"Your Honour, if you will permit me, I will put it another way. You surmise, Mr Havisham, that the doctor who saved your sister's life did so to prove a point. That is your view, is it not?"

"Well, yes. I've said so."

"And you claim that it was obvious that he had committed a 'criminal act', when, as you knew, no crime had, in fact, been committed. In truth, you were the one with a point to prove, weren't you?"

"I don't follow you."

"And you did that by reporting Dr Kemble to the police, didn't you?

"My sister was assaulted by that doctor. Full stop. He knew she didn't want any treatment, including life-saving treatment, and he did it anyway."

"How is it proving a point to report a criminal to the police?"

Matthew felt a sharp pain as the thin chain of his rosary beads snapped between his fingers. He was beginning to wonder whose side Angus was actually on, which was a little unfair given how things were going. It hardly helped Matthew's nerves that his mental picture of a successful cross-examination involved the witness breaking into hysterics five minutes in. "And you had no other reason to want your sister to be left to die other than your conviction that she had the right to die?"

William Havisham looked palpably disgusted. "Of course not. What sort of a question is that? Do you honestly believe that anybody wants to see a loved one die? But if you really love somebody, you have to be prepared to let her go if that is her choice. That has always been my position with my sister. Of course I never wanted her dead, but it wasn't about me. It was about what she wanted."

"The fact that Daisy stood to inherit the lion's share of your family's estate has nothing to do with it, then?"

To Matthew's relief, the question had the effect of making William Havisham appear a little embarrassed for the first time, and he shifted position slightly as though trying to make himself more comfortable. "That can't possibly have anything to do with it", he said immediately, but his tone was noticeably quieter than before. "The will had already been made in her favour. There was nothing I could have done to change it." He hesitated, then shook his head violently. "This has got nothing to do with the case! Our father is still alive. Neither of us has inherited anything. The only money Daisy possesses is what she has earned. She doesn't even own her own home."

"In fact, Mr Havisham, as you well know, you stood to gain a great deal if your sister died before the death of your father."

Angus paused for effect. William Havisham remained silent and looked ahead. "If we can turn please to page three hundred and seven in the bundle, Your Honour?" He waited until the judge had found the appropriate page. "This is a copy of David Havisham's last will and testament; please note the first sentence of the fourth paragraph down." He looked back at William. "Your father's last will and testament states quite clearly that Daisy is to be the primary beneficiary of the will—and clearly once she has inherited, she may do what she wants with the legacy—but if, and only if she were to die before your father, the entire inheritance would pass to you automatically on the occasion of his death."

William Havisham's knuckles were white with the pressure of keeping his composure. "How was I to know that?"

"But you did know, didn't you?"

"How could I?"

"Then you deny knowing it?"

"Yes, of course."

"Could you, perhaps, have forgotten what you knew?"

"How could I forget what I never knew?"

"Very well, then. I think that is clear enough, members of the jury. Now, if I could ask you, please, to turn to page three hundred and thirty-three? Do you have it, Mr Havisham, in the witness bundle? Yes? Good. Have you seen that letter before, Mr Havisham?"

"No, no. I don't think so."

"You see, it's a letter from your family solicitor, Craddock, Passmore and Henshaw. They were your father's solicitors, weren't they?"

"Erm, yes, I think so."

"And can you see to whom the letter is addressed?"

"It's, well, it's addressed to my father."

"Let's read paragraph four of it, shall we? Here's what it says, members of the jury: 'In accordance with your instructions, I have drawn up the will, taking care, as you wanted, to ensure that your family were informed by me separately and had the terms fully explained to them. I was able to explain the terms to both your son and daughter. Your son, William, in particular, asked me what the position, relative to him, would be if your daughter predeceased you, and I explained this to him fully, as you had instructed me to, that he would, upon your death, inherit your estate in full.' Well, Mr Havisham, do you recall that interview with Mr Passmore?"

"I think I vaguely remember meeting with him, yes."

"And you asked him to explain the terms of your father's will to you?"

"I can't remember."

"No, indeed, Mr Havisham. You haven't forgotten what you never knew—you have just forgotten. Is that what you are telling this court?"

"Yes", he almost whispered.

"You forgot that you stood to inherit your father's estate. Is that it?"

"Well, no, no, of course not. I had just forgotten about the other part."

"You mean the part that said you would inherit it all if your sister predeceased her father? That part?"

"Yes."

"You see, Mr Havisham, whatever your family's historic beliefs, your own reasons for wanting your sister to slip away were not chiefly motivated by her supposed right to die with dignity, were they?"

"This is ludicrous!" exclaimed William. "You have no idea what my motives were!"

"And it was you who persuaded your sister to draw up a living will, wasn't it?"

"No, I wouldn't put it like that. No."

"As soon as she mentioned the subject to you, you saw an opportunity. You pestered her and nagged her to get on with it and convinced her to specify that she did not want to be treated ..."

"No ..."

"And from your knowledge of campaigning, you were able to provide her with doubtless many case examples about people who were being burdened with 'unwanted treatment'..."

"Absolutely not, I would ..."

"Perhaps you drew her attention to emotive cases of that nature in the press ..."

"Mr Wetherby, please let the witness answer!" The voice of the judge sounded explosive in the quiet of the courtroom, giving the impression of a referee physically separating two boxers before one of them could beat the other unconscious. William Havisham was beginning to perspire visibly.

Angus nodded to the judge and waited in silence for William Havisham to take advantage of his right to answer, but he stared fixedly at his feet and shook his head. There being no further reply, Angus sat down.

"If I didn't know better, I'd say the judge was biased", declared Matthew, as they drove with deathly slowness through the city's rush hour traffic. "He seemed to find all the evidence inadmissible."

"Don't take it personally, old chap", said Angus. "It's always like that. Endless interruptions to quibble over points of law. Was it much slower than you expected?"

"Excruciatingly so. Apart from that cross-examination, it was like watching paint dry."

Angus chuckled. "Well, at the rate I'm going I'll entertain you all by getting myself reported."

"I suppose it might be nice to have some company in jail."

"Good heavens, they won't send me down for making a nuisance of myself. You're on your own there."

"Matthew ..." Jonathan began, but could not be bothered to continue.

Maria felt more than usually aggrieved when they left Angus' chambers after a lengthy conference and Jonathan asked her to get out of the car near his office and make her contribution to legal history by going in search of a cheap source of food. *I love the way it is always me doing the fetching and carrying*, she grumbled to herself as she stormed in the direction of an Indian takeaway she liked, but she had a feeling Jonathan and Matthew were headed for a blazing row, and they were both old-fashioned enough not to like swearing in front of a lady.

The Taj Mahal Tandoori had a gloriously gaudy shop front clad in imitation marble with a vast overhanging sign sporting a print of the famous mausoleum. A bell clanged noisily as she threw open the door. "Ah, hello, darling, how are you?" Ravi greeted her from behind the counter. "You look tired."

"Exhausted", said Maria. She paused as the kitchen door was flung open and a man in whites stuck his head out and began shouting at Ravi. At least, she assumed he was shouting; he might just have been talking very loudly. There was a brief exchange she did not understand, then the chef's head disappeared and the door slammed shut. "Business all right?"

"Not bad, not bad, darling." He handed her a menu, but she waved it away.

"I come here far too often", she admitted. "I need something quick. How about a lamb biryani, a prawn curry—no actually, not prawns ..." On second thoughts, she suspected Matthew and Jonathan might be meat and two-veg gentlemen who would only eat the tamest possible dish on the menu. "Let's make it two chicken kormas with pilau rice."

"Anything else?"

"Maybe a couple of rounds of naan and some samosas?"

"Great. I'll throw in some bajjis."

"Thanks!"

"No problem. You're trying to save that poor doctor, aren't you? I read about it in the *Metro*. What is the world coming to when a doctor has to leave a girl to die? That'll be £31.90, please." Maria rummaged in her handbag for a debit card and placed it in the card reader he held out to her; she could feel her stomach rumbling. "I tell you something, Maria, if my sister went and took an overdose, I'd want a doctor to save her. All this legal nonsense—whatever happened to common sense?"

As Maria was putting her card away, eagerly awaiting the arrival of the food, she heard the clank of the shop bell ringing and looked up to see a woman stepping timidly inside. When she was asked for a description afterwards, she found it very difficult to remember exactly what the woman had looked like, her appearance was so completely unremarkable, but that had perhaps been the point. She looked like hundreds of thousands of English girls, fine blonde hair tied back in a ponytail to reveal a pale, dumpy face, not particularly attractive but not ugly either. It was not even very easy to guess how old she was; anywhere between early twenties to late thirties was possible.

"How may I help you, madam?" asked Ravi as soon as she had closed the door, but she ignored him and looked instead at Maria.

"You're the one I saw on television, aren't you?" she said guardedly, almost whispering. "Coming out of court with that doctor."

"That's right", said Maria, feeling her heart racing. "Why?"

"I need to speak to you—alone. Will you come, please?"

Maria shuffled uneasily. "Can't we talk here? I'm waiting for some food."

"No." She came as close to Maria as she dared so that she could drop her voice even further. "There's somebody with a guilty conscience who really has to speak to you. *Please.*"

Maria stepped towards the counter, where Ravi was fidgeting nonchalantly with the till, pretending not to listen. "I don't suppose you could have my food delivered, could you? Something's come up."

"To Adamston and Kirkpatrick?" he asked.

"Yes, please, Ravi; it's going to be a long night." She fumbled in her pocket for some change but found nothing. "If you ask Jonathan, he can pay the extra for the delivery."

"Don't worry about it, darling. I'll get my son to drop it over. It is only around the corner."

"Thanks."

Ravi glanced at the intruder, who had turned her back and was looking out of the window. "Everything all right?" he whispered.

"Yes, yes, no problem at all."

As soon as Maria and her new companion had left, Ravi called up the stairs, and a gangling teenage boy came thumping his way into the shop. "Aw, Dad, not another one", he moaned. "I've got an essay to finish."

"If you didn't leave it to the last minute, you wouldn't be in such a hurry", Ravi retorted. "It's all right, this one is very close. Just around the corner. Ring the bell and ask for Mr Jonathan. Tell him—no, wait a moment. Better write it down, or you'll only forget it."

He searched for another scrap of paper then scribbled hastily: "Maria asked for this to be delivered. She went off with some woman who wanted to talk with her. Something about a guilty conscience. Thought you ought to know. R."

Ravi folded the paper and handed it to his son, along with a hot, heaving bag of food. "Quickly!"

19

"What's your name?" asked Maria, as she followed her guide down the still-teeming street. "Where do you want to go? I really can't be too long."

"You don't need to know my name", came the answer. "It's not far. This won't take long."

As they walked, a little faster than Maria was comfortable with, her mobile phone was ringing frantically, but she had forgotten to switch the sound back on when she left the court and could not hear Jonathan desperately trying to get in touch with her. Nor did she hear the subsequent calls from her voicemail, which would have revealed Jonathan's voice shouting at her: "Maria, stop! Wherever you are, come back now. Do you understand? Come back *straight away*!" And another message, left two minutes later: "Maria, where the hell are you? Switch your blasted phone on! Don't go anywhere! Do not go off with this person on your own!"

They arrived at the Albert Hotel, one of those massive complexes with mahogany revolving doors and a sumptuous lobby replete with leather sofas and porters in livery. At this time of the evening the lobby was quite crowded, with guests congregating for predinner drinks before heading into the dining hall, but Maria's companion walked determinedly through towards the stairs. "This won't take a minute", she promised over her shoulder. "She just needs to give you something."

Every inner voice told Maria to stay in the crowded lobby, but her curiosity always won in any contest with common sense, and she walked uncomplaining up a flight of stairs and part of the way along a corridor, noticing the pleasing tread of a thick red pile carpet beneath her feet. The woman stopped outside room seventy-five, knocked twice and pushed open the door, gesturing politely for Maria to step inside ahead of her.

Maria was too taken aback by the sudden darkness inside the room and the sound of the radio playing a little too loudly for comfort to notice immediately that her guide had not entered the room behind her and had simply left the door to slam shut. There was no time to ask why. Before she could turn around, she felt something heavy slamming against the small of her back, and she was thrown to the ground, winded and disorientated.

In her confusion, she could just make out that there were two people in the room, though in the semidarkness it was impossible to see their faces. She felt somebody grabbing hold of her arm and dragging her over onto her back, then the stifling sensation of what felt like a dry face cloth being forced into her mouth. "Which bit of 'back off' is it you scum just don't understand?" demanded one of the men, kneeling over her close enough that she could feel his moist, hot breath against her face. A second later, she felt a pain worse than anything she had never experienced as a fist came down against one side of her face. "You're going to stop, understand?" Another bone-splintering pain, this time from the other side, and a scream was strangled by the cloth trapped between her teeth. She tasted blood in her mouth and desperately tried to spit out the cloth, but it was impossible. "You and your mates are going to stop. Do you understand the meaning of the word 'stop'?"

Maria tried to speak, but she was overcome by the terror that she was going to choke to death, as the cloth became soaked in blood and saliva and began to fill her mouth. This was her worst nightmare; she was suffocating. Her hands went to her face, but the crack of a boot hitting her ribs forced her onto her side. "This is going to end tonight." It was the last thing she remembered either of the men saying. In the minutes that followed, she was so overwhelmed by the shock of what was happening to her that all she was able to do was to curl into the foetal position and pray that they would stop before they did her a permanent injury. For months afterwards, she was tormented by the memory of her own helplessness, writhing around on the floor to the tune of Helen Shapiro belting out *Walking Back to Happiness* at full volume on the retro radio channel they had chosen to muffle the sound of what they were doing. But at the time she felt nothing at all, only the torment of fighting for breath as she coughed and gagged repeatedly.

And all the time, unbeknown to Maria, her voicemail was ringing and ringing with the messages of warning from Jonathan.

Then quite suddenly, as if by an invisible signal, they stopped and stood up. She cowered in a heap on the floor whilst they paused briefly to uncover their faces before slipping nonchalantly out of the room and down the corridor. She was vaguely aware of something being pushed into her jacket pocket as they left, then the sound of retreating footsteps and the door closing above the infernal racket of her own heartbeat. She stayed absolutely still until she was sure that they had gone, then ripped the face cloth out of her mouth and struggled onto her knees a moment before her body went into rebellion and she vomited repeatedly all over the carpet. She had to get out before they returned. All Maria knew as she forced herself to her feet, grateful that the shock had left her so numb, was that she had to get herself somewhere where there was air and light, where there were other people. She remembered afterwards that she started shaking so convulsively that she fumbled and struggled to turn up the collar of her coat so that it would cover up part of her face and that it took a superhuman effort to pick up the pashmina that had come off when she fell so that she could wrap it around her head like a hijab before leaving the room. So carefully concealed, Maria walked along the corridor, down the stairs and through the busy lobby into the cool evening air without anyone appearing to notice her.

Jonathan had to give Maria credit for her dramatic timing. As she walked dizzily back in the direction of his office, Maria finally remembered to take her phone off silent mode and rang Jonathan to tell him she was on her way. "Where on earth have you been?" he demanded. "We've been worried sick. Whatever were you thinking of?"

"I'm absolutely fine", she said as convincingly as she could, which was not very even by her standards. She was not sure exactly why, but she was finding it really quite difficult to breathe. "I'm on my way. Is my curry still warm, or have you eaten it?"

"Still warm, and there's plenty left for you. Where are you?"

"Coming."

Shortly afterwards, as Jonathan was polishing off the last morsels of Ravi's takeaway, and Matthew was struggling to make a start on his, Maria appeared before them like an image from a domestic violence poster. She had uncovered her head on her way up the stairs because the texture of the pashmina was beginning to chafe her skin, and they could clearly see that her face was swelling into a patchwork of what would soon be bruises, her lips cut and bleeding. In spite of her best efforts, she was limping and found that she was unable to stand up straight. The two men jumped to their feet. "I thought you said you

147

were absolutely fine!" thundered Jonathan, as Matthew helped her into a chair. "What happened to you?"

Maria slumped into the squashy office chair and closed her eyes. She suddenly felt lightheaded and a little confused. "I had a litigious appointment", she said tonelessly. "I'm awfully hungry. Is there anything to eat?"

Against Matthew's voluble protestations, Maria insisted upon eating something before doing anything else. A long day and it stresses, coupled with the shock she had just received, made her desperate to pretend that everything was all right, and in any case, she did feel desperately hungry after being so sick. "This is a classic trauma reaction", said Matthew, watching as she gobbled her way through the biryani they had left her. "She's in denial. Maria, we really should get you to a hospital."

"It's just a few bumps and bruises", she said, surprised by how slurred her speech had become, but the space inside her mouth appeared to be shrinking somewhat. "You'd get worse on a rugby pitch."

"You know it's pretty typical", Matthew continued. "As a doctor, I spent half my time trying to persuade hypochondriacs that there is nothing wrong with them and the other half trying to persuade sick people that they really need to do something about it. At least let me take a look at you, Maria."

"Can you tell us what happened?" asked Jonathan. He could not help thinking that Matthew's sharp return to doctor mode was also a form of denial; he was turning Maria into a case study rather than the victim of a violent crime he would certainly feel partly responsible for causing. "Maria, who beat you up?"

"No idea", she answered, opening a bottle of water one of the men had left on the desk. "Couldn't see a bloody thing."

"Can you guess?"

The terrible point was that it could have been one of a number of people she had antagonised and been threatened by over the course of this case and others; indeed, it might or might not be an unfortunate coincidence that one of the men in that room had used an expression she remembered one of Daisy Havisham's circle using to her: "Which bit of 'back off' is it you don't understand ..."

"I think I'm going to be sick", she said, helpfully lurching to her feet.

"Get out of my office then!"

She turned towards the door and took several unsteady steps, giving them just enough time to catch her as she passed out.

Matthew tried to focus his attention squarely on Maria as they walked behind her stretcher back to a free cubicle. By a not unpredictable misfortune, the ambulance had brought Maria to the very Accident and Emergency unit where Matthew had been on duty when all his troubles had started. He stoically avoided eye contact with any of his colleagues as Maria, by then conscious and protesting, was examined, X-rayed and generally patched up, but he half wished he had taken up Jonathan's offer to go home when Dr Harry Anderson appeared, enthusiastically brandishing Maria's notes.

"You'll be glad to know the CT scan came out normal", he told Maria, with an amiable smile. Matthew thought that Harry's bedside manner was coming along beautifully, but it might have helped that his patient was a young woman. "It's mostly cuts and bruises, a largish burn on your arm . . ."

"Burn?" repeated Matthew.

"Friction burn it looks like." He turned to Maria. "Were you dragged along the floor?"

"I might have been."

Matthew winced, half stifling a groan behind one hand.

"Besides that, you've a few fractured ribs, which is why you are finding it painful to breathe. Not much we can do about that, I'm afraid. Your ankle is a little swollen, but it's not broken. Just a slight sprain from falling awkwardly." Harry glanced up at Matthew. "Dr Kemble, I wonder if I could ask . . ."

"It's no good asking my professional opinion, sonny", Matthew put in immediately. "I'm on gardening leave, remember?" *I shouldn't be so hard on the poor boy*, Matthew thought to himself, but a small part of him still bore a grudge against Harry for so conspicuously dropping him in it when he had found himself in an awkward situation.

"Of course, Doctor, I mean Sir . . . I mean . . ." Harry reddened and speedily turned his attention back to Maria's innocuous person. "Given the battering you've had, particularly because you passed out, we ought to have you admitted to a ward tonight."

"Absolutely out of the question!" Maria declared emphatically, trying to sit up. "I've got a trial to attend."

"I really think you should do what the doctor suggests", said Matthew, when Harry had backed out of the cubicle, too desperate to avoid paternalism to have an argument with her. "You've taken quite a kicking this evening, Maria. It probably is best that they keep an eye on you, and the police will want to talk to you."

"What about the trial?"

"I think we'll manage", said Jonathan sardonically.

"Jonathan, don't", said Matthew, taking Maria's hand. "I very much appreciate you wanting to be there, but I really do think you should stay in hospital for the time being."

Jonathan, feeling a little chastened, turned to Maria. "Can you tell us exactly what happened? I can't believe you went off with a complete stranger like that."

"If it had been a bloke, I would never have gone with him", she said, eyes closed. "I was suspicious, but somehow because it was a woman it didn't really occur to me how dangerous it might be."

"Did she tell you her name?"

"No, she said it wasn't important."

"All right then, what did she look like?"

"Difficult to say."

"Tall—short—fat—thin—blonde—brunette—old—young . . ."

"Middle height, blonde, not overweight, not underweight, I'd guess in her late twenties."

"Well, that narrows it down to about four million people, I should think."

"That's the thing", Maria mused, eyes still tightly closed. "She just wasn't the sort of person you'd remember; you wouldn't give the poor girl a second look. She was boring, nondescript, not even ugly. I remember thinking that as soon as I saw her. She wasn't even striking enough to pick out in an identity parade."

Jonathan sighed. "They really knew what they were doing, didn't they? They sent a woman to you to keep your guard down and such a boring woman you can't even remember what she looked like. Where did she take you?"

"The Albert Hotel. Again, I didn't really suspect anything because hotels are such public places. The lobby was heaving with people about to have their dinner. She led me up to a room, then walked away as I was going in. It all happened very quickly."

"Who was in the room?"

"There were two men."

"Did you get a description, Maria?" Maria had to be the most unobservant, useless witness in the whole of legal history. "What did they look like?"

"I couldn't see a thing. It was dark inside. I think their faces were covered. Look, they didn't mean me to be able to see them!"

"All right, all right. Did you call for help?"

"I couldn't. They put something in my mouth, and the radio was blaring. No one would have been able to hear."

"Did they steal anything perhaps? Say anything?"

"No, they didn't touch my handbag, and they said ..."

"Yes?" Jonathan had the sense they were finally getting somewhere. "What did they say? It could be important."

Maria looked nervously at Matthew, who was hanging on her every word. "I'm not sure I should really be ..."

"Just tell us what they said, Maria", demanded Jonathan, brutally. "Matthew is a big boy; I'm sure he can cope."

"I think they said something about people not understanding what 'back off' means and we were to stop. Scum, they said." Matthew whimpered almost inaudibly. "That's a point. I could have sworn they left something in my jacket pocket."

Jonathan seized on her jacket and rummaged in the pockets until he pulled out a folded piece of paper. "What does it say?" asked Matthew.

Jonathan retained his poker face admirably. In handwritten block capital letters, the note read simply: "Our compliments to Adamston and Kirkpatrick." "Nothing", said Jonathan, putting the paper into his pocket. "You remembered wrong, Maria; it's just a piece of paper. A receipt or something." He moved towards the entrance of the cubicle and noticed two police officers walking towards them. He motioned for Matthew to follow. "We'd better get home, Matt. We've got another long day tomorrow, and it looks as though Maria's got company."

"You can't leave me here!" wailed Maria. "I don't suppose you could have a word with the doctor, could you? I'll go raving mad in this hospital."

"That really is in awfully bad taste", commented Matthew, looking back at her. "Of course I can't have a word with the doctor. Do me a favour, my dear; get some rest and be a good patient. *Please.* If they want you to stay here, it's for a reason."

As soon as they got into the car, Matthew went into one of his characteristic explosions of panic. "It's because of the case, isn't it?" he blustered. "I knew they'd try something else—you said they wouldn't. I knew it! I knew they'd come back!"

"Who's 'they' exactly?"

"You tell me; you're the blasted lawyer! Oh, and another thing, I know perfectly well that there was something on that piece of paper you didn't want me to see. You weren't remotely subtle."

"Well, all right, of course it was about the case. But my cases don't usually involve bricks being thrown through windows and members of my team having the living daylights beaten out of them. Just—just for goodness' sake, try to put it out of your mind for the moment."

"They didn't rob her; they didn't rape her. They knew exactly what they were doing."

Jonathan glared fixedly at the road ahead of him. "They were just trying to put the frighteners on, Matthew, and yes, you were right. It didn't work the first time, so they tried again. I'm sure it was the same men. But this time it wasn't you they were trying to scare off."

Matthew did not appear to have heard. "Why didn't they beat me up? To be honest, after everything that's happened, I think it would have bothered me less than all those assassinations by media."

"Precisely", answered Jonathan, unwaveringly. "Do you think they hadn't worked that out? For a start, if you went into the court tomorrow battered and bruised, it would be rather counterproductive, wouldn't it? Poor victimised doctor, et cetera et cetera. You'd get the sympathy of the jury, and that's not what they want at all. It might have aborted the whole trial, for that matter. Maria, in terms of the public face of the trial, is entirely insignificant. She is a dogsbody, an idealistic girly running to and fro. As it happens, she's a good deal more than that, though I'd never admit it to her, and they don't know that. More than that, she's so junior we could never prove that it was definitely related to the case."

"We know perfectly well it was to do with the case! She said they told her to drop the case!"

"Which case? Do you think yours is the only controversial situation Maria's got herself involved in?"

"You know they meant mine!" He almost whimpered the words.

Jonathan did not miss a beat. "Knowing it won't prove it. She's so talented at antagonising absolutely everybody that there could—theoretically, at least—be a number of people who might have done it. Realistically, the connection is pretty obvious."

Matthew was leaning back with his head pressed against the restraint. "Jon, I can't go on with this", he said. "What sort of people would lure a defenceless, unsuspecting woman into a hotel room like that? It's just the idea of those two men lying in wait for her—it's so despicable, the coldbloodedness of it, I mean. You've no idea, Jonathan. Kicking and hitting like that in the darkness, they could quite easily have killed her if they'd slightly misjudged a blow. People are more fragile than you think—they *break*. If that were my daughter ..."

"Oh, Matthew, don't." Jonathan glanced at him momentarily before looking back at the road. "What is it? Are you *shaking*?"

"It's nothing. I thought ..." It was a failing, but he had a tendency to take his cases personally. It was not emotional involvement as such, or so he would have said, but whenever he was attending a child or a young person, particularly if they had been the victim of violence or misadventure, he always found himself thinking, *But what if that were my son or daughter?* He knew he had said it or thought it many times before, but even so ... He shook his head before the memory could erupt all around him. "Perhaps I am a paternalistic monster after all."

"You care, Matthew, that's all. It's important that you do. No one wants a doctor who's a mere facilitator."

"If they want to send me down, they can send me down. They probably will anyway. I should never have fought this in the first place."

Jonathan pulled over without checking his mirrors, so aggressively that the car skidded a few yards before coming to an abrupt halt. "Matthew, will you for the last time pull yourself together? I am not prepared to have this conversation with you again."

"Look ..."

"I know you never set out to fight anyone, but the fight came to you, and you have to face it. In a few days' time, it will all be over one way or another." Jonathan looked at his friend and saw that he was sitting with his hands covering his face and would never give him an answer even if he wanted to. He took a gentler tack. "Listen, Maria is such a master at getting people's backs up that there is an outside chance this had nothing to do with your case ..." Matthew opened his mouth to respond. "Unlikely, I'll grant you, but as I've said, this is not the first or only controversial case we're involved in, and there is a *chance* that attack was payback for something else."

"You know you don't really believe that."

"I think it highly unlikely, but let's be generous with the possibilities, shall we? Assuming it was entirely to do with this case, whoever rigged that situation this evening knew—as you so rightly say—exactly what they were doing. They know you're an old-fashioned English gentleman and you'd fall apart at the idea of a woman half your age going through an ordeal like that on your behalf. That's why they did it."

"So they were right, weren't they?" came the muffled reply. "If she were my daughter ..."

"Oh, no, you don't, Matthew, not again! She's not your daughter; she's nobody's daughter. You have to stop this. As I think I've told you once or twice before, you are not just fighting for your career now. Maria is safe and sound in hospital being very well taken care of. They didn't do her any lasting harm; they never meant to. She will recover."

"Actually, she'll be haunted by that attack all her life."

"She will recover. If you must keep thinking about the whole sorry business, think in fighting terms. Say to yourself: 'I'll show these thugs. I won't let them have the victory here.' "

"Something really unfortunate has just occurred to me", mused Matthew, as Jonathan turned the key in the ignition and the engine roared reluctantly into life. "If those hooligans are ever arrested—which I don't suppose they will be—they might face similar charges for beating a woman to what I'm facing for treating one."

"Clang."

"Excuse me?"

"I thought I heard a gigantic penny dropping out of the sky."

"But it's absurd."

"Yes."

"Like something Kafka would have written."

"I was thinking of *Alice in Wonderland* myself, but choose your own literary metaphor. If it helps they'd be on a GBH charge, but point taken."

Jonathan drove off again with Matthew still staring out of the windscreen, resembling a small, startled bunny rabbit with a waistcoat and pocket watch about to be flattened by an oncoming truck.

Maria lay in her hospital bed and studied the ceiling above her. She had a horror of hospitals, and now that the police had left, she began to feel restless and panicky. She was in a large, open plan ward with perhaps another ten patients suffering from various conditions. The closed curtain offered a certain amount of privacy but did nothing to block the incessant noise: the coughing and groaning, the sound of patients pressing the bedside alarm and the constant chatter of the nurses sitting in the nursing station at one end of the ward. She would not have minded getting a book out to read, since the lights were still on and it would have been too bright to sleep even if she had been calm enough, but of course she had nothing with her. *Be a good patient.* Maria grimaced, wondering for the first time whether she hated being any kind of a patient because it involved the word "patient".

She closed her eyes and breathed deeply, but she could still feel her heart racing, and the images of earlier that day raced through her mind. It was strange the things that haunted her, like the slightly sweet smell of the air freshener in the hotel room and the sound of the door closing a second before they descended on her. She remembered again the terrible, maddening thought that had gone round and round her head as she writhed on the floor of that room, that there were so many people around, people above and below her, people in the adjoining rooms just inches away who could have intruded and made it all stop if they had only realised what was going on. People relaxing and watching the television, people preparing for dinner. People going about their innocent business without knowing the disaster that was befalling her right under their noses.

The gentle rustle of the curtain being pulled back caught Maria's attention, and she glanced towards the sound to see a nurse stepping inside. She was almost glad of the interruption, if only to have the company of another person for a minute or two. "Evening", she said.

The nurse stepped wordlessly up to her bedside and placed a brown envelope in her hands. "I really want you to have this", she said quietly. "I think you could do with something to read. Jenny told me to delete them after what happened to Daisy, but I just couldn't quite bring myself to get rid of them, so I printed them out first." Before Maria could question her, she turned around, stopping only for a second to say. "I'm so sorry."

Maria gritted her teeth and forced herself to sit up, a painful and difficult exercise under the circumstances in spite of the drugs she had been given. Inside the brown envelope were several sheets of A4 paper, each containing dense print on one side, and a memory stick so small that she almost overlooked it. She could see at first glance that whatever it was she was looking at had been sent in email format before being printed out, and through sheer curiosity she began to read. She read and read until she was shaking with adrenaline, then put the pages carefully back into the envelope and lowered herself off the high bed onto her feet. *Thank you, Our Lady of Ta 'Pinu*, she said under her breath, swallowing a spasm of pain as she began to dress. *Thank you, Saint Robert Southwell.* She tried to remember who the patron saint of lawyers was, couldn't remember, so added for good measure, *thank you, Saint Thomas More.*

20

Back at the Kirkpatrick residence, Freya was hurriedly putting together a late evening drink whilst Matthew attempted to make himself useful and Jonathan held a lengthy telephone conversation with Angus, drawing his attention to the evening's events and discussing possible courses of action. Freya was halfway through suggesting that they ought not to be long out of bed when the doorbell rang.

"Who on earth could that be at this hour?" mused Freya, making for the door.

Jonathan sat up sharply. "Wait, why don't you let me ...?" But she had already opened the door, and they heard the sound of a "good heavens!" before Maria appeared in the sitting room, closely followed by a stunned Freya.

Jonathan sprang to his feet, thundering, "What the hell are you doing out of hospital? Have you gone raving mad?"

Maria opened her mouth to make some kind of an explanation, but was drowned out by the extraordinary sight of Matthew shouting. "I distinctly remember telling you to stay in hospital! You're in no fit state to be anywhere else! I've half a mind to take you right back there this minute!"

"There's something I had to show you", said Maria blandly, holding out the brown envelope to Jonathan like a libation to appease a disgruntled deity. "Take it."

Jonathan, suitably diverted, snatched the envelope from Maria's hands and went over to his desk with it. "You'd better have a damned good reason for discharging yourself from hospital, my girl. This is beyond a joke. You never *ever* learn!"

Maria took her jacket off and sat down. "Just a moment", said Matthew, grabbing hold of her wrist. "What's that?" Maria looked down at the back of her hand, where an incriminating bright blue cannula sat embedded in a vein, carefully stuck down with elastoplast. "Is that NHS incompetence, and they let you go without removing that thing, or did you by any chance discharge yourself from hospital without telling anybody you were leaving?"

Maria had never seen Matthew angry before and was bewildered by the sound of his raised voice. "I thought there might be an argument", she tried, but it sounded so lame. "I didn't want any unpleasantness. Anyhow, it wasn't as though I was sectioned or something. I was perfectly at liberty to leave."

"You ought to be bloody sectioned, carrying on like this! Get up!" he said, barely noticing how much she winced and gasped as he hauled her to her feet. "This is totally irresponsible. You might at least have done the doctor the courtesy of telling him you wanted to leave." He looked over his shoulder at Jonathan. "I don't suppose you have a first-aid box anywhere in this house?"

"There's a medicine drawer in the bathroom if it helps", suggested Jonathan, stunned to see Matthew taking such aggressive control of the situation.

"Good." He advanced in the direction of the bathroom, still holding onto Maria's wrist. "You were told you needed to stay in hospital—is that really so difficult for an Oxford graduate to get her tiny mind around? Doesn't anybody listen to doctors these days?"

"I should think the answer to that is obvious," answered Maria tartly, "given your current situation." She drew back as they stepped through the door. "Actually I'd rather ..."

"Look, were you planning on keeping that venflon in situ as a fashion accessory? Lovely sight they are when they get infected."

She gave in and sat on the side of the bath whilst he rummaged in a drawer for a plaster and an antiseptic swab. He found a rather dusty-looking box of plasters and made do with a bottle of antiseptic and some cotton wool.

"Jonathan!" Matthew called out, causing Maria to jump. Jonathan put his head round the bathroom door. "Do me a favour and give the hospital a ring. I don't know if you'll get through to the right person, but it's worth a try. I have visions of some poor little nurse stumbling upon Maria's empty bed in the middle of the night."

Jonathan went back to his desk and switched on his computer to look up the number of the hospital. From the emergency field hospital of the bathroom, he could hear the sound of Maria's vociferous protests.

"Ouch, that really hurts!"

"That's because you've let your hands get dry in the cold weather. Ever heard of moisturising cream?"

"I do not need lecturing on hand creams by a middle-aged man, thank you very much! Ouch! You did that on purpose!"

"You've been beaten to within an inch of your life today, and you have the audacity to say 'ouch' because I'm trying to take a plaster off?!"

"I'll make as much noise as I like! I don't have anything stuffed in my mouth this time."

"It could be arranged. Oh, will you for goodness' sake keep your hand still!"

"Nice bedside manner you've got, Doctor."

"You're not in bed!"

"I've a right to bodily integrity! I have a right to refuse burdensome treatment!"

"Anyone would think I was sawing your hand off, for pity's sake! Do stop making such a fuss!"

"I'm not bloody English; I don't have to fake a stiff upper lip!"

"You know, Freya", said Jonathan, when he had left a message with the hospital. "In all these years, I don't think I've ever heard Matthew lose his temper like that. I don't know why I find it amusing."

"The stress is getting to him", said Freya.

"I know. In some ways it's not such a bad thing, Maria erupting on us like this. Having a minor medical situation to deal with is taking his mind off it all." He glanced sheepishly in her direction. "I hate to say it, darling, but she'll have to stay here overnight. It really isn't safe for her to travel back to her digs at this time of night in the state she's in. In any case, I don't really want her to be alone after what's happened. What if there's some complication or something?"

Freya shrugged her shoulders. "We'll squeeze her in. Always room for one more. I'll put the camp bed out in the box room. It'll be rather a tight fit, but it'll do."

When Maria emerged from the bathroom minus the venflon with a somewhat calmer Matthew apologising awkwardly for being so cross, Freya persuaded her to go to bed. "Have you read those pages yet?" she asked Jonathan, as Freya busied herself finding a nightie for her to wear and her last spare set of bed linen. "You must look at it now. There was somebody else who would have liked to see the back of your casualty."

Maria heard Freya calling her and followed her into the box room. It was a tiny space, meant for storage, and the camp bed Freya had set up for her only just fitted in amongst the bits of old furniture, the overflowing cardboard boxes and stacks of old books they had never managed to fit into their bookcases. "I'm terribly sorry this is the only place we can put you up", said Freya, gingerly guiding Maria to the bed. "I just thought you'd need a bit of privacy, and I'm afraid we don't have very much space."

"This is perfect", promised Maria, and she meant it. She would rather have been pretty much anywhere other than hospital, and though she would never have admitted it, she was a little afraid that something else would happen to her during the night and felt reassured by the thought of going to sleep so near to friendly people. She luxuriated in the sense of being coddled, with Freya tucking her up in bed and ruffling her hair affectionately as though she were six years old. Now that she thought about it, no one had ever done that when she was six years old. "Thanks for everything", she said, taking Freya's hand before she could slip away. "It's almost like having a family."

"Don't mention it. Sweet dreams."

Back in the sitting room, Jonathan was opening the brown envelope. "Anything useful?" asked Matthew. "By the way, I really am sorry I was so severe with Maria. She must be feeling awfully fragile, and there was me having a go at her. I really ought to have known better. It's just you've no idea how frustrating it is for a doctor . . ."

"Sssh. Hang on a second, Matthew", said Jonathan, without looking up. "Dear God, this is more than I could have hoped to get my hands on. I'd never say this to Maria, but it was almost worth a beating. I wonder if she'd mind being a sacrificial victim every time I'm in need of a miracle."

"What are you blethering on about?"

Jonathan laid out the papers very carefully in front of him. What Maria had been given was a printout of a series of emails between Jennifer Little and another woman, Carrie Anderson, who had obviously been the third occupant of the house in which Daisy Havisham had lived and where she had eventually made her bungled suicide attempt. The email stream read:

from: Jen Little ⟨jentinyone@fishnet.co.uk⟩
subject: (blank)
to: Carrie Anderson ⟨cashncarrie@girlpower.co.uk⟩
23/01/2009 22:03

Hi Carrie,
Have had enough. Daisy evidently too stupid or arrogant to get
the message any other way. I thought she might've seen sense
when she got my note and I started cold shouldering her but I
guess my friendship never meant much to her. Are you still on
to make the move? Let me know asap so I can get the ball rolling re letting agents.

Jen xx

————————end of message————————

from: Carrie Anderson ⟨cashncarrie@girlpower.co.uk⟩
subject: getting mildly worried
to: Jen Little ⟨jentinyone@fishnet.co.uk⟩
24/01/2009 9:42

Jen,
appreciate ur mad about Daisy's attitude prob but this is killing
her. She burst into tears all over me this morning when Chris
rang and hung up as soon as she answered, saying she can't take
much more of this. It can't be v nice living in a house where
somebody scowls and turns their back on you every time you
enter the room and I feel like such a fake pretending to be friends
with her so she won't suspect I'm part of this.

CA

————————end of message————————

from: Jen Little ⟨jentinyone@fishnet.co.uk⟩
subject: Re: getting mildly worried
to: Carrie Anderson ⟨cashncarrie@girlpower.co.uk⟩
24/01/2009 14:32

THERE'S NOTHING WRONG WITH THE STUPID KID,
SHE'S JUST PLAYING FOR SYMPATHY. This is her own

stupid fault and if she wanted to patch up our feud she could, but she's a selfish cowardly little witch who can't face up to herself. Im the victim here. Are you on or not?

Jen

——————end of message——————

from: Carrie Anderson ⟨cashncarrie@girlpower.co.uk⟩
subject: ok
to: Jen Little ⟨jentinyone@fishnet.co.uk⟩
24/01/2009 20:42

OK OK will you calm down? I know its her prob & everything and i want to get out of this house too. Just hadn't expected she'd take it this badly. She looks AWFUL, like she hasn't eaten &/or slept for weeks. Don't think she's putting it on at all. Ive seen her taking pills at night and can't help noticing shes constantly shaking. Not saying she doesn't deserve it, but maybe you've gone too far.

——————end of message——————

from: Jen Little ⟨jentinyone@fishnet.co.uk⟩
subject: Re: OK
to: Carrie Anderson ⟨cashncarrie@girlpower.co.uk⟩
25/01/2009 10:12

Soz Carrie, but I don't care if the selfish cow throws herself under a bus. Fat lot she cares about anybody else. What about ME?

BTW the agent says theres loads of 2-bed flats going in town at the mo. We could move out tomorrow if you like.

Jen

——————end of message——————

from: Carrie Anderson ⟨cashncarrie@girlpower.co.uk⟩
subject: Re: Re: ok
to: Jen Little ⟨jentinyone@fishnet.co.uk⟩
25/01/2009 19:58

ok, let's do it. I asked her earlier when she's off on holiday. It's 2–7 Feb. Quite funny in a way, she doesn't suspect a thing. Kept saying stuff about could I water her plants. Wonder if shes just in denial. Just glad I won't be here when she gets home to an empty house.

Carrie xx

—————————————end of message—————————————

from: Jen Little ⟨jentinyone@fishnet.co.uk⟩
subject: flat
to: Carrie Anderson ⟨cashncarrie@girlpower.co.uk⟩
27/01/2009 12:22

Saw a really cool flat this am, well within budget. Have provisionally booked, but you might like to take a look on yr way home this evening. Pop into Sheen's on High Street and mention my name.

—————————————end of message—————————————

from: Carrie Anderson ⟨cashncarrie@girlpower.co.uk⟩
subject: Re: flat
to: Jen Little ⟨jentinyone@fishnet.co.uk⟩
28/01/2009 14:49

ok Jen, put down my share of the deposit this morning. Final moving in date 4 Feb.

Jenny, I know you don't like me going on about this, but I am REALLY worried about Daisy. She said she'd been off sick with stress for the last couple of days which is why she's been around so much. I kept saying it doesn't matter you're having a nice relaxing holiday soon. I feel lousy about this. She'll lose everything. She'll come back to an empty house, she'll know we've been plotting behind her back as well as everything else. She'll never be able to pay the rent on her own or get anyone else in before she runs out of money. Jen she'll lose EVERYTHING. She'll finish up with no home, no money and a bad credit record for not keeping up with the rent payments. I'm not sure I can live with this.

—————————————end of message—————————————

from: Jen Little ⟨jentinyone@fishnet.co.uk⟩
subject: ⟨blank⟩
to: Carrie Anderson ⟨cashncarrie@girlpower.co.uk⟩
28/01/2009 17:02

Let me make one thing clear. I couldn't care less. She's had
plenty of warning I was at the end of my tether and a fat lot
she's ever cared about anyone else. This is a last resort. Some
people just have to learn the hard way. Personally, I wish I
COULD see the Oscar-winning performance she'll give when
she gets home from her posh holiday and finds we've gone.
Serves her right, it's the least she deserves. I hope it hurts. I
hope she cries her little eyes out. I owe her absolutely NOTH-
ING. I'm not going to leave her so much as a light bulb. STU-
PID STUPID STUPID MORON. Can't believe I was friends
with that thing once.

———————————end of message———————————

"Maria!" Jonathan shouted. "Maria, come in here a minute."

"Darling, you can't drag her out of bed", protested Freya. "She's
only just gone."

Jonathan ignored her. "Maria!"

When Maria finally stumbled into the sitting room, Jonathan could
not help laughing out loud at the sight of her. She was dressed in one
of Freya's old Laura Ashley nightdresses, complete with matching dressing gown, which made him somehow think of one of those frilly
dollies old ladies sometimes have in their bathrooms to cover the toilet roll. "Maria, who gave you this?"

"A nurse came in and handed it to me. She said Jenny told her to
destroy the emails but she couldn't quite bring herself to so she'd printed
them first. The memory stick presumably contains a backup copy."

"Have you any idea who she was?"

"I think she was definitely a real nurse ..." She trailed off. "Actually, I'm not sure if she had a name badge. Or perhaps I just didn't
notice it."

"Had you ever seen her before? Maria, this is very important."
Jonathan was beginning to understand why interrogators in films always
ended up losing their temper with their subject and slapping them
across the face. "Do you know who she was?"

"From what she said she's obviously Carrie. I suppose ..." Maria battled to concentrate on the facts. Tired and still in shock, she was finding it more difficult than usual to focus her mind. "Just a minute, I had seen her before. Or rather heard her. She was the woman who lured me into that room."

"Maria, sit down quickly", said Matthew, getting up and pushing her in the direction of an armchair, because she had begun trembling all of a sudden, almost as though she had suffered an electric shock. "Are you sure? Stop it, you're hyperventilating. Nice deep breaths, please."

"Of course I'm sure", she panted, but it was no good. There was something filling her mouth again, smothering her throat. "Of course I'm ..."

"Breathe normally, you're panicking. There's nothing to stop you breathing. You just need to calm down." He turned to Jonathan. "I don't suppose you've got a paper bag I could have, do you?"

"Eh?"

"It would help if she could breathe into a bag. Oh, forget it. Maria ..."

"I'm so—so sorry, I can't—I can't ..." She felt Matthew's hand resting on her shoulder and knew he was trying to reassure her, but part of her still imagined that her panic would be greeted with a sharp slap on the cheek and a command to snap out of it. She buried her head in her hands, willing herself not to go to pieces, but as soon as she blinked she felt tears overflowing down her face. "I promise—I—promise—I'm not doing this on purpose."

"Please don't apologise. None of this is your fault", said Matthew, with the guilty tone of a man who generally believes himself to be to blame for everything. "It's all right; it's just a reaction to the shock. Nothing to worry about."

"I'm sorry ..."

"Ssh. It's all right. Concentrate on your breathing." He noticed that her hands had curled into protective fists and carefully removed them from her face. "Try to relax. You're perfectly safe here; no one's going to hurt you."

Jonathan shrank back into a corner, a man who had squared up to some of the most bullying individuals in the legal profession but was too embarrassed and overwhelmed to go anywhere near a distressed female. He waited, chewing his knuckles, whilst Maria's remaining

165

energies trickled away, her breathing slowed down and the sound of convulsive sobbing gave way to quiet, whimpering gulps. The near silence felt slightly worse, and Jonathan made a dash for the kitchen, busying himself pouring her a glass of water, which he somehow thought ought to help. He almost collided with Freya on the way out. "For pity's sake, let her go back to bed!" she scolded. "You should never have dragged her up. She's overwrought."

"Yes, thanks, I can see that", he snapped, pushing past her with the water. "I promise this won't take long, but some conversations just can't wait."

"Gently then", warned Matthew, taking the glass from him. "Five minutes."

Maria lay slumped back in her chair, hot and disorientated. "I'm awfully sorry", she whispered, uneasily. "I do feel stupid."

"It's quite all right, Maria", promised Jonathan, pulling up a chair to face her. "Don't worry about a thing. I'm sorry to have to put you through this, but I need to ask you: Are you certain the woman in the hospital was the same one who lured you into that trap?"

Maria nodded. "I know it was her", she said with a surprisingly forceful tone. "You know—remember the way I said before that the woman had been the sort of person you never notice, and she really was like that. But when you're a patient in a hospital, you don't notice much about the nurses and doctors either. They're kind of part of the furniture ..." she looked up at Matthew. "Sorry, but you know what I mean. You're expecting a nurse or doctor to pop in every now and again, so you don't suspect them."

"How would you know it was the same person then?" asked Jonathan.

"She had the same accent. I remember because I recognised the way she spoke the last time." She noticed Jonathan raising an eyebrow. "Sorry, I did some linguistics when I was at university. I studied varieties of English. That's why I noticed that man Barry's voice sounded wrong. I find it quite easy to pinpoint different accents, and it was the only distinctive thing about her. Her voice."

Jonathan sat back in his chair and leafed through the papers again. "So there was another missing link", he mused out loud. "This person is obviously the sort to get caught up with other people's plans rather easily. This time, she found herself involved in one nasty escapade too many, and she had a crisis of conscience, but not quite enough of a crisis to come forward as a witness. Unless she thought it was a little late." He looked at Maria. "I'm very proud of you", he said. "I'll have to use you as bait more often."

Freya appeared. "Bed", she said, taking Maria's arm. "Darling, do you need anything?"

"I'd love another coffee", said Jonathan. "It's going to be a long night. I need to give Angus a ring."

"Oh, he'll really thank you for that."

"He certainly won't be sound asleep by now, I assure you. I'll need to update him and let him know the latest developments. You'd better get some rest, Maria. Don't worry about this now, I'll deal with it."

Freya tapped Matthew on the shoulder. "Why don't you give me a hand with the cups?" she asked, in what she imagined to be a subtle ruse to get him out of the room. "Maria darling, you get yourself settled, and I'll bring you a nice cup of cocoa. How would that be?"

"Thanks. I'm not sure I'll sleep a great deal tonight."

"Are you in pain?"

"Not really. All that hate. I keep thinking about it."

"Don't think about it tonight." Maria had a dreamy way of talking at times when something struck her as particularly interesting. "Just relax."

"But all that hate, it's what's driving the whole case. All those horrid things in those emails, the rage in that room this evening. The way those protesters have behaved, the comments on the radio programme, even bringing the case in the first place. It's never had anything to do with anyone's rights; it's just *hate*."

"I know, Maria. Let it go for a few hours."

Maria leant against the door frame. "But where does it come from? That's what I don't understand."

Freya personally marched Maria back to the box room, half expecting that she would put herself to bed in the bath by accident without a minder. When she got back to the kitchen, Matthew was boiling a kettle. "Does she have concussion?" she asked him.

"I don't think so. She's just a bit upset."

"Shock then?"

"Well, yes, but that's hardly surprising. In fact, I'd think it odd if she wasn't a little unsettled after what's happened." Matthew hid his discomfort behind the business of filling the cafetiere with boiling water. He would have thought it unprofessional to tell Freya that, when he had been removing the venflon from Maria's hand, he had noticed

167

a discreet little scar on the side of her wrist, which he suspected was the relic of a self-inflicted wound.

"She will be all right, won't she? She looks *awful*."

"Oh, yes. She's taken an almighty beating, but I suspect she'll fight another day." It was almost like being a doctor again. He was being asked his professional opinion. "The thing is that the attack was obviously quite carefully planned. If they'd wanted to kill her or cripple her for life, it would have been very easy for two men to do it—I was telling Jon that it was quite lucky they didn't do it by accident—but they obviously just wanted to hurt her enough to make a point." He jumped at the sensation of boiling water splashing across his hand and felt the horrors of the day smothering him like a moulding fire blanket. "And they certainly did make a point, didn't they?"

"Matthew, if you don't mind me asking," Freya put in cautiously, "why did you tell her nobody was going to hurt her? Surely she felt safe here?"

He focused his attention on putting the lid on the cafetiere. "She needed reassurance; she was having a panic attack. It's just something one says." He knew from her silence that Freya was dissatisfied with the answer. "Look, I knew she thought somebody was going to hurt her, I could feel it. Talk about a coiled spring." He clutched the side of the work surface to steady himself. "I don't want anyone to get hurt. I've never wanted to hurt anybody; I'm a doctor, for pity's sake!"

"Don't cut yourself up about this, Matthew. There's nothing you could have done to prevent it."

He stared dejectedly at the yellow kitchen cupboards in front of him. "I still wish it had been me."

21

"Remember what I have told you before", said Jonathan, as they prepared to get out of the car outside the court. "Don't show any emotion. Don't answer any questions. Just walk in nice and calmly."

This was easier said than done, as the entrance to the court appeared
to have turned into a circus overnight. Matthew looked through the
car window at the reporters with dictaphones and the cameramen poised
like snipers for his appearance; in the background, the group of protesters with their banners, angry chants and terrible fashion sense
appeared to have grown. He recoiled visibly. "I'd rather walk through
a snake pit", he said.

"Wouldn't we all", Jonathan retorted. "Hang on a minute, I've an
idea. Maria? I wonder if you could do something really, really useful
for the case and step out first? I know we'd normally get out together,
but I can't help feeling it might be better if we gave you a little head
start this morning."

Overnight, Maria's face had become covered in grey and purple
blotches, and she had found when she had woken up that it was still
impossible to walk without a slight limp. "What, to add a certain
pathos?"

"So to speak. A certain *diversion* is perhaps more the word. Don't
worry, I know what I'm doing. Get out first and lead the way."

"I feel like a lamb to the slaughter."

"Just get on with it!"

The ruse worked perfectly. As soon as she stepped out of the car,
a murmur ran across the assembled gathering. The protesters, who
had been about to start shouting, fell into a strangled silence and
watched in confusion and horror as she limped in front of them.
The reporters hesitated, then began manically taking photographs. None of them had the slightest notion of whom she was
other than that she had something to do with the trial, but that
was hardly the point. Distressing sights sold papers. They were so
distracted that by the time anyone had remembered why they
were there, Matthew had been safely and quietly shepherded into

the building. "Told you I knew what I was doing", he said, patting Matthew on the back.

"Why don't you just throw the girl to the wolves and have done with it?"

"Ms Little", began Dudley. He was not circling Jennifer as he generally did and seemed to be at cringeworthy pains to make her feel as at ease as possible. "Perhaps you could tell the court in your own words precisely what happened on the night your friend attempted suicide?"

Jennifer was immaculately dressed as Matthew remembered the first time he had come across her, but much more formally now in a carefully tailored maroon business suit that showed off her legs very prettily without appearing flirtatious. "I was in the process of moving digs at the time. I had shared with Daisy and another girl for over a year but had recently moved out. I had arranged to pop in and collect my post that evening."

"Do you recall what time you arrived?"

She paused. "Well, I was rather delayed that day. I think it was around eight o'clock."

"And what did you find?"

Jennifer closed her eyes; it was plain for the whole court to see that the memory of that evening had haunted her ever since. "I unlocked the door and walked into the kitchen. There was a post tray there, you see. I didn't find any post, but when I turned to leave I just thought something was wrong. I had expected Daisy to be in, but it was so quiet."

"You suspected something then?"

"Yes, I can't quite explain it, but there was a funny feeling to the place. I don't know, bad vibes or something. I went up to her door and knocked, but she didn't answer. So I opened the door and stepped inside." She held her hands together almost in prayer and pressed her lips against the tips of her fingers. "She was lying in bed, and you would have thought she was asleep, but you see her position was all wrong. The top half of her body was leaning over the edge of the bed as though she hadn't got into bed in time before she fell asleep, and there was a terrible smell. I think that must have been what I noticed when I stepped inside the front door, now that I think about it. She had been terribly sick." Jennifer began shaking her head as though trying to stop herself from breaking down, but her eyes glistened.

"What did you do then?" asked Dudley.

"I took out my mobile phone and dialed 999. They told me to unlock the door so that the paramedics could get in, so I went to the front door and left it ajar. Then I went back in. That was when I noticed a piece of paper folded on her desk. I thought perhaps it was a suicide note, but when I opened it I noticed it was her living will."

"Had you been aware that she had a living will?"

"Oh, yes", said Jenny emphatically. "A whole lot of us had decided to take one out when the law changed. There'd been one of those conversations in the bar. You know what I mean?" He nodded encouragingly. "There'd been some documentary on recently about people in comas or something. Everyone was talking about it, and we were all saying how we wouldn't want to be forced to be treated or anything like that if we got really ill. I think the others forgot about it quite soon after the conversation. You know the way people talk and then just forget they ever said it, but Daisy and I chatted about it the next day. I never got round to making one in the end, but Daisy told me some time later that she'd been to a solicitor and got one."

"Why do you think she was so keen? Surely she was rather young to be worrying about such things?"

"Oh, she was a very determined person", Jenny explained, with the tone of a person who knows that the worst part of the ordeal is over. "Once she had put her mind to something, she was—well, she was obsessed with being in control of her life. You know, she was the sort of person who, like, if the doctor wanted to prescribe something, she would want to know exactly what was in it and what all the side effects were before she took it. It was a good thing, don't get me wrong. She was independent, very—very strong."

"Did her suicide attempt come as a surprise to you?"

"Of course it did!" she exclaimed. "Everyone asks that. Of course it was a surprise. You never expect anyone you know to try and kill himself, do you?"

"You couldn't think of a reason she might have done that?"

"No, she had everything to live for." Jennifer shook her head again. "*Everything.* She was from a wealthy, privileged background; she had a nice boyfriend, a good job. I can't think what drove her to do such a thing. No one can. We've all been asking ourselves."

"What happened next, when you got to the hospital?"

"I told the doctor she had a living will and didn't want any treatment. He said he would have to ask a colleague. Then Dr Kemble came in."

"Did you tell him about the living will?"

"I did, of course. I told him she didn't want any treatment."

"Did he look at the living will himself?"

"Yes, I handed it to him, and they went off to talk about it."

"With whom did he speak?"

"Sorry, the other doctor. Dr Harry Anderson—the first one who saw her, I mean. Then Dr Kemble just went ahead and treated her."

"Did you witness this?"

"Yes. He said I could leave because people find it distressing, but I couldn't bring myself to walk out on her like that." Her face clouded over. "It was terrible. He was so rough and arrogant. I knew she'd have hated someone going against her wishes like that. It was—it was a *cowardly* way to behave."

"That's a rather strong word."

She was working herself up to a massive emotional outburst, thought Angus bitterly, whilst behind him he could hear the horrible sound of Matthew grinding his teeth. "But it *was* cowardly. She was unconscious; she couldn't resist him. He knew perfectly well she didn't want to be treated, but he just carried on and rammed that bloody tube down her throat. I just wanted to force him to stop!"

Jennifer was clutching her head and had finally given in to tears. Matthew had moved on from grinding his teeth and had stuffed his knuckles into his mouth. Yet again, he was being forced to sit helplessly by whilst he was portrayed as a heartless, arrogant tyrant, but hearing his actions put like that, he rather felt like one. "That will be all, Ms Little. Thank you. Please wait there as there might be some further questions."

Angus raised himself to his feet whilst Jennifer was asked whether she wanted time to compose herself, but she valiantly shook her head and—it could not be denied—looked most attractive as she regained her dignity. By the time Angus had reached the witness box, she had wiped her eyes and stood calmly and stoically awaiting his questions. "I realise that this is very distressing for you, Ms Little," said Angus, with impeccable courtesy and a winning smile, "so I will be as brief as possible."

"Thank you." Matthew was surprised to see that she returned the smile with a brave attempt of her own.

"Had you known Daisy Havisham a long time?"

"Yes", said Jennifer. "Some years now. We were students together."

"Would you describe your friendship as close?"

She hesitated. "Yes, I suppose I would. We'd had our differences, of course, but we went back a long way."

"You mention that you found Daisy Havisham unconscious when you returned to pick up your post, having recently moved out. May I ask your reasons for moving out?"

"I fail to see the point of this line of questioning", the judge broke in.

"If you will allow me to continue, Your Honour," said Angus, "all will become clear." The judge nodded reluctantly, poised to interrupt again. "Ms Little?"

"Well, as I have said, we had had our differences, and we both felt that it was time to move on. I guess I just needed space."

"Would you say there were any hard feelings between you?"

Jennifer was beginning to fidget just a little bit, which Angus clearly found encouraging. "Not on my side, I assure you."

"Do you know a woman by the name of Carrie Anderson?"

"Yes, of course. The three of us shared digs—Daisy, Carrie and me, that is. Then Carrie and I shared a flat for three months."

"Have you ever corresponded with Carrie Anderson?"

She looked at him in amusement. "We were living together; we talked!"

"Did you ever correspond in any other way? By letter perhaps?"

"No, nobody writes letters anymore."

"By email then?"

"I suppose so. I write emails all the time."

"Ms Little, do you own your own computer?"

"Of course I do."

"Does anybody else have access to it?"

"It is password protected."

"Do you use a computer at work?"

"Everybody does!" She was positively flustered now. "There are dozens of computers at my place of work. Everybody uses computers."

"Is your work computer also password protected?"

"Yes."

"The same password?"

"No, different from my home computer."

"And does anyone else know your work computer password?"

"I guess the IT department must know it. I don't know—I suppose they must have a right to access the computer if necessary. I'm not sure."

"May I ask where this is going?" interrupted the judge again.

Angus turned to the judge. "All will be clear presently, Your Honour." He turned back to the witness. "Do you use any other computers?"

"Sometimes."

"Any other devices to access or write emails?"

"I use my mobile when I'm traveling, but it's quite expensive."

"To the best of your knowledge, Ms Little, did you engage in an email correspondence with Carrie Anderson in January of this year?"

"I—I might have done. I don't think so. Look, I send dozens of emails to people every day!"

"But you do not think you sent emails to Carrie Anderson in January?"

"I really can't tell you! I'm pretty sure I didn't, but it was ages ago!"

"Indeed." Angus handed a heaving file to Jennifer Little, open about three-quarters of the way through. "Would you please take a look at this page, Ms Little?" He turned to the judge. "It's page nine hundred and twenty-four E in the bundle, Your Honour." He paused whilst the judge flicked through his own copy of the evidence, coming to an abrupt halt at the appropriate page.

"Do you recognise this document, Ms Little?"

Jennifer looked positively disorientated and refused to return Angus' glance. "It—well, it looks like an email."

But Dudley had risen to his feet, and Angus was forced to sit down. "Before my learned friend goes any further, I have a brief submission to make about this evidence."

"Is it about admissibility?" asked the judge.

"Yes, Your Honour."

"In that case, members of the jury, I must ask you please go with your usher for a short break. Ms Little, please return to the witness room. Please ensure that you talk to nobody about the case or your evidence during this break. You will be called when you are next wanted."

Angus waited in his place whilst the jury were led out of the court, judiciously avoiding Jennifer Little's glare before she too was escorted out of the room, looking every bit like a prisoner enjoying a brief reprieve.

"It's no good", said Jonathan to Matthew. "We can't prove those emails are genuine."

By the time counsel had finished making submissions and counter-submissions, it had been a few minutes before one o'clock, and the judge had sensibly decided to break for lunch. The defence team sat around a table together in a desultory huddle around plates of food none of them seemed particularly inclined to eat. "What we have are a series of emails—or alleged emails—printed on a few pieces of paper. We can't prove they're real; we can't identify the source."

"It's not so bad", Maria volunteered. "The judge allowed the evidence."

"Well, yes, Maria", Jonathan replied.

"Surely it's fairly obvious that the person who handed them to me must be Carrie Anderson?" said Maria desperately. Even after a dose of painkillers, the previous night's attack was making its painful presence felt, and she was beginning to feel that this was yet another unfortunate escapade that had borne no fruit at all. "If we can only trace her somehow . . ."

"But dammit, how? And how can we be sure it is her? Think about it. As far as you know, some random stranger just happened to put a large envelope into your hands. You couldn't identify her, a recognisable accent doesn't count, there are plenty of people from—Preston, was it?—residing in this country. She told you that she had been instructed to delete the emails but had made copies beforehand. You can be sure Jennifer removed all evidence of their existence from her machine."

"The very fact that she responded the way she did when she looked at that page must count for something?" asked Matthew. "She was white."

"Not enough is the simple answer to that." Jonathan looked across the canteen. "Who the Dickens is that coming towards us? Some flame of yours, Maria?"

Maria glanced up and saw Rick walking towards them, armed with the sort of bunch of roses Salvador Dali might have handed his girl-friend. Nevertheless, she felt an unfamiliar but pleasingly squirmy feeling inside her and smiled. "Rick, how nice to see you", she said, playing it all as demure as possible. She thought she heard one of the men snort unhelpfully.

"I hope you won't think it forward of me", he almost stammered, thrusting the bunch of flowers at her. "I saw the photograph of you on the news, and I just had to find out if you were all right."

Tragic to say, but Maria had never been given flowers by a man before, and the squirmy feeling quickly erupted into a warm, dull ache, even though she was not entirely sure now that she had been given flowers in the strictest sense of the word. The roses, which had looked from a distance like a bright array of red and yellow buds about to burst into full, glorious bloom, were in fact made of wood. "Thank you", she said, wondering if there was some joke in there somewhere that she just hadn't got yet.

"I hope you don't mind", said Rick, defensively. "I got the impression you were some kind of trendy green Catholic who wouldn't approve of real flowers if they'd been imported. So I got you these."

Angus roared unashamedly with laughter. "How romantic, dear boy! No woman could possibly resist."

"Oh, but they're lovely", promised Maria. "Why don't you join us?"

"Thank you." Rick pulled up an empty chair and waited patiently whilst Jonathan and Matthew shuffled apart to make space for him. "So, how's your asylum case going? Did you get the removal orders canceled in the end?"

"She's dead", whispered Maria, her shoulders drooping.

"Oh—oh, I am so terribly sorry", said Rick, looking as ashamed as if he had slapped her in the face. "I really am sorry. Whatever happened?"

"She was knocked down by a bus trying to escape her escorts."

Maria stared fixedly at her glass of lemonade. She had lost control of herself once too often over the past few days, and she was damned if she was going to break down in front of a group of men again. Having given him a frosty welcome, even Angus found it impossible not to feel sorry for Rick. "I don't suppose you're any good at modern technology, are you?" he asked.

Rick took the lifebelt without any further prompting. "Actually I quite like technology", he said. "What particular kind of technology were you thinking of?"

"We've got a little problem with emails you might be interested in. We have a printout of a correspondence between two young ladies, and let us just say that one of the young ladies has rather serious reasons to deny she ever wrote them, if you catch my drift."

"Can't you simply get the other woman to vouch that she did write them? If it's a correspondence . . ."

"Very good, son, we had thought of that. The problem there is that the other young lady has done a runner. She has refused to come forward as a witness. She simply dumped the evidence with our young friend here and fled the scene."

Rick considered the situation. He was keen to impress Maria, particularly after making such a disastrous mistake, and was the sort of person who generally liked to be useful to people. "Do they have webmail accounts?"

"Yes", Maria put in, because Angus was looking askance at him, and she knew he wouldn't have a clue what the man was going on about.

"That's a pity. If she had used a work email address it would be so much easier to trace. You can still trace people's identities if they use webmail accounts, though it's much harder, but not impossible."

"Good", said Jonathan. "How quickly? We're not inundated with time at the moment."

Rick made a slightly annoying sound, drawing a sharp intake of breath through his teeth. "Not that quickly, I'm afraid. You would have to get the police involved, I suspect. You would need to ask whoever it is who hosts the account to hand over her details. When she signed up for the account, she would have given things like her name and possibly her address."

"Well, thank you, that's very useful", said Jonathan, trying hard not to sound churlish but failing. "I'm afraid we don't have anything like that much time, and it would be a bit much to try to get the trial adjourned for that reason."

Rick looked rather shattered, thought Maria, and she instinctively put her hand on his arm as though to assure him that she had valued his contribution if nobody else had. "It doesn't matter", she said, giving Angus a smile. "The witness doesn't have to know that we haven't had time to do all that, does she?"

Angus' bulldog face broke into a mischievous grin. "How gloriously sneaky you Catholic girls are."

"Actually, it's called casuistry."

22

"Ms Little," said Angus, "before the luncheon adjournment, we were at page nine hundred and twenty-four E. Looking at the top of that page, we have an email ..."

The brief break had restored Jennifer's self-confidence, and she glowered at Angus with evident contempt. "I'm sorry, but I don't know what this is all about."

"If you would just bear with me, Ms Little. Please read out the first line."

"It says, 'from Jen Little ⟨jentinyone@fishnet.co.uk⟩'".

"Is that your email address?"

"Yes, but I didn't write this."

"Continue reading, please."

"'subject: Re: getting mildly worried.' Then in the 'to' field it says 'Carrie Anderson ⟨cashncarrie@girlpower.co.uk⟩'". She was reading with the cringing reluctance of a schoolgirl being forced to read out a catty note about a hated teacher in the presence of her entire class with the teacher concerned breathing down her neck. "Then there's the date line. Twenty-fourth January, 2009, time 14:32".

"Now, would you please read the second sentence of the email?"

"I don't have to do this!"

"I'm rather afraid you do, Ms Little. Please proceed."

"This is absurd. I won't do it!"

"Would you prefer me to read it out?"

"No! No, I ..." she floundered miserably. "I never wrote this."

"Just read it."

She stared fixedly at the page before her. "This is her own stupid fault and if she wanted to patch up our feud she could, but she's a selfish cowardly little witch who can't face up to herself."

"Do you deny writing that?"

"Of course I deny it", she answered, a little too slowly.

"Perhaps we can move on to the following page?"

"I didn't write it!" She sounded close to tears. "Anyone could have hacked into my account ..."

"From the top, if you please?"

"No."

"As you wish", conceded Angus. "Then I'll read it. 'from: Jen Little. Email address: jentinyone@fishnet.co.uk . . .' "

Every muscle in Jennifer's face was taut to snapping point, but it was impossible to know whether she was angrier with him for the humiliation he was putting her through or herself for making such an obvious tactical error. The jarring combination of girlish choice of email address and vicious female vitriol sounded all the more detestable spoken with Angus Wetherby's dry, sardonic tone. "'Soz Carrie, but I don't care if the selfish cow throws herself under a bus.' Ms Little, are you in the habit of using language like this about your close friends?"

"I didn't! I would never have said those things about her!"

"You deny writing those words?"

"Yes, I do."

"Ms Little, I must say this to you. You wrote these emails to Carrie Anderson, and they are an entirely accurate reflection of your hatred towards Daisy Havisham."

"I've never seen these emails before."

"Whatever your past friendship with her, you felt nothing but hatred and malice towards Daisy Havisham in the days leading up to her suicide attempt . . ."

"Actually . . ."

"You had no qualms of conscience whatsoever about defaming her to a mutual friend."

"Will you *stop*?" Jennifer froze as though surprised to have heard herself shouting, before looking wearily in Angus Wetherby's direction. "Once and for all, I have no memory of writing those emails."

Angus gave a generous smile. "You do realise, of course, Ms Little, that it is perfectly possible to trace a person's identity and indeed to verify whether or not they sent certain messages at certain times? This is true even if the person deletes the emails to cover their tracks. You knew that, didn't you?"

Jennifer swallowed hard and seemed to be weighing up a decision in her head. This was the moment in films, thought Matthew, when the false witness breaks down in sobs and confesses everything. He waited for her to crumple up in front of him, tearful and distraught, filled with contrition, but she stood up straight and looked coldly at Angus with the air of a soldier preparing to make a final, doomed advance. "As I have already said, my account could have been hacked, couldn't it? Some malicious person who wanted to frame me could have spoofed my address and written all sorts of things."

Angus showed no flicker of emotion. He was used to remaining cool under the pressure of an unhelpful or hostile answer and showed no sign of panic. He returned Jennifer's death stare with a calmly confident look of his own. "Are you seriously asking the court to believe that these emails were generated by a third party so cleverly that the person to whom they were addressed believed them to have come from you?"

"I don't—I don't know."

"And if that were the case, is it not a little strange that Carrie Anderson shows no surprise at the way you describe Daisy Havisham?" He waited for an answer, but she simply shook her head. "Or are you going to claim that the entire correspondence was fabricated simply to show you in a bad light?"

The silence was so protracted and so complete that Matthew was almost afraid to move in case he brought all hell crashing down on him. "Our quarrel had nothing to do with it", she said quietly. "She was such a mess. Something would have pushed her over the edge eventually. And I had nothing to do with that living will. I just—I noticed it after I'd called the ambulance and guessed she'd meant it to be found. If I hadn't cared about her, I wouldn't have called the ambulance at all. I would've tiptoed out and left her."

"Or perhaps, Ms Little, it would be truer to say that you were afraid that if she died and there was an inquest, the fact that you had walked away and left her to die might come to light along with your dislike of her."

Jennifer stared at her questioner, but no response came.

"By calling an ambulance, you made sure nobody could claim that you did nothing to help her, and her death would be someone else's problem. Is that what you were thinking?"

"No", she said, but there was no energy left in her voice. "I know how it looks, but when someone's hurt you, you just want to hurt them back. Really hurt them, but even when you know they're cracking up, you never really think anything's going to happen. When I found her, I guess I just panicked and called the ambulance. I never thought she'd actually do it, however bad anyone made her feel." She looked suddenly angry again. "Look—it was none of my business. I had my own life to think about! I'm—I'm not really sure what I was thinking after that."

"Thank you. Wait there, please. There might be further questions." And Angus sat down.

"You know, I almost felt sorry for her", said Matthew later that evening as he sat with Jonathan, Freya and Maria at the Kirkpatrick residence.

"Don't", said Maria. "She's a nasty little bully."

"But she might well not have realised how much harm she was doing."

"Perhaps she didn't", Maria conceded. "But I'm not sure that's so important. Bullies are parasites."

"Ouch!" Jonathan put in. "Hit a nerve, has he?"

"Well, they are! They leach the life out of people for the sheer, malicious pleasure of it. Maybe it's a power thing, maybe that's the only way they can feel good about themselves, but don't ask me to sympathise!"

"A few little parasites at your school, were there?"

Maria was aware of Jonathan's needling tone but could not resist allowing herself to be riled. "It's a perfectly valid analogy, I think you'll find."

"I would have classed it as a metaphor."

"Bullies are parasites! Neither ever mean to kill their objects. What's the point of that? But sometimes they do. They can't bring themselves to stop and end up going too far."

The subject was obviously so personally hurtful to Maria that Freya found herself clumsily changing the subject. "I've got some terribly nice shortbread if anyone wants some with their coffee?" she asked, with a grating false cheerfulness. "My sister-in-law sent me a tin. They were on a walking holiday in the Highlands."

Maria smiled to herself. The world where bullies thrived seemed quite far away from the security of this little home. "I've never been to Scotland", she said lamely, but it set an invisible ball rolling.

"Beautiful countryside", said Matthew. "I was taken on a fishing expedition once when I was a boy. We caught the biggest salmon I've ever seen . . ."

Maria was relieved to be distracted by the sound of her phone ringing, and she scurried away into the box room. It was Rick. "I really feel awful about your asylum seeker", he began before she had even had the chance to say hello. "You know, I didn't see anything about it on any major news site."

"I don't think it was reported outside London", said Maria. "Who cares about some little Chinese girl dying like that? I still haven't heard if they were able to save the baby."

"I don't suppose my information was of any use to you, was it?"

"Oh, yes, it was very useful. Whether it will help in the long run is a little more difficult to guess. You know what it's like."

"Well, let's hope the jury can be swayed. Your doctor comes across as a nice chap. You never know, that might be enough to clinch it."

"I'm not sure anybody cares about nice chaps anymore!" Maria burst out, but her rant over dinner had left her smouldering with rage. "Let's face it, when we were growing up, being nasty to everyone was practically a virtue. It was like you had to prove you could outbully everyone to show how assertive you were."

"That's a bit harsh", Rick began, but he couldn't face having an argument with Maria. "I do know what you mean, but I don't think it has to be that way. Anyway, I wondered if you'd read Hansard today?"

"No, of course I haven't. I've been in court all day. Why?"

"Well, I just happened to be on the Parliamentary website looking up some information about an MP . . ."

"You working on some juicy fraud case or something?"

"No, as a matter of fact."

"Of course, you know how many MPs have got into trouble with the law in the past, don't you?"

"Not as many as are going to be if the Fleet Street rumours are true. Anyway, I noticed that your Dr Kemble has been mentioned in dispatches, so to speak. An MP asked a question in Parliament about the law regarding living wills, citing his case specifically."

"Who was it?"

"Reg Conlon."

"*Conlon?!* But he supported the wretched bill that got us into this mess in the first place!"

"I thought you'd be delighted by the man's bare-faced cheek", laughed Rick. "He actually stated that this terrible situation was precisely the sort of disaster he and his colleagues had predicted when the bill was being debated."

"But they *supported* the bill!" Maria raged down the phone. "They sold out. They said over and over again that it was a very good bill. It just required a few amendments, and those of us who opposed it were either heartless or stupid! The bloody, *bloody* nerve!"

"Really, Maria!" exclaimed Freya, who had just poked her head round the door to see if Maria needed anything. "Do you honestly have to use language like that?"

"Barrack room language", Maria replied, over her shoulder. "Your husband's a bad influence."

"That's it", boomed Jonathan from the other room. "Blame somebody else."

"Look, Rick, could you send me the URL?" asked Maria, closing the door to block out the background commentary. "I'd like to take a look at it myself."

"Certainly. I'll email it to you."

Matthew, Jonathan and Freya were looking expectantly at her as she put the phone down and rejoined them. "Reg Conlon MP mentioned you in a parliamentary question", explained Maria, "as an example of what he claims he warned Parliament would happen if the End of Life Care Bill went through."

"Well, one has to admire the man's nerve", said Jonathan with a smile. "He went on record as saying it was a very good bill. I seem to remember it being suggested that people who opposed it were heartless extremists."

"Yes, and if *I* remember rightly, his best mate called those of us who opposed it 'wicked' and 'crass' with 'laughable' views. Wasn't some reference to the Mad Hatter made at one point?"

"You mustn't take that sort of thing personally, Maria", said Jonathan, for the millionth time. "You're far too thin skinned to be a politician."

"Oh, would that be the only barrier?" she enquired, throwing herself into a chair, only to flinch with pain. "I thought honesty might be a bit of a handicap."

"Come, come, not all politicians are dishonest." She snorted with derisive laughter. "You shouldn't be so cynical at your age."

"I've been called cynical since before I knew what the word meant."
The lie did not come into the world through me . . .

She closed her eyes and thought of the horrible divisions that had crept into an already divided movement in the runup to the vote, the endless little insults and side swipes that had been exchanged. She had been working full time as a campaigner then, and the battle against the bill had dominated her every waking hour. She vividly remembered leaving a particularly bad-tempered meeting one afternoon and her counterpart in another organisation latching onto her as she glided up the escalator at Victoria Station. He was wearing his very best endearing smile. "Aren't these divisions a pity?" he said.

"Yes, Jerry, they certainly are", she answered.

"You know, it really doesn't have to be this way", he continued, apparently undeterred by her noncommittal tone. "Our people are very keen on cooperation. It's just that your boss doesn't want to. Isn't that so sad?"

It was childishly manipulative, so much so that she found herself blushing with embarrassment when rage ought to have been in order. "I'm not sure I know what you mean", she managed to say.

"Of course, of course." Now he was embarrassed. "I was just wondering if you could have a little word with him for me, but you probably don't know anything about this."

He was talking to her—unwittingly, she suspected—as though she were a feather-brained female incapable of understanding the political intrigues of the big, scary male world of lobbying and campaigning. She felt no qualm of conscience about playing along. "No, I'm afraid I don't, really. Maybe you should speak to him yourself."

"Yes, yes, I suppose I could. Could you arrange it? Just a friendly, informal chat." He laughed awkwardly. "We're all on the same side in the end, aren't we?"

By a desperately unfortunate example of bad timing, they had arrived at Maria's office on the stroke of one, when Gavin, the director, always stopped for a brief lunch break, and he stepped unsuspectingly into their path before Maria could prepare him for what was coming. "Hello, Maria", he said cheerfully. "How was the meeting?" He was a large, amiable individual who was still capable of optimism after thirty years of campaigning for the rights of Britain's embattled Catholic minority. He recognised Jerry and nodded. "Afternoon, Jeremy. Have you come to see me?"

It was a great misfortune of Jerry's that he was the sort of man who did not cope well with being put on the spot, and he went into what Maria could most charitably call autopanic. "Why won't you cooperate with us?" he demanded without so much as a "good afternoon" to break the ice. "We're nice people, we're decent people and you're determined to ruin everything!"

"Erm, Jerry ..." Gavin began, looking down at him in utter bemusement.

"We've been in this business longer than you; we know what we're doing. Our senior activists gave up well-paid careers to stand up for the truth ..."

"Jerry, what might you be talking about?"

Jerry was scarlet and scowling; Maria suspected that he was just seconds away from stamping his foot. "You actually said that doctors would be forced out of practice. Scaremongering nonsense! We all know that with the right amendments ..."

The tirade went on and on. At one point, Maria attempted to slip away, but Gavin gestured for her to stay where she was. She realised afterwards that he had wanted her to hear every hysterical word to make absolutely sure she was not left in any doubt as to the state of things. And she had watched and listened and fallen into utter despair. *Divide and conquer*, she thought. *We divide, and our opposition conquers ...*

"Don't take it too hard, Maria", said Jonathan. "It's quite flattering, really. They're trying to rewrite history to make it look as though they saw things the way we did. It just goes to show that our position was right after all."

"The fact that Matthew here is in the dock shows that we were right after all", she retorted. "But it's a bit late in the day for 'I told you so', isn't it? I just wish they'd had the humility to listen when it really mattered. That way we wouldn't be in this mess, and Matthew would be practising medicine and not having to apologise for saving somebody's life."

"I'm not apologising," said Matthew, reminding them that he was still there, "and I won't forget easily where the real battle lines were drawn. I still have a copy of the letter Reg Conlon sent to Bishop McEvoy, moaning about meddlesome people who were going around suggesting that the bill was fatally flawed. He mentioned me by name then as well."

Matthew distracted himself by biting into a piece of shortbread in the shape of a thistle from a tin that had evidently been left overnight with the lid off. Like Maria, he felt an overwhelming sense of betrayal that Jonathan would never quite be able to understand. He knew that Maria felt angry because she had suffered the frustrations and humiliations of being branded a "militant" and a "lunatic" when she had known that she and her colleagues were simply telling the truth, but in his case, there had been the same sense of frustration coupled with fear. The fear, however abstract at the time, that he would inevitably find himself precisely where he now stood. "I suppose I shouldn't be afraid anymore", he mused out loud. "My father always said that soldiers stopped being afraid as soon as they were in the thick of the battle. They wouldn't sleep a wink the night before. They'd be in a terrible state as they got ready, but when they were in there with the bullets flying about, they just fought. He saw men get shot in the arm or the shoulder—some nonfatal injury—and they wouldn't even notice. The adrenalin kept them going. Then once it was all over, they would realise they were injured and die of shock before he could treat them."

"You can start to relax soon, Matt", said Jonathan, patting him on the shoulder. "We'll soon be starting the case for the defence, and we'll be on the home straight. Just make sure you don't drop dead with a heart attack after you're acquitted."

He thought it inopportune to mention that Matthew still had to step into the witness box and that, unbeknown to the poor innocent, the success or failure of the case might well hang on precisely how well he coped under cross-examination. He did not need to know about the bullet lodged in his own arm just yet.

23

The day was not going swimmingly well. The prosecution's final witness had been the solicitor responsible for helping Daisy Havisham draw up her living will, and Angus had had very little opportunity to unsettle the man. Being a lawyer, he was not a typical witness, felt less sense of awe or nervousness at finding himself in the witness box and answered the questions of both sides with a cold sense of boredom. Yes, the living will had been drawn up correctly; yes, it was legally binding; no, he had had no sense whatsoever that the lady in question did not understand what she was getting into; no, he did not believe she had been coerced into making the living will.

The only time a flicker of mirth had crossed the solicitor's funereal face had been when Angus had suggested that living wills could be against the Human Rights Act because they forced medical professionals to act against their consciences. "I think the majority would regard an individual's right to autonomy to be rather more significant than the perceived right of a doctor to obey a quasi-religious impulse." Someone in the public gallery had actually applauded, prompting one of the ushers to command him to be quiet.

Things began to brighten up a little—and it really was only a little—when the defence opened its case with an expert witness who took the stand with confidence and began to talk about mental illness and the very grave difficulties associated with undiagnosed cases of depression. "There is a very serious possibility that Daisy Havisham was suffering from depression at the time she made the living will", he said, in the soft Scottish lilt of a man accustomed to putting neurotic patients at ease. Professor Reid was a short, wiry man with jet black hair and pale, almost translucent skin which marked out his long Celtic heritage, and Angus had to admit that he cut an impressive figure in the witness box. It was what came out of his mouth that was more uncertain. "A very serious possibility, particularly as she went on to make a suicide attempt."

"Can you prove she was suffering from depression at the time she made the living will?" demanded Dudley. "Surely that is the sticking point? She might have become ill with depression ten minutes after she left the solicitor's office, but what evidence do you have that she was suffering from depression *when she made the living will?*"

"None. That is the whole point", said Professor Reid. "Depression is an invisible condition. Many of my patients go for years concealing the symptoms before they seek help. She might not have had depression; alternatively, she might have done, but in the end a doctor in an emergency room has to make an on-the-spot decision. If there is any doubt at all about the patient's state of mind when they drew up the living will, the doctor must err on the side of caution. He must err on the side of life."

Dudley gave an indignant laugh and shook his head as though the witness were so misguided it was as much as his life was worth not to lose control. "But surely if you were to obey that principle, you would have to query the legitimacy of *all* living wills? One could never be sure that a person was making an entirely free and rational decision to refuse treatment."

"Quite so", continued the professor, relentlessly. "That is one of the major arguments against euthanasia—passive or otherwise. In the end, a doctor can never be entirely certain that the patient is making what you have called a free and rational decision. And it is better, surely, for ten living wills to be disregarded than for one vulnerable patient to be left to die?"

Dudley by now was grinning like a Cheshire Cat. "If you believe living wills should be routinely disregarded, Professor Reid, perhaps you could tell the court what legal status you imagine they should have—if any?"

Jonathan swallowed hard. It was a very obvious trap, but the witness might not be aware of it until he fell headlong into it and broke his neck. "I am a doctor, not a lawyer", answered the professor. "I was called here to answer questions relating to medicine. It is my professional opinion that living wills are highly dangerous because of this question of how to ensure their validity from a medical point of view. How Parliament—and indeed the courts—choose to act upon that medical question is another matter."

Jonathan relaxed but knew that the answer was unlikely to have been good enough. Unusually, however, Matthew was clearly quite pleased with the way things were going when the court adjourned, and Jonathan kept his reservations to himself as Matthew and Professor Reid chatted over old times. "Would it be twenty-five years, Nigel?" asked Matthew, taking the much-needed drink his friend passed him.

"At least", he answered. "I haven't seen you since you fell into the fountain in Trinity Great Court the day after graduation."

"You know, I wasn't even drunk. My foot slipped on a patch of moss."

"Now they all say *that*, sweetheart."

Matthew and Nigel had completed their clinical studies together, those exciting but nerve-racking years when medical students are allowed contact with real patients and get to negotiate their way around real hospitals. Nigel had taken such offence at being patronised by middle-aged nurses that he had got into the habit of coming into hospital dressed in a three-piece suit, which made him look ten years older and caused other medical staff to behave towards him as though he were a consultant. This did wonders for his self-confidence, if not his skills, and looking at him now, with the ravages of middle age finally hitting him, Matthew could still feel the sharp pain in the back of his hand as his eager friend had practised fitting a venflon and the needle had missed the vein a full five times. In fact, he had never succeeded in hitting his target, as Matthew had passed out on the fifth attempt, and never lived the humiliation down.

"Well, I never guessed if we met again it would be here", mused Nigel, looking at his friend's haggard face. "Of all the people from our year, I would never have imagined you ending up in court. It's a mad world."

"There are lots of things we never imagined back then, I suppose", said Matthew, draining his glass. Jonathan signaled to Nigel not to fill it again.

"It's taking its toll, isn't it?" Nigel persisted. "You look hideous."

"Thanks. You don't exactly look like a bunch of petunias yourself."

"Are you taking anything?"

"Certainly not!"

Nigel gave an exasperated smile. "Now isn't that just typical of a doctor? Ravaged by stress, not sleeping a wink—I daresay not eating much either given your suit looks a wee bit big on you—and you've not sought professional help."

"It's not a medical problem, Nigel, it's just circumstances."

"If you fell out of a window and broke your leg, you wouldn't say it was just circumstances, now, would you?"

Matthew looked wearily past Nigel's head, unwilling to make eye contact with him. "It doesn't matter. In not very long at all, this will all be over one way or another."

Nigel shrugged. "Och well. I'd better hang around until after the verdict in case I need to bash your chest in."

"Thanks."

Matthew had never understood when he was young why older people became nostalgic, but he supposed that most young people did not understand the notion. Sitting with a man who formed one of his only links to his student days, Matthew felt the ache of growing older and the bewilderment of knowing that many years had passed in what seemed to be the blink of an eye. It all felt so fresh and yet so foreign— Nigel in his ridiculous suit looking like a kid who had put on his father's clothes because he wanted to play at being a grownup, the raucous laughter that had greeted him when he came round in the hospital corridor with his legs propped up, the punishing night shifts and the exhilaration of rushing out of an exam room. The hope ... so much hope, futures being planned and prepared for as though the years to come could simply be rolled out and enjoyed.

Maria dropped in briefly to pass Jonathan a message before slipping away again. "What happened to her?" asked Nigel. "She looks as though she's had the stuffing kicked out of her."

"She has indeed had the—had seven bells beaten out of her", said Matthew numbly. "Some thugs were trying to get my legal team to drop the case—or so it appears, anyway. There's no way of proving it had anything to do with it, but I know it was." So many peculiar things had happened in his vicinity over the past months that he could not process the information properly any more.

"Good God, really?"

"Yes, really. Unfortunately, she has no idea who they were. They had their faces covered."

"It surely wouldn't be that difficult to find out?"

Matthew sighed. "It's in the hands of the police, Nigel. If she's lucky, she might eventually see her attackers brought to trial, but I have a feeling that file will be quietly closed."

Nigel looked at him in stunned silence. "You have got yourself into deep waters", he said.

"Not by choice, I assure you. As far as I can make out, all I did was to rinse a patient's stomach out."

Matthew's good spirits evaporated at the memory of Maria's dramatic appearance in the office and the emergence of every horrific detail. Nigel evidently sensed the change in him. "Cheer up, mate", he ventured. "The reluctant heroes are always the best."

Nigel wondered how many years the ordeal had taken off Matthew's life and how much worse it was likely to get. When Matthew slipped out to find the men's room, Nigel turned to Jonathan and Angus, who had discreetly moved to an adjoining table to give them the chance to talk more privately. Maria, he noticed, had slipped back in. "What are his chances?" he asked. "I need to know. If that man goes to prison, it'll kill him. If he loses his career . . ."

"I honestly couldn't tell you", said Angus, as bluntly as the question had been asked. "I think it unlikely he will get a custodial sentence if he is convicted, though if the judge is feeling particularly vindictive or wants to make an example of him, he might."

"How likely is a conviction, in your professional opinion?"

"Well . . ."

"Yes?"

"I would say that the whole case rests on a knife edge. If we could have persuaded a few more people to stick their necks out and give evidence on Matthew's behalf, I would say we would have had the case in the bag, but it has been complicated by people's prejudices and fears. If it had been twenty years ago . . ."

"So you think there's a strong chance he'll be convicted?"

Angus grimaced, aware of Jonathan and Maria glancing icily in his direction. "Matthew Kemble is one of the most honest and genuinely innocent men I have ever come across, and I do not deal as a rule with honest and innocent men. But I wouldn't wager my career that he will walk away from here without a stain on his name."

"It's obscene", snarled Nigel. "The state doesn't want honest, hardworking, conscientious doctors. It wants automatons following procedures."

"Indeed. That's the irony of it", said Angus. "There have always been miscarriages of justice; I've witnessed a few during the course of my career. But if Matthew is convicted, it will be the first time a client of mine has gone down *because* he was honest and innocent."

Matthew stood in the doorway and listened to his case being discussed in the contrasting tones of Nigel's cool, calm Edinburgh lilt and Angus' 1950s English accent, which somehow conjured up images of port and cigars even as he reflected upon the noose around his client's neck. There was something about being outside a conversation concerning him that made Matthew feel especially helpless, but it was only a reflection of his case itself. All the way through, since the fateful night it had all been set in motion, Matthew had had the sense of being outside of things: the doctor with scruples about a piece of legislation his colleagues had barely noticed, the renegade doctor who had graced newspaper headlines and radio programmes for doing what he regarded as his duty, the doctor out of touch and out of time, whose values and convictions belonged to another generation, another world which had long ago slipped into history.

Never in his life had he felt adrift like this; never had he felt so lost. He felt himself sweating and trembling. He knew his breathing was too shallow and too rapid, but his chest felt so tight it was as much as his life was worth to catch his breath at all. Some invisible adversary was trying to crush the life out of him once and for all; he felt his heart racing, faster and faster until it seemed to be ready to burst. Moments before his vision blurred, he saw Maria's bruised face turning to look at him. "Hey! What is it? Are you all right?"

He slumped against the door frame, hitting his head as he fell. There were people all around him—his friends, who believed in him even though they thought his case was hopeless, but he was still alone. The ground beneath his feet had disintegrated; he was sinking beneath invisible waves, and he was going to drown. "Eva", he whispered. "Eva."

24

Matthew came round to the sight of Eva's tearful face looking down at him. He recognised the clinical sounds and smells of his workplace and realised that he was lying in a hospital bed with his arm attached to a drip. "It's all right, my darling", she said, stooping forward to kiss his face. "I'm here. I came as soon as I heard."

"What happened?" He felt an overwhelming sense of weariness, as though some practical joker had tied weights to his limbs whilst he was unconscious. Even his head felt too heavy to move.

"You collapsed", she said. "They've brought you here."

"The trial . . ."

"It's all right. Don't think about that. It's been adjourned."

"I feel so tired."

"I know. Just rest, my darling. Don't think about anything else."

He felt a pang of guilt that she was in tears, and it was all his fault, but he suspected she had cried a great deal during his hours of happy unconsciousness. He struggled to reach out to her, and she took the dead weight of his hand; he was astonished to find that it was an effort simply to curl his fingers around hers, and he quickly gave up trying. "I'm very sorry, Eva", he lisped, but his mouth felt dry. "I'm so very sorry I'm causing you such worry."

"Don't be silly. I just want to see you well again. Sleep now; don't fight it."

Matthew felt himself nodding off to sleep again; it was so impossible for him to keep his own eyes open. He felt protected as he always did with his wife by his side like an Amazonian warrior, guarding his rest. He knew he could sleep peacefully with such a fiery guardian watching over him; he could sleep without fear of harm or disturbance. He could rest for eternity if it came to it, safe in the knowledge that even the devil could not touch him if she were there. *To sleep, perchance to dream* . . .

And Eva held his hand as he drifted off before placing it carefully on his chest and pulling the white sheets up to his chin. She felt horribly as though she were sitting at his deathbed and had been left alone to take her leave of him whilst a priest waited for her outside. "*Oh, God*", she whispered. "Please, God, give him back to me."

"It's killing him!" shouted Eva, causing Jonathan to back away from her. "This whole case is killing him! Not enough for these cretins to try and get him locked up. They won't stop until he's in the ground!"

As soon as Matthew had been asleep long enough for Eva to be sure he would not wake up again for many hours, she had agreed to go with Jonathan to his office to discuss the situation. "It wasn't a heart attack, Eva", said Jonathan. "You heard the doctor say that. Your husband is exhausted and stressed and at the end of his tether. That was why he collapsed."

"It was a warning though, wasn't it? Next time it might be a heart attack."

"He is in good hands, Eva. The doctors are saying he just needs a couple of days' rest and some peace and quiet."

"And then what? You'll drag him back into that snake pit to be humiliated and—and bullied, and . . ."

"Eva, I assure you I'm not dragging him anywhere", answered Jonathan, as gently as he could manage. "The Crown Prosecution Service dragged him into this situation, egged on by a small group of vindictive people with axes to grind. All I'm trying to do is to ensure he gets out of this unscathed. There are plenty of people who would like us to drop the case."

Eva covered her eyes, and Jonathan prayed she would not break down in front of him. He had already been forced to bear the terror of a distraught female crying her eyes out in front of him once during this case; a second time, and he would surely go to pieces himself. "I know", she whispered. "God help me, I *know*. I just can't tell you what it feels like to see the man you love being dragged through the gutter like this."

"I understand."

"I'm scared to death I'll lose him."

"You won't, Eva. He's far stronger than he seems. And he's in the right. You know what they say: the truth is its own protection."

Eva sniggered bitterly. "Tell that to Edmund Campion; tell that to Maximilian Kolbe! Tell that to the millions of people who've been shot, hanged, tortured, locked up and God knows what else in the name of the truth!"

Jonathan took her hand. "Eva, I do appreciate what you're going through, but would you honestly have it any other way? You know he was right."

"Of course I do!" She slumped over the desk in front of her and burst into tears. "Of—course—I—do! I just don't want him to suffer any more. I don't want him to be a martyr."

Jonathan counted to ten silently in his head and then to twenty whilst Eva composed herself again and sat up, looking expectantly in his direction. "He isn't going to be a martyr, Eva. In a few days' time, Matthew will be well enough to return to court, and the trial will be completed. And if I have anything to do with it, he will be acquitted. I don't think I have ever cared more about the fate of one of my clients before. It's a matter of honour."

"I know. I'm sorry. I'm really not ungrateful."

Jonathan noticed the grey smudges under her eyes. "You should get some help yourself, Eva. It's taking its toll on you too. You're bound to feel the strain."

"Oh, I'm all right. It's resisting the urge to kill the swine that's the real strain."

"Would you like me to accompany you back to the hospital?"

She shook her head. "It's all right. I'll be fine. Really."

Jonathan helped her on with her jacket, kissed her on the cheek and watched as she left the room with characteristic poise and dignity. He wondered how he would feel if Freya found herself fighting to clear her name in court, the sense of panic and outrage he might experience if he were called to the hospital to be informed that she had collapsed and been brought there unconscious in the back of an ambulance. It was not an entirely implausible scenario given Freya's previous campaigning activities, but unlike Eva he would at least be in a better position to fight in her corner.

Maria walked in. "Why didn't you want me to meet Mrs Kemble?" she enquired.

"Because I didn't want her to see your face", he explained. "She might well have seen the pictures in the papers, but she didn't mention it, and I didn't want her to start asking difficult questions. She's on edge enough as it is without knowing about your little misadventure."

She shrugged. "I suppose that's sensible. How's the good doctor bearing up?"

right. Not making a great deal of sense at the moment,
to be expected. It might even buy him some sympathy.
you never know."

ake a few people examine their consciences."

at would be asking far too much. The really nasty sods
will say ~ got no one but himself to blame; the marginally less vile
ones will say it is unfortunate but can't be helped. I can almost hear
them saying it. 'Can't be helped!'"

Maria could hear them saying it. She could see their cold smirks or
scowls, the complacent shrug of the shoulders, the dismissive tone of
voice. As a person who found it difficult to negotiate her own emotions at the best of times, she could tolerate virtually any emotional
excess from rage to tears, but to be capable of feeling no emotion at
all was entirely beyond her understanding. It was so inhuman, so contrary to her belief in love as the greatest force holding together the
frail human condition. It was so, so very *English*! All these frosty people trapped behind their own ironic detachment, too cowardly to reach
out and empathise with any other member of the human race—let
alone someone of whom they did not approve—until they had forgotten how it felt to feel the stirrings of human affection and solidar-
ity. *If we do not burn with love*, Francois Mauriac had put it, she seemed
to remember, *many will die of the cold*. If the Solzhenitsyn quote had
not been her motto for life, it would have been that.

"I half hoped he would be unfit to stand trial and they'd drop the
whole thing", admitted Maria.

"Now that would be a disaster", said Jonathan. "That's the last thing
we need at this late stage. The case has become a public spectacle, or
a matter of public interest, if you prefer. If the court fails to reach a
verdict, poor dear Matthew will never be able to walk away and get
on with his career. It will plague him for the rest of his life. He is also
likely to have to face the General Medical Council."

"He might have to face them anyway."

"Not necessarily, if he's acquitted."

"If."

Next morning, having spent much of the intervening time fast asleep,
Matthew woke up feeling a good deal better. As he munched his way
through three slices of toast smothered in butter, Eva mused that it
was the first time he had greeted the appearance of food with any

enthusiasm since his first contact with the police. "I wonder if they'll discharge me today", he said. "Perhaps if I ask very nicely."

"Don't rush things", said Eva, handing him a cup of tea. "You did bump your head rather hard when you fell."

Matthew rolled his eyes. "If one of the children fell and bumped his head, I'd kiss it better."

"Not if they were out cold you wouldn't. Come on now, you know it was more than that. You might be feeling better now, but it will take a while before you're up and about again."

"I wish I'd managed to hold my nerve a little longer", he said. "I feel so ridiculous getting myself into such a state. I ought to know by now how to look after myself."

"You didn't make yourself ill with stress", she countered. "You owe it to yourself to recover properly."

He knew she was torn between relief at seeing the improvement in him and fear about him being forced to return to court. The hospital offered a sterile kind of sanctuary to them both. He was tucked up safely in bed with drugs to force him to sleep if he couldn't make himself relax; he was protected from television and radio and newspapers and court appearances. The door to his ward had an alarm on it to prevent impostors getting in, and in his case that meant journalists with their dictaphones and campaigners with their attitude problems. Out in the ugly world of everyday life, all kinds of calumny might be being spoken against him, a lynch mob could be stalking the streets baying for his blood, but he was cushioned from it all.

"I'll have to face it all sooner or later", he said. "If I hadn't passed out like that it might be all over by now. I won't be able to relax properly until it's over and done with."

There was a rustle of curtains being pulled back, and a young female doctor with what Matthew would have termed a convict haircut stepped inside the cubicle. "Good morning", she said brightly, pausing to pick up the medical chart clipped to the end of the bed. "How are you feeling today?"

"Much better", said Matthew, with as much enthusiasm as he could muster. "I was wondering whether you might let me out today?"

"Hmm, well, that depends." Eva held her breath, praying the answer would be no. "Fortunately, in spite of how it first looked, you didn't have a heart attack."

"Yes, I know that! I do feel rather a fraud actually, getting myself into a state like that. If I'd been conscious I would never have let them call an ambulance."

"Dr Kemble, you certainly weren't a fraud." The doctor pulled up a chair and sat at his bedside. "Collapsing with severe stress is never a good sign, as you know. When would you say was the last time you had an unbroken night's sleep?"

Matthew closed his eyes and shook his head. "I've no idea. Months, I suppose, and sometimes I have not slept at all."

"Quite. What about your eating habits?"

"It's difficult. I'm afraid I feel constantly sick. Look, it's entirely psychosomatic. I know perfectly well what this is all about! I just have to pull myself together for a few more days until the trial's over."

The doctor scribbled something on his notes. "Well, we can't do anything about your circumstances, obviously, but you'll need to do more than pull yourself together before you can go anywhere near a courtroom."

"I need to get on with this. I can't have it hanging over me indefinitely. I'll go stark raving mad."

"I quite understand. My suggestion would be this." She sounded, thought Eva, like an inexperienced diplomat about to step into the middle ground between two clashing extremes. She was just unsure as to who represented the other extreme. "All being well, you'll be discharged after four o'clock this afternoon. I'm going to prescribe you some medication to help you sleep at night and to deal with the anxiety during the day."

"Those pills are terribly addictive. I'd really rather . . ."

"I'm aware that sleeping pills are addictive, Dr Kemble. I'm going to prescribe enough to last a fortnight. Just enough to see you comfortably through the rest of your trial. As soon as it finishes, you need to make an appointment with your GP and see what he suggests. It might be a while before you start to get back to normal again."

"Thank you."

Eva hung her head, refusing to acknowledge the doctor as she left. "I suppose we should be grateful for small mercies", she said quietly, staring fixedly at the corner of the bed.

"I can't hide out in hospital forever, darling", he said. "Some things just have to be faced."

"The trial?"

"Yes."

"Prison?"

Matthew shuddered. "Well, let's hope it doesn't come to that." He heard the clatter of invisible keys again and felt the old harbingers of panic taking him over. He lay back in the bed and tried to control his breathing. "Perhaps the tablets might stop me going round the bend after all."

Eva patted his arm. "I'm sorry, I'm hardly helping, am I?" she said. "Think of the holiday we'll have after this is all over. We'll take the children somewhere special, wherever you want to go."

"The Isle of Wight", he said without hesitation.

She laughed. "You're so *boring*!"

Matthew smiled without opening his eyes. He exceled at boring. In fact, he had made boring a subject of such intense study during his long life that he had virtually turned it into a martial art. And it was his most desperate hope—once his fifteen minutes of notoriety had passed and the media had some other fall guy to pester—that he could go back to being boring, and nobody would mind.

25

Matthew was guiltily grateful for the sleeping pills. Not only did they ensure he got a decent night's sleep, but during his waking hours he was left feeling curiously detached from the world around him, as though he were a visitor from another planet or he were encased in a vast glass tube which obligingly hovered about him everywhere he went. "I don't see why you should feel guilty", commented Jonathan, watching as Matthew swallowed the helpful little white pill with a few sips of water. "You're a doctor, for heaven's sake."

"Yes, I know, but I'm really strict about prescribing stuff like this to patients."

It was eleven o'clock at night, and the trial was due to resume the following morning. Freya and Maria had both gone to bed, but Matthew could hear the sound of tossing and turning from the box room that had become Maria's temporary bedroom and the occasional, indistinguishable shouted word. "There's somebody else who could do with some sedation", said Jonathan, getting up to close the sitting room door and muffle the sound. He was not sure why, but listening to a person having a bad dream felt a little too much like eavesdropping.

"Oh, dear, does she often have nightmares?"

"I've only noticed a couple since she's been here. They might not be nightmares, of course. Seeing how highly strung she is, she's probably just dreaming about everyday life."

But Maria was trapped in a dream world so terrible she would have begged to be woken up by force if necessary, if she had only known she was dreaming. She was being wheeled down the eternal corridor again, with its terrible familiarity and menace, desperately protesting that she wanted to be left alone. They were heading for that room at the end as they always were, where some monstrous threat lay in wait for her, but she could not stop. She could never stop. She felt herself moving faster and faster, shouting that she wanted to be left alone, only to find herself skidding to a halt in the room calling out to nobody.

The doctor was not there. The room was as it always was in her nightmares—searing light everywhere, machines she could not name—but she was alone, and the doctor's face did not appear. She looked around and realised that even the people who had pushed her down that corridor had deserted her as soon as they had entered the room. She opened her mouth to call for help, but she could not catch her breath, and somehow she knew, with the bizarre omniscience dreams gave, that she had been left alone for a reason, and that no one would come even if she screamed at the top of her voice. It was a motif for her entire existence: trapped in a place she did not want to be without companionship ... without comfort ... without hope.

The lights were going out, one by one. There were a series of clicks as switches were pressed by invisible hands, and the room went from blindingly bright to pitch darkness within seconds. She lay in the mortuary darkness and knew that her own life was being switched off like so many lights and there was no one there to witness it and there was no one to stop it ...

"Open your eyes."

"Dark! It's too—I—I can't—breathe ..."

"Wake up. Bad dream; just a bad dream."

She was lying in the darkness, aching all over, hemmed in by the outlines of boxes and furniture. She was aware of a figure standing in the doorway who had talked her out of her nightmare, but she was too confused to say anything. She heard the figure say, "Good night now", before slipping away and closing the door, but she had no idea which of them had rescued her, and when morning came she was too busy and too ashamed to ask.

It could have been a worse start to the morning. Mrs Olga Mallia, a highly attractive fifty-year-old whose late husband had been one of Matthew's patients, made a most charming character witness. In fact, Matthew felt palpably embarrassed as she purred—in the sensual voice of a retired dancer—about how very kind he had been to them both when her husband had received a terminal diagnosis, how dedicated, how generous with time, how impossible it was for her to exaggerate his professionalism. Matthew had grown so accustomed to being de-monised by complete strangers that he was completely overwhelmed, and by the end of it, he wondered whether he would ever be able to look her in the eye again.

If nothing else, it made up in some measure for Rebekah's performance. No one could go so far as to say that Rebekah did not provide the jury with some useful information, particularly casting doubt on earlier accounts of Daisy Havisham as a strong, independent-minded character, determined to be in control. That said, it was impossible to overlook the fact that Dudley had done a really quite professional job of making her look uncertain and even confused. By the time she was allowed to withdraw, neither Angus nor Jonathan felt very hopeful.

Matthew, in contrast, felt his courage coming together at just the right moment, aided by his drug-induced glass tube. The sight of other witnesses faltering had made him keen for the first time to tell his side of the story, on the grounds that he could not possibly do a worse job and would finally be given the chance to fight in his own corner. When his name was called, he held his mended rosary beads in his pocket like a lifeline and stepped into the witness box.

"I swear before Almighty God that the evidence that I shall give shall be the truth, the whole truth and nothing but the truth ..." His right hand slipped off the copy of the RSV Catholic Bible, and he looked down at Angus, who made a comradely nod in his direction.

Angus opened with an icebreaker. "Give the court your full name and address, please."

"Dr Matthew Joseph Kemble. 26 Eliot Road, Richmond."

"Dr Kemble, please describe your movements on the night Daisy Havisham was admitted to hospital."

Matthew took a deep breath, like an opera singer about to begin a well-rehearsed aria. "I was on a night shift in A+E when a colleague asked for my advice regarding a patient who had been brought in after taking an overdose. It was a fairly standard case, I felt: a young woman accompanied by the friend who had found her, and to start with I wasn't sure why I had been called."

"Are such cases common in your experience?"

"Yes, very. There are between eighty and one hundred thousand suicide attempts every year in this country, and those are only the ones of which we are aware. A casualty unit might see one or two a day."

"Are they usually drug overdoses?"

"Those are very common." Angus could sense Matthew getting into his stride with the gentle stream of medical questions. He was on his own territory, in what the younger generation might call his comfort zone, and he evidently felt secure there. "Others include deliberate self-harm—cut wrists, that sort of thing—but deliberate overdose is very common."

"Have you treated such cases before?"

"Many times."

"What does it involve?"

"It depends upon the particular case. In rare occasions, if a poison is ingested, there might be a specific antidote, though that is unusual. The patient might need a gastric washout, or that might be unnecessary. In some cases, it is simply a matter of the patient sleeping it off, being kept under observation."

"What happened in the case of Daisy Havisham?"

"I needed to rinse her out."

"Did she resist?"

"She was unconscious throughout." The memory flicked past his eyes as though his own life were flashing before him. He remembered opening her mouth and inserting the tube, guiding it down her throat and into her stomach. It was the most straightforward, the most mechanical of procedures, made considerably easier by the fact that the patient was not in a condition to fight him off, which the patient sometimes did in spite of himself even if he wanted to be treated. The distress involved in submitting to such a procedure and the self-preservation instinct that automatically fights off encroaching pain or bodily invasion could be almost impossible for the patient to stifle. "They very often are unconscious or at least not capable of communicating much."

"Were you made aware that she had a living will?"

"Yes, that was why my colleague had called me over. Her friend handed it to me."

"How did you respond?"

Matthew could feel his chest tightening, but even his own stress symptoms seemed curiously separate from him now. "There was no time to seek legal advice; I felt I had to act immediately. I could have tried to find a loophole somewhere, but my first concern was for the patient. I simply did not feel there was sufficient time to waste."

"Did you suspect that she would have wanted to be treated?"

"In my experience, even when a suicide attempt is made, the overwhelming majority do not have a fixed wish to die and are relieved when they're saved. We call them parasuicides. There is no way of distinguishing between those who claim they want to die and those who genuinely want to die. Even with a living will, I could not be sure that at that precise moment she would not have wanted to be treated, so I went ahead. In the end it came down to erring on the side of life, which I am duty-bound as a doctor to do."

"Thank you, Dr Kemble. Please wait there. There might be some further questions for you to answer."

Angus hoped it was not transparently noticeable to the jury that he had not asked the most obvious question: If you had known beyond any reasonable doubt that the living will was legally binding and that she had meant every single word, would you still have gone ahead and saved her life? He could almost see Dudley homing in on Matthew's jugular as he sat down and his learned friend rose to his feet. It was out of his hands now.

"Dr Kemble, would you say that this case is about a great deal more than the fate of one patient?" asked Dudley immediately. Because of his black robes and wig, Matthew could not help thinking of a large vulture fattened by the carcasses of many previous kills.

"I'm really not sure what you mean by that", answered Matthew.

"I mean, Dr Kemble, that you opposed the law you are accused of breaking from the very start, did you not?" Jonathan bristled. He had expected Dudley to play this card, but not quite so early in the cross-examination, and Matthew appeared blissfully unaware of the coming danger. "Your views on the End of Life Care Act are very widely known."

"As far as I understand it, I have not been charged with breaking the terms of that act. I have been charged with assault and battery."

"A charge which could never have been made against you if it had not been for this act. Did you or did you not put your name to a letter published in *The Times* prior to the passing of the act in which you stated your opposition to it?"

"I might have done. I can't quite remember what I said."

"Well, Doctor, let me refresh your memory." Dudley was having the time of his life, thought Jonathan, watching in growing dismay as his adversary opened up a lever arch file. "Page four hundred and sixty-eight in the bundle, Your Honour." He handed the file to Matthew.

"It is a copy of a letter to *The Times*, isn't it?"

"Yes."

"It has your name at the bottom of it, doesn't it?"

"Well, yes."

"Third sentence of paragraph one. Do you see it?"

"Yes."

He handed the file to Matthew. "Would you care to read that sentence aloud?"

Matthew glanced uneasily in Jonathan's direction before giving an unhelpful shrug and reading: "This is a dangerous and wholly unethical bill which will place doctors in an impossible situation, potentially forced to act against the best interests of the patient."

"Did you or did you not write that, Dr Kemble?"

"I can hardly deny I wrote that."

"You are quite a prolific writer, in fact, are you not? Some might say that you were a bit of a *campaigner*." He had managed to say the word as though it were some form of disgusting sexual perversion, but again Matthew did not appear to have noted Dudley's tone and did not respond. "You expressed some fairly strong opinions in the *Christian Medical Quarterly* six months before the End of Life Care Bill was passed, did you not?"

"I can't remember exactly."

"Please look at page four hundred and sixty-nine of the bundle."

The judge looked quizzical.

"At page four hundred and sixty-nine in the bundle, Your Honour. Dr Kemble, please read out the first sentence of the second paragraph."

"This bill, in the name of empowering patients, is the first step to legal euthanasia, which will attack the rights of the most vulnerable and might force Catholic doctors to leave the profession."

"Do you deny writing that, Doctor?"

"Of course I do not deny it."

"Then there was a letter published in the medical magazine *Heartbeat*. Page four hundred and seventy-three in the bundle, Your Honour. First paragraph, second and third sentences, if you please, Dr Kemble."

This had to be the worst nightmare of anyone who had ever had a piece of writing published—being forced to account for every word in a court of law with the barrister from hell bearing down on you. "This is a dangerous and unacceptable bill which will have far-reaching ramifications for the medical profession. Doctors, faced with an advance directive or attorney demanding no treatment, will be left with the choice of either withdrawing from the case and abandoning their patient, going against their own conscience or breaking the law."

"Do you deny writing that?"

Matthew had begun squeezing the bar in front of him with his free hand so that his fingers looked white beneath the lined flesh. "Of course I do not deny writing these things; they are in print with my name attached to them."

"In the eighteen months preceding the passing of this bill into law, you did in fact write hundreds of letters and articles stating your opposition and encouraging other members of the medical profession to adopt your position. I have here also the transcripts of several lectures you gave on the subject at conferences organised by anti-choice extremists . . ."

"That's a gratuitous insult!" snapped Matthew, feeling a surge of anger for the first time. "I have never been associated with extremists. You have no right using that word simply because you disagree with my position."

"There are many people out there, Dr Kemble, who might regard a doctor who refuses to obey the law on a petty point of principle as an extremist. Public opinion . . ."

"What people out there think is pretty irrelevant!" Matthew almost shouted. "Public opinion may construe my actions any way it chooses. You must construe them according to the law."

Jonathan put his head in his hands; he was beginning to realise that much of Matthew's psychological preparation for his trial had involved watching Robert Bolt's *A Man for All Seasons*.

"I must say this to you, Dr Kemble. Your decision that night had nothing whatsoever to do with the welfare of your patient. You had been looking for a means to test the law from the start, and you were prepared to use a dying woman who simply asked to be left alone to make your point. Can you deny it?"

Matthew felt a little unsteady on his feet. He tried to catch his breath but felt every muscle in his body tensing to tearing point. He counted silently to five, commanding himself to calm down, but he had always been hopeless at dealing with confrontations. And Jonathan looked steadily up at his friend, willing him not to break down. "You are quite wrong", said Matthew quietly, and if the courtroom had not been so completely silent he would have been impossible to hear. "It is true that I think this is a ludicrous law, and I stand by everything I have written on the subject, but ultimately I am a doctor. The first tenet of the Hippocratic Oath is 'first, do no harm'. It would have gone against my every instinct as a doctor to leave a suicidal young woman to die when there was the chance of saving her life. Moreover, it was clear to me that her living will was ambiguous and did not appear to reflect her genuine will at that moment."

"A ludicrous law", Jonathan repeated, rather unkindly imitating Matthew's cut glass English accent. "A *ludicrous* law. Whose bloody side are you on?"

"Well, what on earth did you expect me to say?" demanded Matthew. "I had only expressed that opinion a couple of times in print."

"I do wish doctors would leave the campaigning to the campaigners and get on with taking patients' blood pressures or whatever else it is you do for a living. I mean, maybe you should broadcast your opinion on the BBC just to make the prosecution's case as watertight as possible."

"Funnily enough, I did an interview on BBC radio, but they don't seem to have picked that up."

"Well, why don't we drop Dudley a line and tell him about it? He might even play us the tape in court, just to entertain the jury."

"Do leave him alone, Jonathan", Maria interrupted. "We need conscientious doctors to nail their colours to the mast, or our campaigns don't stand a chance."

"How much did that campaign fail by in the end? Landslide vote by Parliament, wasn't it?"

"I'm not sure you're in a position to throw many stones in that direction!" Maria exploded. "How many of Freya's campaigns have been resounding successes either, for that matter? Perhaps you'd rather we all went home to die quietly whilst our society collapses?"

Jonathan threw his hands up. "All right, sorry. We're on the same side. At least I think we are. Let's get home and calm down before we kill one other. Matthew?"

"Yes", answered Matthew sulkily, fully aware that the only one among them who was fit to commit a murder was Jonathan.

"Good." He pulled over near the entrance to the Underground station. "You and Maria go back to my place. I need to talk over one or two things with counsel before tomorrow."

"Oughtn't I to be there?"

"You've done your bit, Matt, you can relax now." He hesitated to leave. "By the way, before I forget, you ought to pack a small bag. Just in case."

Matthew glared at him. "In case of what?"

"In case they send you down."

"I thought you said there was next to no prospect of that?" he thundered. "You—you've been so confident, I *knew* you didn't really believe it!"

"It's just a precaution, Matthew," said Jonathan, with infuriating ease, "but on the off chance the jury are a bunch of cretins, you don't want to be transported to the nick without a spare pair of undies and a toothbrush, do you?"

"It's standard procedure", Maria pointed out, as she and Matthew stood on the downward escalator.

"He thinks I'll be convicted."

"He has to say that in every case. It's just a precaution like he said", promised Maria, but she knew she was wasting her time. Matthew suspected, as she and Jonathan and Angus and their very few supporters were beginning to suspect, that the trial might have been a mere legal formality after all, and Matthew's innocence or guilt had been determined before he ever stepped into court. "There will probably be the chance of an appeal", she ventured, but even mentioning the appeals process before the conclusion of a trial sounded horribly like a counsel of despair. She made a feeble attempt at humour. "I'll come and visit you."

26

Freya's little home had never been quite so full. When Eva had rung her up to ask if there was any chance she could stay over the night before the final day of her husband's trial, she had hardly felt as though she could refuse. What with Matthew's nasty little brush with hospital and the stress he was under and the prospect that it might be the last night Matthew and Eva would spend together for some time if the prosecution got its pound of flesh ... She contemplated briefly turfing Maria out of the box room, but she still resembled one of those models who stare accusingly at commuters from the grey landscape of a child protection poster, and she did not have the heart to send her home either.

In the end, she made up her own marital bed for Eva and Matthew, prepared the sofa bed Matthew had been sleeping on for her husband and weighed up the possibilities for herself whilst she awaited Eva's arrival. The sofa bed was technically a double if it were being used by two svelte twenty-somethings, but she did not fancy her and Jonathan's chances of surviving the night without killing one another. She could always put some blankets and cushions down in the enormous cast-iron bath, which would be more comfortable than most people realised, but it might prove awkward if anyone needed to pay a visit to the bathroom in the middle of the night—and poor Matthew had pretty much taken up residence there himself since his arrival at the house. Since it was likely to be a clear, dry night, it occurred to her that she could put her one-man tent up in the communal garden. It appealed to her retired Girl Guide sense of adventure, and she was not a person who minded enormously what the neighbours would think, which was probably that she was out of her tiny mind.

Freya was still contemplating where to lay her head for the night when Eva arrived at the door, laden with shopping bags. "I come bearing gifts", she said. "You are going to let me cook dinner, aren't you?"

"Don't be silly, Eva", said Freya, helping her take the bags into the kitchen. "I wouldn't hear of it."

"Come on now, my husband's been eating you out of house and home for days. It's time I made a contribution."

"Hardly out of house and home, the poor darling", commented Freya. "He's barely eaten a thing." Eva began taking various purchases out and placing them on the counter. Minced meat, porridge oats, a big block of cheddar cheese, avocados, a couple of onions, a large tin of sweet corn, spices and tubes of tomato puree and garlic paste that terrified Freya just to look at them. "What are you planning?"

"Mexican beef; you'll love it." Freya looked visibly uncomfortable. "It's all right, it won't blow your head off. I'll omit the chilli peppers. Matthew doesn't like his food too spicy either, and neither do the children."

Freya pointed Eva in the direction of a chopping board and vegetable knife. Whilst Eva chopped up the onions, Freya washed up the frying pan she had used the night before and left in the kitchen sink to deal with later. "Do you want me to fry the mince?" she asked, pouring a quantity of olive oil into the pan and placing it on the gas burner. Freya's cooking habits had become set in stone around 1970, and she had no idea how much olive oil she really needed or indeed how she was supposed to know when it was hot enough, but she was too embarrassed to admit it.

"Yes, please."

"Do you miss home much?" asked Freya, smiling at the pleasing sizzle of meat hitting the hot pan. That sounded just right. "I mean, do you ever go back?"

"It's not really home for me", said Eva, blinking away tears. "Wretched onions always sting my eyes so much, I hate them! I've never been to Mexico, I only have one Mexican grandmother, so it doesn't really count for much, and my parents left Spain just a few years after I was born. They were children of the Civil War, and I'm afraid they grew up very bitter after everything they'd been through. They didn't want me to have anything to do with the country and, well, I wasn't even allowed to learn Spanish."

"That's a pity. I've always thought people should stay close to their roots if they can."

"Me too. I thought it very cruel of them at the time, but then I suppose it's difficult to understand what a civil war does to people unless you've been there. And they were very young and impressionable. Do you have a slotted spoon you could take that mince out with? I need to fry the onions in the juices. This has been the first time I've wished there was another country we could turn to."

"You'd like to emigrate?"

"Well, wouldn't you?" Eva had begun scooping the cooked mince into a bowl, seemingly oblivious to the specks of boiling oil spitting at her as she did so. "My husband has worked hard all his life to serve others. They march him out of his own home in handcuffs and subject him to this gauntlet of hate. Why would anybody want to stay in this disgrace of a country after this?"

"I'm sure I can think of a few good reasons!" Freya blustered.

"I can live without Marmite. I've never liked it."

Freya could not help feeling hurt. She still viewed Eva as something of a foreigner, even though she had grown up in England and came across as completely British. It was irrational, but she felt personally under attack in a way she would not have done if someone ethnically English had made exactly the same remarks. "You can't just run away like that! Britain needs families like you so badly."

"We've done our national service", Eva retorted, squeezing tomato puree out of a large metal tube. It splattered all over the interior of the pan like arterial blood. "If Matthew is convicted, if he is struck off, we'll make a fresh start somewhere else." Freya found herself taking a step towards the doorway as Eva threw the meat back into the pan with an unnerving aggression. "When a country loses its head, it is always the people who really care about it who get driven out", she continued. "Would you please put the kettle on?"

"I beg your pardon? I mean yes, yes, of course." Freya picked up the kettle and placed it under the tap as though she had a gun to her head. She suddenly had an overwhelming sense that she needed to do whatever Eva wanted with every possible speed. "Sorry, you were saying?"

"That it's always people who love their country who get hurt—just in case you think I'm an ingrate."

"No, no, of course not. I wouldn't dream of . . ."

"When my husband was a medical student, there were a whole lot of young, newly qualified doctors from Malta working in London. They'd had to flee Mintoff's glorious utopia when they were students because they had protested against their government—like students across the world do—and so they sought refuge in England and made very fine doctors here. Do you imagine they did not love their country? Do you imagine they would not have preferred to minister to their own people given half a chance? It's the same for Matthew. He's as English as they come. If you asked Central Casting to send you a stereotypical example of the Land of Good Manners, they would send you Matthew. All he wants is to get on with being a doctor, but if we're so unwelcome here, we'll go somewhere else."

Freya absorbed herself in the petty details of making up a jug of beef stock and opening a packet of oats for Eva to use. "Smells wonderful", she said without any enthusiasm.

Eva peered through the steam that was filling the tiny room and sighed. "I'm sorry, I know you don't want to hear me ranting like this. I just feel so ... I don't know what exactly. I've never been so angry in my entire life."

"I understand." *I don't understand at all*, thought Freya miserably, carrying the weight of a blissfully sheltered life on her shoulders. She had no idea what it would have been like to come to England as an immigrant and grow up haunted by the traumas lived out long ago by two battle-scarred parents. She could not begin to imagine how it would feel to witness a member of her own family put through such torture and to have to face the prospect of losing him at a time when she might have imagined that life had settled down happily ever after. Freya did not understand at all and felt like a liar pretending otherwise.

"I wish it was me", said Eva. "My mother used to say that when I was a child and something went wrong. I used to get angry and think 'but it isn't you, so stop going on about it!' Now I know exactly what she meant. I don't think I would mind nearly as much if I was the one facing being taken off to prison tomorrow or at least having to stand there being convicted and told I was a disgrace to my profession."

There was the sound of a key turning in the lock, and the front door creaked open. "Perfect timing", said Freya, suddenly feeling more cheerful. "I'll lay the table."

Freya realised later that the idea of eating together had been an embarrassing mistake. The five of them sat around the cramped dining room table, desperately trying to be positive, whilst Jonathan inwardly agonised about the possible conclusion of the trial, Maria battled the continual low level of pain she was still suffering, Matthew pictured himself being pronounced guilty over and over again and Eva imagined her husband being marched out of her sight by two burly police officers without being given so much as a chance to say goodbye. And Freya herself felt an unfamiliar knot of anxiety in her stomach at the thought that her husband might be about to lose the most important case upon which he had ever embarked and would never forgive himself if his old friend were wrongfully convicted, whatever his pretences at professional detachment. All in all, it was like attending a wake in anticipation of the unhappy event, and Freya was relieved when Jonathan got up to clear the plates away, releasing them all from their obligations to sit together any longer.

"Would you mind awfully if we retired?" asked Matthew, getting up. "I'm feeling a little—tired."

"Absolutely not", said Freya quickly. "I've made up our room for you tonight so that you can have a bit more privacy."

"I ought to wash up", said Eva, moving towards the kitchen.

"Don't be silly. You cooked", said Freya. "Maria and I will wash up. Go and relax."

Eva gave a relieved smile and led her husband out of the room. There was something almost girlish about her taking his hand and leading him away from them, as though they were a courting couple demurely walking out for a date and he were just a little nervous of being alone with her.

"I'm sorry I'm being like this", said Matthew, sitting on the bed, which immediately began sinking beneath him. "I can't stop thinking about tomorrow. It's childish, but I keep wishing I could press a fast-forward button or something."

Eva smiled and started undressing him. Helping him off with his jacket and tie, she fought off the painful notion that she was behaving more like a nurse than a lover. "It's all right. Did you enjoy that dinner even a little bit?"

"I did. Thank you. It's one of my favourites."

"I know." She tried to stand up, but he placed an arm around her waist, stopping her in her tracks. "It's all right", she said, letting him draw her towards him. Her head came to rest against his shoulder. "It's all going to be all right. I know it's all going to be all right."

He lowered her very carefully onto the bed, watching her sinking into the soft, lumpy cushions and blue tartan bedclothes like a small child. "If I'm convicted, we'll have to sell the house. If I go to prison, I want you to stay down in Wiltshire with the children. You'll need family round you."

"Not now, darling. We don't have to talk about it now."

"We have to be prepared for the worst."

She smiled sadly and reached out to embrace him. He thought for a moment about how easily she could have been made to laugh once. She had been a terrible giggler when he had first met her, constantly bursting out laughing as though she saw signs of the world's absurdity everywhere, but it was such a long time since she had thrown back her head and laughed, really laughed uproariously. He wondered if she ever would again or whether the time for merriment and silliness had disappeared forever with the sound of police boots stamping through their door and the lurid sight of endless damning newspaper headlines.

"We are prepared", she said, easing his head onto the pillow beside her. "Just get through what's left of the trial. You don't know you're going to lose. You've always been a terrible pessimist. If I'd believed you every time you said the situation was hopeless, I would have lost the will to live by now!"

"I'm a realist."

"Fatalist. Have a little trust in your legal team."

"I know. I do trust my team; it's the system I don't trust at all. I suppose I feel it's best to assume the worst in a situation like this. I know Jonathan thinks . . ."

She placed a finger over his lips. "Whatever happens tomorrow, they're not going to hang you. You'll live to fight another day."

"It's just the thought that . . ."

"Be quiet."

She pressed her lips against his and felt him shudder before breaking off. "Did I see you lock the door?" he asked softly.

"You certainly did."

He buried his face in her hair and kissed the elegant curve of her neck. "Thank you, my darling."

And somehow, slowly, hesitantly, they made love. Matthew let himself surrender to the waves of heat and light that overwhelmed him, promising a future where life in all its loveliness and beauty might yet go on. There was still such a thing as passion, not the rage and indignation of protests and public meetings and trials, but in the most intimate of encounters. Hidden in the tender embraces of his wife, he knew simply that he loved, that he had loved, that he would always love . . . and that there was still one impulse left in their lives that could not be regulated or condemned by the omnipresent machinery of the state. The blood thundered through his veins like a melody of life, rich, ecstatic, intoxicating and he gave into it with a sense of glorious, giddy abandon.

27

"Judgement day, Dr Kemble!" called one of the protesters, as Matthew stepped out of the car. Matthew wondered, looking at the demonstration in front of him, whether anyone would ever call him Dr Kemble again without an audible taunt in their voice. He hesitated as he always did, but his eye was caught by what appeared to be a counterdemonstration alongside the right-to-die rent-a-mob. A smaller but visibly younger group made up of mostly women, he noticed, stood under a series of banners they had evidently cobbled together the previous night, with messages such as FIRST DO NO HARM and STOP PERSECUTING DOCTORS FOR SAVING LIVES. Matthew blushed deeply at one banner which read: DR KEMBLE IS A HERO NOT A CRIMINAL.

"Where on earth did they come from?" asked Matthew, who, in spite of his embarrassment felt his back straightening and a certain spring appearing in his step.

"Maria's address book, I think you'll find", chuckled Jonathan, acknowledging their presence with a discreet wave of the hand. He recognised some of them from medical ethics forums and the many Catholic youth groups that proliferated around London. "There, you see, you've got a much prettier fan club than the prosecution anyhow."

Matthew smiled and was photographed smiling as he stepped away from the jamboree outside into a building he sincerely hoped he would never have to look at again.

"Members of the jury", began Dudley. The atmosphere in the room was noticeably less tense than in previous days, but the public gallery heaved with every specimen of the population—activists from both sides, friends and supporters, a gaggle of medical students curious to see what the outcome would be and what the implications were for their own careers, a few voyeurs keen to see what was going to happen like the reader of a trashy novel rushing straight to the concluding chapter. Somewhere in the midst of the throng, Matthew knew that Eva was sitting, watching and listening. Praying.

"Members of the jury, this is a case which has betrayal of trust at its very root. The abuse of authority by a professional in whom great trust is placed is a serious matter, and what profession enjoys greater trust than the medical profession? Indeed, it is necessary that such trust should exist between doctors and their patients when the stakes are so high. Patients when they are at their most vulnerable, their most needy, have the right to be able to put their trust in doctors and to know that their reasonable wishes will be taken seriously. Long gone are the bad old days when doctors were free to manipulate and bully their patients without being held to account. And Dr Kemble is being held to account for his actions. In February of this year, a defenceless young woman was brought to a hospital in this country and treated entirely and explicitly against her will. She was not sectioned under the Mental Health Act. Her wishes regarding treatment were clearly stated in an advance directive drawn up in the presence of a qualified solicitor. The defence has made numerous attempts at muddying the waters, claiming that Daisy Havisham was coerced into making a living will or, indeed, that she was suffering from underlying depression at the time, but there is no suggestion that Daisy Havisham lacked capacity at the time she drew up her living will. It has been stated over and over again in evidence that Daisy Havisham is a strong-willed, independent and intelligent young woman who was more than capable of making decisions regarding her future treatment. You have heard the solicitor who assisted her in drawing up her living will—Mr West—state categorically that she knew what she was doing and that the document in question was legally binding.

"The defendant has claimed that he had to act as he did because he had reason to doubt that the living will represented her will at that particular moment. The terms of the living will were abundantly clear, and Dr Kemble's attention was drawn to the terms of that living will more than once before he commenced treatment of Daisy Havisham. He has suggested that she might have been a so-called "parasuicide", but the evidence suggests precisely the contrary. The living will stated that Daisy Havisham did not want to be treated should she become incapacitated. It went so far as to state that this refusal included life-saving treatment, and the fact that the living will was left by Daisy Havisham near her body where it would be easily noticed leaves no doubt that she intended it to be found by whoever discovered her to ensure that she would not be treated against her will, however well meaning—or otherwise—the motive.

"The End of Life Care Act was passed to affirm the rights of patients such as Daisy Havisham to exercise sovereignty over their own bodies, a human right with which few would disapprove. Dr Kemble's opposition to this law is well established. He has described it as 'dangerous', 'unethical' and 'unacceptable'. In your presence, he has spoken of it as 'ludicrous'. He has played the part of a caring physician duty-bound to err on the side of life, whose concerns were only for the safety of his patient. In reality, members of the jury, Dr Kemble had actively sought an opportunity to challenge the law, and he found that opportunity in the case of Daisy Havisham. This was not a compassionate decision made in the heat of the moment; it was a calculated and deliberate attack on a young woman who was powerless to resist and had asked only to be left alone."

Anyone would think I was a rapist, thought Matthew, closing his eyes to avoid having to look at the man who was apparently enjoying the act of destroying him.

"Whatever your views on the act, the facts of this case remain crystal clear. On that night in February, Matthew Kemble treated a patient against her will. He admits readily enough that he knew about the living will, that he knew the legal implications of ignoring the patient's wishes and that he continued regardless. Daisy Havisham's wishes were clear; the law itself is clear. If a competent patient does not give consent to treatment, the doctor commits assault if he proceeds. In this case the patient was unconscious and incapable of making her wishes known to the doctor, but she did not need to. The whole point of a living will is that it allows individuals to withhold consent for burdensome treatments they want to be spared. That living will should have protected Daisy Havisham from the indignity of being subjected to treatment against her will, but it failed to do so because of the paternalistic views of a doctor who believed himself to be above the law. Members of the jury, you must consider all the evidence and decide whether or not that is so, and you must decide it so that you are sure of it. If you are not sure, then you cannot convict. But the Crown's case is that you can be sure. On the evidence that you have heard and read, members of the jury, you can be sure that Dr Kemble is guilty of exceeding his role as a doctor, of treating his patient against her express wish and thus of committing an assault and battery."

"I don't know why they don't just show me into a room with a bottle of whiskey and a revolver", Matthew whispered, turning to Jonathan.

"Don't tempt fate", Jonathan whispered back. Dudley and Angus passed one another like two eighteenth-century gentlemen engaged in pistols at dawn, acknowledging one another briefly as Dudley sat down and Angus took the stage. Matthew found it extraordinary to think that after all this was over, the two men might well sit down together for a drink without any hard feelings at all. For now, however, they were the keenest of adversaries, kept tactfully apart by the centuries of judicial ritual and protocol that demanded professional courtesy from all its players.

"Ladies and gentlemen of the jury", Angus began. Matthew closed his eyes again, this time out of sheer terror, rather in the way a child might hide behind the sofa when the hero of the science fiction film finds himself facing two or three slavering aliens. "The man before the court, charged with assault and battery, is Dr Matthew Kemble, a medical professional trained and wholly committed to the care of the sick. He has worked as a doctor for twenty-five years, and he has an entirely unblemished record. Never once has a single complaint or question been raised as to his professionalism or good character. You have heard him described in evidence as a hard-working, dedicated, generous and compassionate professional, a man prepared to go that extra mile for his patients and their families. The prosecution would have you believe that Dr Kemble is a paternalistic busybody who treated a young woman as a campaigning tool to challenge a law he opposes. You are looking at a man who does a difficult and demanding job and does it well. You are also looking at a pillar of the community, a decent and worthy citizen who simply desires to get on with his job serving the community as a doctor. Does it seem likely that a man at the peak of his career, who has a reputation for treating his patients with unwavering respect, would act so entirely out of character in this one instance? Is it credible that Dr Kemble would have risked his career, his good name, the well-being of his young family, simply to defy the law?

"I suggest to you that this case should never have come to trial. Indeed, I suggest that it should never even have been reported to the police. The evidence that has been presented to the court has demonstrated that, contrary to what the prosecution would have you believe, Daisy Havisham did not draw up her living will freely or in an entirely rational frame of mind. Let us not forget the evidence of her friend Rebekah Walter, that Daisy Havisham was emotionally fragile but had learnt to conceal it, that she had a tendency to low self-esteem and even to depression. Let us not forget the evidence of Jennifer Little, who admitted under cross-examination that Daisy Havisham was, as she put it, 'a mess'. You will recall, members of the jury, how she told us that 'something would have pushed her over the edge eventually'. You will, I am sure, have been particularly struck by that rather sad reflection on her state of mind. There can be little doubt that she was given to bouts of emotional turmoil and even instability. Indeed, members of the jury, the evidence strongly suggests that she was suffering from undiagnosed depression at the time the living will was drawn up. You will recall the evidence of Professor Reid."

He paused for effect to give the jury time to recall the professor's testimony.

"As Professor Reid explained in his evidence, depression is an invisible condition the symptoms of which are relatively easy for a patient to conceal if they are determined to do so. In this case, the patient concerned had attempted suicide, an act which, Professor Reid told us, in eighty-five percent of cases is made by individuals suffering from undiagnosed depression. And in so many of those cases, as the professor told us, there is most often no settled intention of doing away with oneself but rather a sad and lonely cry for help, help that is not always to hand.

"Many people who aren't medically trained who draw up living wills are not aware of the implications of refusing certain treatments. That, we have heard, is particularly likely in the case of those suffering from depression, or emotional instability, who make such instruments. The emotional state of Daisy Havisham was not always stable. We have heard that in evidence. Not stable when she attempted suicide nor, the evidence tells us, when she was planning to make, and did make, her living will. Her solicitor cannot be blamed. Undiagnosed depression is a matter for a doctor, not a solicitor. He could only take her expression of wishes—her instructions to him—at face value. To do otherwise would have been to fail in his duty. But he could not know of her emotional state. That was a matter for a doctor, and no medical report was before her solicitor at the material time.

"In the end Dr Kemble was faced with a choice. An unenviable choice that no one in this room would ever care to have to make. A life and death choice. Consider the events of that night, members of the jury. A patient was brought to him in serious danger of death having taken a cocktail of drugs, including insulin, and he had to make the following choice—save the patient's life or stand back and leave a young woman, with her life ahead of her, to die needlessly. Living wills, like all legal documents, can be complex. They can also be ambiguous or inapplicable in certain situations. In this case, the living will was both, and there was no time to put the matter before a lawyer, still less a court. Was this living will framed so as to apply to the situation of a young girl who had attempted suicide as a cry for help? Or was it rather framed to apply to a situation where burdensome and possibly futile treatments might be given to her after a serious accident or when suffering from a terminal disease? For that, members of the jury, is the common intention behind many a living will, and this one appeared to be little or no different. Can we even be sure that, in her then state of mind, Miss Havisham even remembered that she had made a living will? Yes, the document was found near her, but then she often had it with her for campaigning reasons. The pathway leading to her attempting suicide was unconnected with the living will and more connected with emotional reactions to other events in her life. She was, members of the jury, crying for help. And help was at hand.

"Dr Kemble had to make a quick decision under pressure, and he made the decision that a professional and conscientious doctor would have made in his place. He was sufficiently persuaded that this was a cry for help, that she had no settled intention to end her life, that she was in a state of emotional turmoil and probably depression and that this was not a situation that she connected, in her mind, with the living will she had made much earlier. He moved to save her life as he had been trained to do and as all doctors are trained to do. In simple terms, he saved that young woman's life. Can there be any real doubt that this was the right thing to do, that attempted suicide was not encompassed by the living will, that this was a cry for help and that Dr Kemble, a conscientious doctor, was acting rightly in giving it? It is right, therefore, members of the jury, that I accordingly ask you to acquit this conscientious doctor of the charges that he has been so burdened with. It is right, therefore, that he should be set at liberty by you to return to his practice, where he can carry on conscientiously saving the lives of other patients in his community. Patients—people like you and I—who will be relying upon his professional skill and ethical integrity perhaps to save their lives, also. I therefore ask you to find Dr Kemble not guilty of these charges."

Matthew sat at the table with his head buried in his folded arms. The court had been adjourned over two hours, and the jury were still locked away, arguing over his fate. Matthew imagined a kind of *Twelve Angry Men* scenario, with the entire jury against him save one voice of reason who believed in his innocence and who was desperately trying to win the others round.

"Not long now, Matt", said Jonathan, consolingly. "Not long at all. And remember, even if you are convicted, we'll appeal. The fight doesn't have to end today."

Matthew groaned. "I know I'm supposed to be reassured by that, but I'm not", he said.

"Can I get you another coffee?"

"I'll go rocketing off into hyperspace if another droplet of coffee passes my lips." Matthew sat up and slapped his hands against his cheeks several times as though trying to snap himself out of a bad mood. "I didn't think much of the judge's summing up."

"Oh, I didn't think it was at all bad."

Matthew tried to think over what he had said and was surprised to discover that he could hardly remember a word of the long speech the judge had delivered to the jury before the usher had led them out and the court was adjourned. Shards of half-remembered sentences, the odd phrases here and there that had embedded themselves like shrapnel because they annoyed him or gave him cause for alarm: "No one denies that Dr Kemble ignored the apparent terms of Daisy Havisham's living will ... do not allow yourselves to be swayed by ideological concerns relating to ... the defendant clearly understood the implications ... a young woman lies in a hospital bed ..." "I have to hand it to Angus", he said, sitting up sharply before he could fall into the dark swirling abyss of the worst-case scenario. "He's quite an orator. I'd acquit me."

"So would I", came a bright voice from the doorway, and Maria flounced in, looking more cheerful than any of them had seen her in days. The bruises on her face, Matthew noticed, were still very much in evidence, and she moved with a stiffness that suggested she was still feeling the effects of her battering, but she was peculiarly relaxed. "Just had a call from the hospital. They think Lydia's baby will be discharged later this week. The father has come forward."

"That's wonderful news", agreed Jonathan, standing up to offer her his seat. "There, you see, a life saved."

"Pity the mother had to sacrifice her own though, isn't it?" she answered. "Pity the father only bothered to come forward when she was dead, pity the UK Border Agency . . ."

Jonathan placed a hand on her head, a gesture she would normally have found insufferable. "Steady on, Maria, don't spoil things. The baby lived, and it was the baby Lydia was fighting for in the end."

Maria was about to answer when the clerk of the court appeared, summoning them back in.

"Is it a good sign when it takes the jury ages to make up its mind?" asked Matthew as they rose to their feet.

"Two hours is not a long time, I assure you", said Jonathan, motioning for him to go ahead. "They can be in deliberations for days."

"But is two hours good? Is it a good sign?"

"I really wouldn't try to guess the verdict. You'll know in the next five minutes."

Matthew hesitated outside the courtroom before stepping heavily inside. *Bring it on*, he thought, moving towards his seat, *bring it all on*. He knew Jonathan was right, but it was impossible to avoid trying to guess which way it was all going as the court regrouped. He found himself scanning the faces of the jury for the tiniest clue of what their conclusion had been and read signs of hostility in their most innocuous facial expressions—the slight frown, the look of weary indifference, the exchanged glance or smile. He felt himself becoming unbearably hot and sensed that it showed.

"Stop fidgeting!" hissed Jonathan.

"I think I'm going to have a stroke", whispered Matthew.

"Would the foreman of the jury please stand", said the clerk of the court, making Matthew jump. He watched as a white-haired woman rose to her feet, removing her reading glasses as she did so. "Members of the jury, have you reached a verdict upon which you are all agreed?"

"Yes", she said.

"Members of the jury, do you find the defendant guilty or not guilty of assault and battery?"

Matthew was aware of time slowing down the way it was said to do in the final moments of life. He tasted bile at the back of his throat and felt the hot, dizzying sense of unadulterated terror overtaking him. He looked fixedly at the foreman.

"Not guilty."

"Thank you. Would you sit down, please?"

A murmur rose across the court, hastily silenced by the clerk. Matthew felt a hand patting his shoulder, but he was too stunned to move a muscle and stared downwards, not daring to blink as his sight misted over and he felt the mortifying sensation of tears gathering in the corners of his eyes. He slipped his hand into his jacket pocket and searched for the rosary beads he had succeeded in breaking twice during the days of the trial, clinging onto them until the moment passed and he could trust himself to stand up straight and look the judge in the eye.

The judge returned his glance. "Well, Dr Kemble, you are free to go, and you may walk from this court without a stain on your good name. I appreciate that this has been a distressing experience for you, which has taken its toll on your mental and physical health, but I am satisfied that the correct verdict has been reached and that no crime took place on the night in question. I suspect that those who brought this case knew that too. I agree with the verdict and am also convinced that you acted lawfully, and out of necessity, in a stressful situation in which you were forced to make a quick decision and to act upon it."

"However," he continued without missing a beat, and Matthew heard the unmistakable hardening of his tone, "the End of Life Care Act was passed by a large majority after careful consideration by Parliament. The defendant in this trial was a doctor charged with assault and battery, not the act itself. The act itself is not on trial here. Individual cases might, from time to time, throw up problems with the act that were unforeseen at the time of its passing, but modifications are, of course, a matter for Parliament and not this court."

Matthew found himself leaning against the table in front of him as the judge thanked the jury, witnesses and counsel, and left the court; he forced himself to count to five before slumping back into his chair. "That's that then", he said to the world in general. "It's all over."

"That's right," said Jonathan, "for you, at least. Come on."

Matthew got up, hesitating with the thought that he had forgotten something, then knelt down and picked up his overnight case. A flood of nightmare images from the past weeks washed over him, leaving him paralysed. "Thank God", he said quietly. "Thank *God*."

"Brace yourself to step outside", warned Jonathan, helping him out of the room.

The journalists and photographers who reported the outcome of the trial did not capture any images of victory on the steps of the court building, no Churchillian poses or victory signs. Matthew Kemble stood in silence, flanked by Angus, Jonathan, Maria and Eva, an exhausted and rather insubstantial figure on the shadowy steps of the court. He was still clinging to the beads in his pocket as Jonathan read out a brief statement on his behalf, in which he thanked those who had supported him and expressed his wish to return to work as soon as possible. The statement concluded with a line from the Hippocratic Oath, which was so seared into Matthew's consciousness now that he never needed to hear it again. "First do no harm."

28

Maria always found her belief in eternity returning when she caught a glimpse of the sea on a sunlit day. It was not so much the luxury of being able to look far into the distance rather than just as far as the next building, but the way in which the sea and sky seemed to merge invisibly behind the misty panes of heat on the horizon and the sense of being surrounded on all sides by something infinite, untouchable, unbreakable. It was one of those perfect days in late summer when the air felt warm and balmy all around them and the fields and trees they had passed on the train were still green, but with the first rusty promise of autumn colours to come.

Maria, Jonathan and Freya had come on a day trip to the Isle of Wight to join Matthew and his family, who were having a holiday there. They had picked up the Portsmouth Harbour train at Waterloo station, then the ferry to Ryde, where Freya had pointed out the names of all the different ships that were in port and suggested a visit to the garlic farm if either of them were interested. They weren't, as it happened. After a long, sunny walk along the esplanade and a brief pause to buy ice creams, they had arrived on the stretch of beach where the Kemble family had marked out their territory with beach towels and windbreaks. Whilst Freya busied herself making shambolic sandcastles with the children, Matthew and Jonathan slumped into deck-chairs like two old men at a cricket match, and Eva and Maria went in search of a tea house.

"I feel as though I know you very well", said Eva. They were seated at a table covered in a damask cloth, near a window where they could look out and see the sea not far away. Maria had never been a fan of the British seaside, with its almost inevitable rain showers, gritty sand-wiches and stalls selling whelks. Whenever they had been taken on such trips as children, she had done her best to escape the communal picnics and tiresome beach games that were organised to keep them occupied and fled with her sandwiches in search of solitude. The seas that guarded Britain were meant to be looked at not grappled with, and she had spent many wistful hours looking out to sea, imagining herself embarking on every kind of solitary adventure. And they were always solitary. Today, however, she had to admit that she was enjoying the company of others, and it had meant a lot to her to be included in the whole escapade.

"I know what you mean," said Maria, "even though we have hardly met. I think this must be the first time we've ever had a proper conversation."

"Yes", Eva said. "It's amazing the way an ordeal like this brings people together, and of course Freya and Jonathan have told me so much about you. Matthew told me how much you had fought for him, and I am very grateful."

"It was Jonathan and Angus who did the fighting", said Maria. "I think I just provided the rage."

Eva smiled. "Passion, not rage. And I think that's very important, even in a court case. Listen …" She took a sip of tea, then stared uneasily into the half-empty cup. "Listen, I was hoping I'd get the chance to speak with you alone. This is—well, it's very difficult to say, and I hope you won't mind too much that I know about it, but I realise it must have been quite hard for you to get involved with a case like this."

Maria glanced out of the window. She could feel the unpleasant sensation of every muscle in her body tensing, the way it always did when the past jumped out at her, but she was surprised to find that it was easier to control than usual. "I was just doing my job", she said, but it was such an awful cliché she knew she had to do better than that even if it were true. In all honesty, it was hardly as though she could have turned to her boss and refused to work for months. "It's all right. I really don't mind if you know", she ventured, placing a hand on Eva's arm. "It's not a secret as such, though I don't exactly broadcast it, but as it happens that wasn't the reason."

"I'm terribly sorry. I'm afraid I misunderstood."

"It's all right. Jonathan thinks I'm motivated by my father's suicide too—that's what he told Matthew, isn't it?"

"Yes, I hope you don't mind. Matthew is very discreet."

"I know he is. I've always known that." She paused, aware that this was her last chance to change the course of the conversation if there was any doubt in her mind about proceeding. She could change the subject or find some way to distract Eva until the moment had passed; she was very used to deflecting attention away from upsetting subjects ... but the final doubt slipped away in the safety of that room, and she braced herself. "Jonathan is right, it does have a lot to do with it, but wasn't the reason this time." She noticed Eva sitting up a little and knew it had to be said. "You see, your husband doesn't remember, there's no reason why he should, but he saved my life once."

Eva looked at her in silent recognition. "Good heavens! You know, I should have realised it was something like that. When was it?"

"Some years ago. I was still at school."

Maria's worst memory hovered about her like a looming vulture, waiting for her to break, but for the first time she could remember she felt quite calm as she began to describe the day her life had finally spiraled out of control. It had been on an evening during her final year at school when she had been sitting in her room struggling with an essay on sin and damnation in Marlowe's *Dr Faustus*. She saw once again the cold, institutional study bedroom, the bed against the wall decked in mustard yellow sheets, the shelves lined with her books and files, the sink tucked discreetly next to the wardrobe, guarded by a regiment of little pink bottles. Then there was the desk she had been sitting at overlooking the hockey pitches and netball courts where she had never covered herself in glory.

In the fading light, she felt again that catatonic sense of being quite unable to move, even to get up and walk a few steps to the light switch near the door. Through the paper thin walls, she heard the voices—voices as much a part of the background to her life as the tawdry furnishings of her own room—of two girls from her class gossiping about how utterly lousy she was. She had been here many times before, but it felt very different on that particular evening. She became aware of being completely alone, which was strange since she had always been alone, but at that moment she felt imprisoned by her loneliness, trapped in a sterile impersonal room where the only evidence of human life around her was entirely hostile.

It will always be like this, she told herself, and she saw before her the terrifying vision of the rest of her life, the endless days alone without a single human soul to care about her or to be loved by her. And that was what tipped the balance. Not the thought that nobody loved her or cared about her, not even the thought that nobody had ever loved her or would ever love her, that if she died her passing would barely be noticed. Others contemplating suicide might fantasise about the obituaries and the pictures in the papers, the bouquets of flowers at the death scene, the outpourings of grief by guilty friends, but she knew perfectly well that her death would provoke no such emotional response, and she truly did not care. It was the thought that she would never have anyone to love, that the deepest human need of all, to hold someone, a husband, a child, a sister in her arms and know she loved them more than life itself, might never come to pass. She saw a faint shadow on the wall, ugly, clumsy, insignificant and saw only the way life should have been, the family she should have known, the person she might have become.

Maria reached into a side drawer and brought out a packet of sleeping pills a doctor had been careless enough to prescribe for her when she had complained of insomnia. She had only gone to him in the first place because she was desperate to confide in somebody, but he was a busy man with little time for naval-gazing teenagers and had simply reached for his prescription pad. It hardly mattered now. Maria managed to find the energy to pour herself a glass of water, then laid out the small white pills into parallel rows and swallowed them one by one in what was almost an obscene ritual.

The recurrent nightmare always began after this point, a little time after she had put herself to bed and had to cling to the mattress to fight the sense that she was spinning round and round on a raft in the middle of the sea. Her housemistress burst into the room like a grotesque seagull, all claws and beak and disheveled feathers, demanding to know what she was doing in bed when she was supposed to be doing her prep. Maria reached down into the invisible sea around her, vaguely aware that she had left the empty packet in view, only to feel herself sliding drunkenly onto the floor, quite unable to steady herself any longer. Somewhere nearby the seagull shrieked in panic disguised as anger, "You *silly* girl! Whatever have you done?"

Then there was an ambulance, two men in green overalls carrying her away and the hospital corridor she remembered so vividly, with its unforgettable sense of cold hostility and her own dizzy confusion of panic and guilt and foreboding that she was going to die or be put through an ordeal too horrific to think about for the privilege of staying alive. In the midst of this, she remembered his face—in the tiny detail that a person always remembers the one who saved his life—his otherwise entirely unremarkable face.

"I'm Dr Kemble", he said, gently. "You've taken some pills, haven't you?"

"Hundreds of the wretched things!" came the relentless, squawking voice of the seagull. She handed him an empty packet. "I don't know what the doctor was thinking of giving a girl like that such a large prescription for sleeping pills. I assure you it was entirely his decision. I would never have encouraged her to take drugs like that."

He ignored the woman. "How many did you take? Was the packet full?"

"Yes", said Maria, but her tongue felt heavy. "I had never taken any before. I was saving them."

Dr Kemble drew in a deep breath. "Well, they're pretty powerful. We'll have to rinse you out, I'm afraid."

Maria began shaking her head as vigorously as she could manage, but it only set the room spinning. "Please leave me alone. I don't want this."

"Oh, just do as you're told, you're hardly in a position to argue!" snapped the seagull again. "You've caused enough trouble as it is, sitting about feeling sorry for yourself."

Dr Kemble cleared his throat. "I wonder if you could step outside for the moment?" he asked, with impeccable courtesy. "I'm not sure this is the time for recriminations."

"She didn't have to do that. It's a selfish, cowardly thing to do!"

"Madam, if she were my daughter, I'd think her worthy of a little sympathy."

"She's nobody's daughter, isn't that obvious?"

Maria heard the clatter of footsteps walking grudgingly into the distance and the sound of a nurse preparing equipment out of her field of vision. "You're not sticking a tube down my throat", she said, but what sounded so emphatic in her head came out as little more than a whimper. *"Please."*

"It's all right", he said, softly. "You're going to be all right. It'll all be over soon."

She could feel a pulse thundering in her neck as though her own body were screaming at her not to let it stop, but she covered her face. "Please don't! I'll choke!"

"You won't", he said, very carefully removing her hands so that he could make eye contact with her. "I've done this hundreds of times; I promise it'll be all right."

She grasped the sleeve of his jacket as though she seriously intended to fight him off by brute force. "Just leave me alone!"

He paused, and she marveled afterwards at how he had managed to behave quite so calmly, as though he were a man with all the time in the world. "I know this is very upsetting for you, but if I don't treat you, you'll die."

"I don't care", she said, and she felt tears sliding down her face. In spite of everything, the smallest of doubts was making its presence felt, not enough to make her want to live but enough to make her afraid. This had to be the most wretched hour of her entire life, all the more so because it still seemed quite right that it should be the last. "I don't—care."

"Well, I care", he said, and he managed to sound as though he meant it. "Please try to relax."

A nurse held her hand. Maria felt a tube slipping between her teeth and into her mouth until it touched the back of her throat. She gagged violently and found herself trying to push him away again, but the room was dissolving into mist all around her. "I'm falling", she tried to say, but it was quite impossible now to speak a single word, and she felt her chest tightening with the terror of what was happening to her. Of all the most horrendous sensations she would ever experience, this had to be the most terrible, the most harrowing, but she was being rescued. To her intense relief she felt herself slipping away and knew that the battle for her life would be fought by others as she fell into darkness. But if her life mattered enough, she might wake up again. She might open her eyes and find that the world still held a place for her.

Eva sat in silence for a long time. "Should I tell him?" she asked.

"I don't know", replied Maria. "I don't suppose it matters very much now. Do you think it would help?"

"I think everyone needs to know sometimes when they have done something incredible, particularly someone like Matthew, bless him. All doctors know that they will save lives as they go about their work, but only in the most general way. I think it's quite different when you can point to someone and say, 'I saved that person.' " She laughed lightly. "How extraordinary!"

Maria felt her phone buzzing an incoming text message and reached into her pocket. "Who could this be?" she asked out loud.

"Maria", said Eva, suddenly very serious. "I hope you don't mind me asking, but are you all right now? I mean, since it happened?"

Maria smiled, half at the message in front of her, half at the question. "It's all right, Eva, I'd never try it again, I can assure you, even when I get really miserable ... and I do sometimes."

"Are you sure? These urges can remain quite strong in people sometimes."

"Well, the urge is there sometimes even now, but, well—this is going to sound a bit odd but—well, I know that what he did that time was all in a day's work for a doctor, and he wouldn't have thought twice about it. He told me himself he'd treated hundreds of cases like me before, and I'm sure there have been many more since. But the fact was he did it. He spent time and energy keeping me alive when even I didn't see the point. It was the first time in my entire life that anybody had behaved as though my life was actually worth something." She handed over her phone. "Look at this."

It was a text message from Rick, asking if she wanted to meet up. "Who's Rick?"

"I suppose he might be a suitor", she giggled. "Said he just happens to be on the Isle of Wight today visiting a client in prison. What an extraordinary coincidence!"

"There is a prison here, of course."

"Well, yes, but ..."

Eva smiled. "Listen, Maria, you probably think I'm about a hundred but it's not so long since I was getting nervous phone calls from a terribly nice, terribly shy doctor who just happened to have found himself in my neighbourhood. Why don't you go and meet him?"

"I hardly know him", she said. "He could be a complete weirdo for all I know."

"He might be, but he probably isn't. Why not get to know him before you make up your mind? You've nothing to lose by arranging to meet."

Half an hour later, Matthew arrived, ruddy and windswept from the beach. In spite of his plan to relax and move as little as possible during the holiday, he had been unable to resist getting out of his deckchair and joining in with one of the children's games. There was something so exhilarating about the sea, so inviting that he had run into the icy waves, just to feel the joy of the cold water swirling about his legs and that bizarre, liberating belief that he could go on running forever without anything to hold him.

"What's Maria up to?" he asked, breathlessly. "She's standing outside the door on the phone looking decidedly guilty."

"Leave her alone. She's talking to a young man. I think he's planning to take her out for a few hours."

"What? Here?"

Eva giggled. "Yes, bless his heart. Just happened to be on an assignment in the Isle of Wight today for some reason. He must have moved heaven and earth rearranging his work schedule."

"I say, is he coming to meet her here? Can we be very embarrassing?"

"Don't you dare! I want this to work out for her."

"Of course, of course. He seemed like a nice chap from the brief glimpse I got of him."

"You know, don't you? You remember." Eva looked quizzically at him, but he gave nothing away. "I'm sorry, darling, I forgot you can't discuss these things, but it's all right, she told me everything. You do remember, don't you?"

"Oh, yes", he said. "It took me a while to remember where I had seen her before. I don't usually, but in her case I couldn't get over how alone she was. It was awful."

Eva smiled. "Cheer up. I don't think a lady like that is meant to be alone. You'll see." She waited for him to sit down, but he hovered expectantly. "Well, have you come in search of tea?"

"Actually," he said, "I was hoping to drag you back down to the water's edge. It's rather beautiful at this time of day."

"I'll settle up then."

"No, you finish your tea. I'll pay."

When Maria had finished her lengthy phone call, she realised she had been left behind and wandered lazily back down to the beach to find the rest of the party. The sun was at its highest point, on the cusp of beginning its slow descent into the myriad colours of twilight and blissfully distant night. She was aware of the summer winding down and the thought that it would not be long before the days shortened and she felt the sharp, frosty air cheekily touching her face as she stepped into the street. But for now, she was warm, cocooned in the glow of a feeling she did not entirely understand.

"Not like you to daydream", said Jonathan, walking towards her. "Are you all right?" In front of them, Freya and the children were unpacking a vast picnic made up of a seemingly endless collection of plastic boxes and polythene bags, whilst Matthew and Eva walked together a little further along, two shrinking silhouettes arm in arm, enjoying a few moments of quiet before joining the others.

"I don't want to go to court", she said, not turning to look at him. "I'm really not sure I can face it."

"You don't have to be present if you would rather not", said Jonathan. "The men are both entering a guilty plea. But you might find it helps to draw a line under it, even if you just turn up for sentencing."

"I know. I just suddenly thought of all the other battles waiting to erupt."

"Don't think about it now", he said. "Of course there will be other cases like this; the battle lines are being drawn. Who knows where they will all end when it comes to it? But for the moment, be proud to have been part of a victory—let's face it, there aren't many of them. Matthew is a free man. He can return to his work, and his family can rebuild their lives."

And you can build yours, he thought, when Maria had made her goodbyes and walked out of sight to a meeting she did not want to share with anyone else. *You can build the life he gave back to you once.*